MW01173848

BOOTLEG Vol.3
Bridget Chase

BOOTLEG
Vol. 3
Bridget Chase

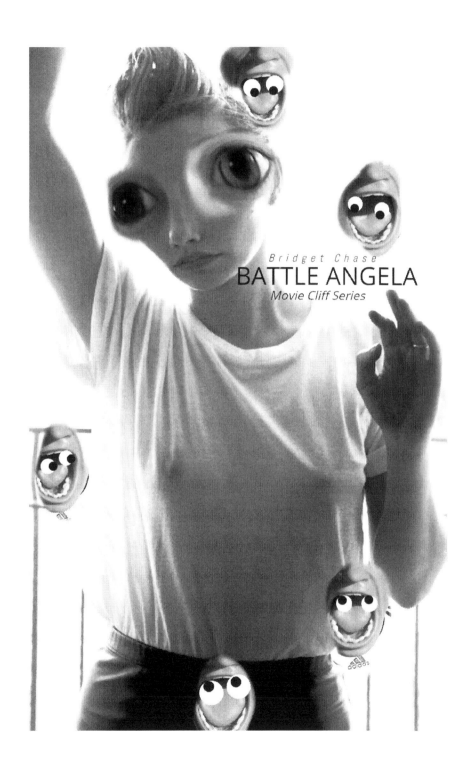

BATTLE ANGELA

Bridget Chase

Hot Garbage Bitch

Well, here I am; just looking through this mess. Never know what I might find.

William trudged through the pile of sci-fi garbage.

The sun was orange and beat down on the steaming piles of discarded robotics that were left unguarded for people to dig through, but no one did, for some unknown reason; well, except for William.

He was an older dude with a friendly face that said hey, let's be friends, and grey slicked back hair that made you know he was old.

"Oh, what's this now?"

Something caught his eye.

Yes, something caught my eye.

He reached in the garbage and pulled out a head.

"Damn you're pretty aren't ya? Hell, she's a real beaut. What a great find. Man 'o man, this one'll be great for givin' me the sucky wucky, slurpy wurpy."

He turned the head around in his hands.

The bust was a woman with silicone skin, but underneath was robotics and wires 'n shit, which hung out from below the neck.

William had a few robot-heads at home that he mouth-fucked regularly, but this one was special.

He looked at its eyes. "Peepers, she looks like the girl next door got mixed with anime. Pretty big eyes you got there; but hell, might get me a good nut off with how cute 'n innocent you look 'n stuff. Yep, no way you're a combat machine with a secret, no sir. Just gonna' be a good nuttin' device."

He dropped her into his side satchel.

"Now let's see if I can find a hot body to go with the head."

He dug around some more.

So, Yeah

William fixed the robot's head on a body.

He was inside his home. His house showed that he wasn't a rich man, nor an important man; but a smart man, well, maybe.

"Too bad I couldn't find you a body with skin."

He ran his hands over her metal plated tits.

"You got all the right curves though, and-,"

William's hand slipped down her stomach and then between her legs.

"Ah, well, at least Roger Rabbit seems to be wet. Now to turn you on."

A hard-on pitched a tent in his grey sweat pants.

BING!

The robot opened her eyes. And they were big 'ol eyes; like almost ridiculous if done in a movie.

"Hi," William said.

She said nothing.

He smiled. "My name is William and I found you; so, now I own you. Anyways, we're in this world where human looking robots are hunted and destroyed; so, you'll need to be inside all-the-time, okay? Oh, and your name is Angela."

He petted her glossy hair.

"Angela?" she asked. She pouted her lips. They were soft delicate and youthful.

Oh, 'Ol Willie's gonna' give that mouth some attention tonight!

"So," he said, "How bout we give ya' a test run, you sexy silicone thang?"

Angela said nothing.

William leaned in for a kiss. He closed his eyes.

Oh, here we go. Man, she looks great. I mean steel tits isn't perfect, but her Sea Otter outta' give me a perfect squeeze. Man, I tightened that shit real tight, anus tight, with a screw driver?

He opened his eyes.

Angela looked confused. "Who am I? What am I? Where am I? I don't even know who I am? Who would I even be if I weren't an 'I'? Please I must go, I have a headache and need answers."

She stood.

"No wait," William said, "Think you could blow me fir-,"

-She pushed past him and went out the door.

"Damn, damn, damn, damn, damn; I knew I should have scrambled her brain and made her semi-retarded. Shit, chicks, man. I better leave myself a note for next time."

He went to the refrigerator and wrote on the dry erase board – *Make sure to scramble brains. Need bimbos, not emotional beings, or machines with thoughts.*

Hunky, Hunky, Butt Cut

He had a butt cut. That is, a butt cut hair cut- like a bowl haircut and parted down the center, like an ass; and it fit him. He was an early twenties, ass.

Billy walked down the exotic market street.

There was shit here,

and there;

some shit over there too.

It was a future sci fi outdoor market with IDK, drapes 'n shit blowing off small stands; but the stands had nondescript technological devices. Fuck, who cares; Billy was outside walking, so he could come across…

"Wow who's that?"

A hot chick milled about the crowd; she looked lost.

And, she looks like easy prey. I mean, a new girl in town, lost? How quick will I be able to get her naked 'n shit? She'll have to rely on me for everything. I better go say, hi.

Billy pushed people out of the way. "Outta' the way you extras; we got a star comin' through here."

The girl bumped around people like a pinball machine on wheels in the back of a U-Haul van driving down a winding road.

She ran into some big guy. He looked angry and turned around and grabbed her.

"Let me go," she protested; because she didn't give permission for the guy to grab her and lift her off the ground; which was unusual, because robots usually like that stuff.

Billy ran up, "Hey beef cake, let the girl go."

"Mind your business little man," the burly man said. He had a shaved head and a huge jaw injected with growth hormones 'n shit. Actually, a needle was stuck in his cheek. Just hangin' there. It's the future, so it was some kind of fashion statement. Sure.

"Let her go, or else," Billy said.

He held the girl by her throat. She kicked feebly.

"Hahah," the guy laughed and, SMACK! Back-handed the girl.

Billy got mad. "I'm mad now." He cocked his fist back and-

-POW! The girl kicked the huge guy.

"Urgh," he dropped her and held his ribs.

The girl took a defensive stance.

The big guy lurched forward. Billy jumped on his back.

"Hey, get off me fucker," the huge swollen man said. "This ain't cool, or fair. Everyone knows I can't touch my back, not with these swollen arms and massive biceps. Have you seen how swollen my arms are? Pretty cool and impressive, huh?"

Billy tried to choke him out. "Man, your neck is thick and strong!"

"Thanks, I work out." He caught Billy and, FLING! Threw him.

Billy flew and, CRASH! Hit a market booth.

"That's my future boyfriend," the girl said. She sprinted and, LEAP! Jumped in the air.

The big guy turned around. "HUH?"

BLAM! Her knuckles rang off his jaw.

The guy stumbled back.

The girl rocketed forward with a knee.

BLAM! It caught him in the stomach.

BARF! Chocolate flavored protein shake splattered on the sidewalk. The big dude's knees buckled, and he fell. He reached a hand and tore the girl's ragged clothes off.

"She's a robot," the big guy said.

"Wow! She's a robot," Billy said.

"I'm a robot," the girl said and, THWAK! Round housed the dude into unconsciousness.

"Wow, you're amazing," Billy said. He walked up to her.

The crowd had parted and formed a circle around the two destined love birds.

"What's your name?" he asked.

"Angela."

"Cool, my name is Billy. Do you like the name Billy? I didn't get to pick it." He reached a hand up and felt her steel tit. He played with her nipple.

"What are you doing?" she asked.

"Oh." He put his hand down. "It's was just a greeting."

"Okay."

Angela lifted her hand and tweaked Billy's nipple through his shirt.

He smiled. "It's nice to meet you. You're cute."

"You are too," she said.

"Hey, want to be my girl 'n shit?"

"Sure, but only if you'll help me recover something from my past and then when assassins come, and I have to fight, get in the way."

"I can do that. So long as we fuck soon. I mean-," Billy combed back his hair with his fingers. "-It won't be super weird because you look mostly human. And, you look young; but you're not human and don't have an actual age. You do have a puss, right?"

Angela looked down. "I think so." She kicked a leg up by her head and held the ankle. "How does it look?"

That steel trap winked at Billy.

"Looks great." He slipped two fingers in.

Angela brought her leg down. The crowd lost interest and milled around. "I'm headed to a crashed ship or a laboratory thingy. Want to come?"

"Yeah, I want to come; and I'll go to the ship as well," he said.

She smiled.

Technology MacGruffin

"What's that?" Angela asked.

"Cum; just keep on jerkin'"

Billy sat on an overturned garbage can. Angela stood between his spread thighs and kung fu jerked his dick.

"It's spittin' at me," she said.

Billy trembled. "Well, next time use your mouth and swaller it."

The last of his hot snot shot onto Angela's steel chest.

She wiped the marshmallow cream into her hair.

"So, about this ship?" Billy hopped down.

"Yeah, I was drawn here by a forgotten memory. Let's go inside."

They went inside

"Wow this place is weird and cool," he said

Angela looked around. "I should pull that lever."

A lever stuck from a control panel. She pulled it.

PSSSH! A door hissed a slid away, revealing, something; like a big orb thingy.

Angel walked over to it.

Billy said, "Hey, don't touch it."

But, touch it she did.

WOOOSH! Her hair went all matrix and information played behind her big eyes.

"I know it all, now," she said.

"What does that mean?" Billy asked. "You're still my girlfriend, right?" *Shit, what does she know? Does she know what I did last summer? No, no that was all just a terrible accident.*

"Yeah, I am. It means people will want, what I know."

Assassin Poop

"She has it; I want it," some guy said. He was rather evil because he planned to use the technology to do bad things to good people. Now, what those bad things were, I don't know; but I *can* tell you that they were, *for sure*, bad. Evil, very evil, like, don't like this guy, evil, okay?

Evil.

A part human, part robot assassin stood in the room with him.

It was like some futuristic, nice office with shit that was black and sleek and made you go ewww, cool future stuff. There was a desk, too.

"You want her dead or alive?" The half human half robot asked. He was an upgraded human with part of his face robotic and a robotic arm. Maybe other stuff too; but we can't really see because he wore a dark leather jacket- open, shirtless underneath, and leather boy band pants. The human robot hybrid had a shaved head and looked like a mean, bad ass dude you wouldn't want to encounter in an alley when you got three hundred dolleroos in yer pocket. You might even cross the street, if you saw him comin' yer way.

"I don't care, either way. Just get her here, Daniel," the mean, oh so bad guy boss, said.

"Will do sir. What does she look like?"

The boss man hopped over to his desk like a little bunny and, typiddy, type, type, typed on the computer. "Here, have a look fer yerself. Man, you'll like this."

Daniel looked over the dude's shoulder.

The Pornhub website was pulled up.

"Battle Yanker?" he asked.

"Yeah, she did some porn at one time; but memorize that face. You need to find that face."

Daniel did, but he also memorized her body.

DA-YUM! Them titties be like, KABOOM! Oh god, oh god, oh god, oh god, oh god, oh god- GIMME!

"I'll track 'er down," the robot human said.

"Good, now get on outta' here. I think I'll jerk it a little; since I have this video up and all. Also, I've been eating pretty good, so got me some test-rone flowing in these forty year old veins."

Yeah, and that was how you knew he was evil. Villains are always a bit older. Older equals evil, okay?

"You got it boss." Daniel left.

"Wait."

"What boss?"

The boss dude looked over at the human robot. "Do you need to poop? You look like you kinda' need to poop."

"No, boss."

"Are you sure? You kinda' have that look to ya'."

"No, I'm sure, boss."

"Okay, well maybe try before you go. You look like you need to poop."

Hmm, maybe I do. "Okay boss, I'll go poop."

"Good; poop and then get the robot girl."

The human robot thingy left the room.

"Ah, at last." The boss pulled his sweaty meat out. "Oh, you're a naughty droid; this is the meat you are looking for. Damn, got me a nut coming real soon."

He watched the girl ride pole like she was a cowgirl on stilts riding pole in a porn video.

"Damn, them are some good 'ol pepperonis, fo' sho'! If they make a movie of this, I bet Hollywood will drop all the good stuff."

The door opened. "You say something, boss?"

"No."

"Okay." Daniel closed the door.

Fight Me Topless

Ah, there she is. Daniel perched atop some balcony overlooking the futuristic streets of a new, New York. It was raining and made it look cool as shit, with neon lights and sleek dark clothing.

Angela walked down the street carrying Billy on her back.

"Oh, this is great, just swell I tell you, just swell." Billy said, "You're like, so strong; ya' know that? So strong. Damn, strongest girlfriend ever. Even stronger than Tina; and she was really strong! You should have seen her; tons of muscle, like the hulk, and stuff."

Angela pranced and picked up speed. Billy laughed like a monkey driving a car on its way to get donuts.

Daniel lept down.

I'll attack her good. She be all, 'Oh I didn't see that coming,' and I'll be like, 'Naw bitch, you didn't.'

SMACK! His feet hit the ground.

Angela stopped running and Billy slipped down her back.

Daniel was a bad looking dude, like eight hundred pounds, all muscle, no hair, tatts and robotics. "Yeah bitch you didn't see that coming."

"No," she said.

"So, yer coming with me," Daniel said, "I pooped and all; so, I'm ready to fight ya' if necessary."

Billy peeked over her shoulder, "You're wrong, bro; this bitch is bad. She's gonna' kick your ass."

Angela turned her head and said, "Step back a little."

He did and said, "See? What'd I tell ya? You're in for *real* trouble now, buddy. Go get him, babe!"

"I'll get him." Angela took a battle stance.

"Ah, little girl; you's stupid. I'm gonna' destroy you. I hope you went poop before coming down this street."

"She did!" Billy shouted.

REEE! A chainsaw looking thing came out of Daniel's arm. WHIR! BUZZ! A thing replaced his eye. "That's a laser sight." He put his finger to it like Cyclops from X-men, BRRRRRR! A fat laser came out.

FLIP! Angela flipped in the air like a video game.

Daniel skipped back. "Naw, come on now; fight me topless."

She landed and looked back at Billy.

He nodded.

"Hmm-kay!" Angela said. She tore that top off. Them little Hamburglers went all free and flying like butter on pizza. HOT Pizza. Man, those nipples were pink; they were!

"Well, Build A Bear titties, let's fight," Daniel said.

He struck a stance.

I sure hope I can win. I love beating up girls, but this small chick might be powerful. I mean, there is no reason why I should think so, but, if she is the star of this narrative and not me, I might get my ass handed to me. On the other hand, I do like beating up girls; so this should be fun. Yep, my fists haven't pounded enough female faces this week.

Angela charged forward fist cocked.

I hope I win. I mean this dude is big. I'm surprised he can even stand up 'n shit; he must weigh a ton. But, I must be some badass fighter or some shit; otherwise, this story wouldn't have happened this way; well, unless the author was a real asshole and I get my ass kicked. But hopefully not, because if I live, I'll do a sex scene with Billy. DO you hear that author? I'll fuck Billy to end this story if you want. I'll be all, bow-chicka-wer-wer.

Daniel swung the chainsaw arm, BRRRRR!

Angel lept. She jumped the weapon arm and struck at his face.

He dodged.

Angela sailed past but, *hey now!*

Daniel caught her by her hair. He yanked her back and threw her to the ground.

The human robot lifted a heavy foot.

"I'm gonna' stomp your face!"

STOMP!

Angel rolled aside. She got too her feet but-

-GRAB! Daniel caught her by the neck. With his other hand, BAM! BAM! BAM! BAM! He pounded her in the stomach.

His fist was almost the size of her torso.

Billy watched. *Is this hot? I think it's hot. Yeah, damn he's pounding her.* He slipped a hand down the front of his pants and tugged his wiener a bit. *Boy, I shouldn't be doin' this. It's kinda' weird, but something's come over me. I can't explain it. WOOO DOGGIE!*

Angela pried the hand off her neck. She somehow did a backflip and, CLAK! Kicked Daniel under the chin.

His head kicked back, and teeth snapped shut, TATTAT!

Angela landed in a cool action pose. Her girls went all swimming like this was a space movie. They were supposed to be steel-tits but in this scene, they looked like tits that were airbrushed to look like metal. So, they swang around 'n shit.

Men in the audience, watching the movie, squirmed in desire. Their balls clenched and demanded to be pumped into something wet and tight.

"Hey what you doing?" Angela asked.

BUDDA, DA, DA, DA, DA, DA, DA- Daniel was seated playing a guitar. "Nothin', playing a guitar."

"Why, I thought we were fightin'?"

"Yeah, we were. I don't know; kinda' decided I didn't want to be an assassin anymore."

Angela put her hands on her hips. 'So, you aren't going to kill me?"

"Naw, I don't want to. Actually," Daniel said while he strummed the guitar, "I kinda' just fell into this line of work. I've always wanted to be a musician; but hell, ya know, got to pay bills 'n such."

She blew strands of hair out of her face. "And you decided this now?"

Daniel's fingers strummed a melody. "Yeah, when you kicked me, I was thinking about my mom. Ya know, when I was a young Lost Boy, she-,"

CLAK! A bullet went through Daniel's brain.

Billy danced around. "Oh! I got him. I got him good. Did you see that? Oh man, BLAM! OH! Got you sucka'! Did you see? Did you see?" He bounced around waivin' the pistol.

Angela smiled. "Yeah, you did real good. So wanna' fuck?"

"Sure," he said, "But isn't there like a main boss we need to kill, so that you can live the rest of your life like a fairy tale?"

"No," Angela said

"Okay; and there isn't anyone you need to see that might have brought you to life, or helped you early on to become who you are now?"

"No," Angela said.

"Really? Didn't you say something about a William, or somebody?"

"No."

"Okay, let's fuck!"

BOOM! Billy's clothes were off.

Fuck A' Blender

Angela walked over, all sexy. The camera caught a nice shot of robot ass. Sci-fi geeks creamed of wheat in their Batman and Robin undies.

She pressed her body against Billy.

His hands went for them titties.

Again, her body *now* looked it was only spray paint and not steel. Especially, when Billy squeezed those oranges, the skin dimpled like soft memory foam.

His Wonkie got all hard and slipped around Angela's stomach. It dripped 'n spit. *Fuck us, fuck us!*

She kissed him. Their tongues played hamsters stuck up asses.

Angela reached down and wrapped her pneumatic fingers around his trembling shaft.

"Oh yeah, like that, WOW!"

She piston jerked that meat. Her hand yanked like one hundred yanks a second.

"Oh, baby, I'm gonna' come!"

"Not yet Purple Velvet. I want you inside me."

She pulled him to the ground.

His cock slipped in that healthy juicer.

"Oh, it's gonna' be a long winter," Billy said. "My groundhogs gone home. Go home buddy. Go home." He thrusted. "Go on home, now."

Angela's legs were all up in the air 'n shit.

People walking down the sidewalk stopped and looked; some took pictures.

One dude tried to mount Billy's ass.

"Don't fight it, now. Just relax; it'll be just fine."

BAM! Angela kicked the dude. He flew in the air, soared over the buildings, and landed in the street three blocks away.

A little girl riding a tricycle screamed when he went, SPLAT! Right in front of her.

END

Bridget Chase

CHAINSAW

CHAINSAW
Bridget Chase

His fingers clawed at the knife blade.

Kelly washed her hands. She checked her appearance in the mirror above the sink. "Yep, I look good." Her brunette hair was styled, and her oiled turkeys pressed at her sleeveless t-shirt. GOBBLE, GOBBLE, YOINKS!

She applied lipstick and left the bathroom.

As the door opened-

"-Give me the mother fuckin money!" A guy shouted.

He held a pistol to the cashier's forehead.

The patrons of this small-town diner trembled in fear.

"Nobody try nothin', ya' hear; I'll shoot this bitch!"

The young, kinda' attractive cashier held back tears and, BING! Opened the register. "Kinda' attractive? Thanks, that's kinda' a compliment. Hey, since I'm young and stuff, think you could *not* have this guy shoot me?"

We'll see…

Kelly looked at her three friends sitting in a booth.

Steph's eyes were big. She was twisted around in her seat. "This should be good."

Liz raised an eyebrow, like asking, what are you going to do? "Even though I know exactly what she is going to do."

Ginger nodded. "This guy is toast."

Kelly smiled at them and approached the robber.

He looked over at her. "Damn! Now you're a piece of jailbait mall ass if I ever saw it. What are ya' fifteen? Shit my god! Look at what you're wearing!"

She wore a very loose t-shirt with the sleeves cut off. Her Sea Biscuits wobbled under the loose top and peeked out the sides. She wore ultra-small painted on jean shorts.

"Them legs; gimme, gimme!"

"Stay back bitch; you don't want any part of this. Though you'd be fun to wrestle with, no doubt! I'd put you in a headlock, for sure."

"Dang," Kelly said and smiled, "Aren't you a handsome piece of shit?"

The guy's pretzel-face crinkled. "Pretzel face? I ain't got no pretzel face. Hell, no one's ever called me handsome before."

The cashier with the pistol to her forehead shook her head. Her eyes were saying don't. "Don't let this guy shoot me. Shit if I live, you can write me into the story later. Hell, I'll do a topless scene or something; just don't kill me."

"Fuck you bitch; you wanna die?" the guy asked Kelly.

Kelly had her thumbs hooked in the pockets of her small shorts. She walked forward with a sexy swagger. Her hips- side to side seductively.

"Here we go," Liz said. She was turned in the booth and watched.

Kelly stopped a few feet from the guy.

She had a girl next door face with flowing healthy hair. Trim with nice hips, soft skin, and perky Pee Wee Hermans just askin' to be tossed around in the sack; and her ass, well, it might as well be Satan himself.

"But, it's not me. Nope; I stopped inhabiting women's asses centuries ago."

The guy swung his arm. The pistol coming towards Kelly.

In a flash, CRACK! She kicked

The heel of her cowboy boot, CLOCK! Caught the guy under the chin.

SNAP! His teeth clicked together, and his head kicked back.

The people in the diner gasped.

The gun flew from the guy's hand.

In slow motion Kelly's foot came back down. The smooth muscles of her legs relaxed.

The guy's back was arched. His eyes rolled to the ceiling; knees buckled.

He collapsed. And the back of his head hit the counter, CRACK! His skull bounced off.

The gun hit the floor.

With a THWAK! He fell unconscious on the ground.

Everyone was silent watching the beautiful girl as she walked over to a nearby table.

"Can I borrow this?" she asked the people sitting there.

The man and woman at the table nodded; their mouths open. "Yeah, I couldn't believe what happened." The man was taken by her danger and beauty. "Yeah, she was dangerous. But, shit; I wouldn't mind a bit of danger in my bed."

"Harry, you scum. That girls could be your granddaughter!"

Kelly took the knife. She went back to the robber. She knelt and in a fierce attack, STAB! Drove the knife into the guy's neck.

SLOOGE! Blood welled in gallons and spilled around the knife.

The guy bolted awake and his finger clawed at the knife blade.

The people in the restaurant screamed and it was a mass exodus.

GURGLE, GURLE, the guy thrashed; his fingers were coated in blood.

Kelly stood up and, BAM! Stomped the end of the knife handle sending it through the guy's spine.

A wet breath escaped his lips and his body stopped moving.

Kelly came back to the table.

The diner was empty.

"Nice job," Liz said. She scooted over for her friend.

"Guy deserved it," Steph said.

"Yeah, you did the world a favor," Ginger said. "He would have fucked people the rest of his life. Good thing you ended it."

Kelly picked up her ice cream milkshake. It had warmed some and wasn't as thick as she liked. She put it to her lips and drank. "Yummy, that's fucking good. Yeah, fucker picked the wrong diner today."

Cars peeled out of the parking lot and police sirens howled in the distance.

BING!

Steph pulled out her phone. "Got a text." She tapped the screen.

Ginger chewed on a French fry.

"What do you think it'll be this time?" Liz asked.

Kelly shrugged her shoulder. SLUPR! She sucked the straw pulling that sugary yummy shit into her mouth. "Hopefully, somewhere other than Texas; its hot as fuck."

A smile spread o Steph's lips; she read the text.

Steph was a gorgeous young girl. Light and innocent, looking but with a body like, WHA-BAM! A wet dream of popsicle condensation in summer.

"It's Montel Williams," Steph said. "Here, we've got to Facetime him."

Liz gestured. She and Kelly got up. They went to the other side of the booth and squeezed in next to Ginger.

Ginger moved over and tossed her golden hair over. It framed her face like heaven.

Steph held the phone out in front of them.

Montel's smiling daytime tv face appeared. "Hey, sexy Charlies Angels kinda' thing… girls."

"Hi Montel," they said in unison.

"I need to meet with you girls. I have a new mission."

"Oh, what is it?" Ginger asked

"I hope it's somewhere nice with beaches," Liz said. "I have this barely there string bikini I want to parade around in and let my girls bounce around in tight jumping twirls."

Montel opened his mouth and drooled, "ARGHGGG!"

Police stormed into the diner guns drawn. "Police! Nobody move!" the guy in front said.

"Montel, we are in Texas, remember. It'll take a couple days to get back to LA," Kelly said.

"No problem," he said, "Head outside; I'm pickin' you bitches up."

A police officer came to the table. "Are you ladies okay?"

"Geez what happened to this guy?" An officer asked. He was bent over the dead man.

"We'll be out in a sec," Steph said to Montel and hung up.

"Yeah, we're fine," Kelly said.

The police officer eyed them. "Yeah you are; shit a lifetime in prison might be worth the squeeze of them ripe lemons. Damn Girl! Sausage Egg McMuffins! Damn them titties!"

Their young cleavage peeked like rabbits in a carrot patch.

"Is anyone hurt," the officer asked. "Actually, I'm hoping one of you is. Then you might lift up your shirt; showing me a tiny little cut under one of them fleshy McGruff crime dogs. I would kiss it for you and make it better. Maybe, I'd put a little band-aid on for ya' too. Oh, you'd be so grateful that you would slurp this police's cock-,"

The girls noticed a bulge in the officer's pants.

(Cough) "Well glad you girls are okay. Why don't you get on outta' here. We'll clean this up. Oh, and lunch is on me."

"Thanks," the girls said and got up.

"You are such a nice police officer," Kelly said. She leaned up on him on her toes and kissed his cheek.

"Damn, the lord! Why can't I land a babe this fine waiting for me when I get home? Just cookin' brisket and wearing nothin' but a small apron. I'd eat my dinner and she would scrub the floor only to give me a show of her swinging sloths and wigglin' that sexy Hamburglar at me. The floor doesn't even need cleaning, but she knows I like to watch."

The girls left, and the officer stood unmoving. The cum in his balls cried, 'Let us free. Let us outta' here. Let us in her!"

Paramedics came in the door as the girls went outside.

One of the paramedics said, "Shit, this looks similar to that dude we found in Austin."

The other paramedic said, "At least this guy didn't have his head removed by a chainsaw."

The girls walked out to the street.

ZOOOOM! A sleek military sci-fi craft flew over their heads and hovered.

Ropes came down.

The girls grabbed a hold and fixed them to carabiners on their belts and, WHISK! Were taken up to the ship.

Montel stood, pulled his hand out, and adjusted his boner.

The ship hovered over McDonald's

The fast-food worker leaned out the drive through window. "SHIT!" Her little minimum wage visor was whipped off by the turbulent air. Her hair went all Matrix spaghetti.

Ginger pressed the recoil button. The little basket with their lunch was pulled up to the craft.

The McDonalds worker watched the ship, ZOOM! Off into the sky.

"Damn, that looks like a fun adventure." She put the mic to her mouth. "Wish I had a life like that. (Pause)What can I make for you today?" She asked for the bazzilionth time.

"Ah, great," Steph said.

Ginger entered the 70's porn-set-style living room aboard the ship. She carried their lunch.

"Didn't we just eat?" Liz asked.

"Shh, its fine," Kelly said, "Shit doesn't always have to make sense."

"No, it doesn't" Montel said. He entered the room. He wore a dark satin robe and smoked a pretentions pipe. The interior lights danced on his black waxed head. "Nope, and this ain't bout to make no sense, either."

The girls opened their respective bags and chomped down on that shit.

Montel puffed the pipe, "You lady-whores are stayin' in this small town a little longer. Seems that guy you killed today was no ordinary crook."

"How so?" Ginger asked. She was a bit thicker than the other girls; but not, too thick. Just that satisfying, cum in her tight cunt, thick. She didn't dress quite as provocatively as the other girls but that didn't matter because there was no hiding them delicious buttery L. Ron Hubbards; no sir! The full weight of scientology sat perky on her chest.

Montel continued. "That guy you killed was the towns minister."

Kelly said, "He didn't seem that godly to me?"

"No, he didn't; but that's because-," Montel sat down on the arm of the couch. He reached a hand down the front of Kelly's top and played with her Oscar the Grouches. "Ah, there's that nipple. So soft and rubbery. PIK-A-CHUUUU! Pika, pika!"

She let him. "It feels nice and he's o boss; besides, what are tits for other than playing with?"

The black pimp continued, "-this town has been infected by some kind of mutagen."

"Everyone in *any* small town looks like mutants," Ginger said.

"True," Montel said, "but this is different." He squeezed that soft lemon. "Oh, these are just great; just great!"

"Different how?" Liz asked. She nibbled on a fry and had her long legs crossed.

"Well," Montel pulled his hand out, stood and adjusted his boner. "This towns about to need some serious saving."

"Because everyone will become a criminal?" Steph asked. Ah Steph, so sexy with milky little cupcakes frosted and peeking out her top.

"No, worse," Montel said.

The live studio audience gasped

"The town is about to turn into *real* mutants," he said.

The audience cheered.

Montel walked off the set.

A few drops splashed his clean shoe.

The police Sergeant didn't like this. "No, I don't like this one bit-,"

"- Not one bit."

He continued to watch the monitor.

"What violence."

The girl on the scream gagged. Tears pilled from her eyes and she dry heaved.

"This is really bad. Bad, bad, bad…," The Sergeant couldn't look away.

The guy in the video shoved his cock back in the chick's mouth and abused her face with his powerful Cross-fit hip thrusts.

"Sergeant," An officer came in the door. "You need to see this."

The Sergeant hit pause. "I might watch the rest later. Shit, gotta' know if the guy nutted. What's the matter?" he asked.

"The prisoners sir; come 'n see."

"Uhg," the Sergeant hefted his weigh and got out of the chair. His manly gut pressed at this tucked shirt. He was built solid with thick arms and a bristly face.

He followed the mousy officer. "This fuck better not be bent outta' shape for nothing. If it's another cute cat video, I'm killing him."

The racket coming down the hall made clear this was serious.

The Sergeant made it to the holding cell.

Three other officers stood with their backs to the wall giving the prison bars the largest breath.

"DAMN, what's happening here?"

The guy they had locked up, for the night for indecency at the park, thrashed around in a violent rage fit for a Slipknot concert.

VOMIT! The guy threw up. It volleyed through the bars.

The Sergeant stepped back. A few drops splashed his clean shoe.

The inmate let out a weird sharp sound and then grabbed the bars and thrashed like a wild animal.

"What's wrong with his skin?" The Sergeant asked.

The officer that had called him over said, "I don't know; he's been changing slowly for the last hours."

"We better call paramedics. Something isn't right."

The inmate screamed and thrashed on the bars. Patches of his hair were falling out and large pustules were forming on his oily sardine skin.

"He wasn't a looker before; but the sight, makes me want to lose my dinner. Disgusting."

The prisoner began to tear his clothes off.

"Oh, come on; don't do that."

Her clothes were torn off and she tried to escape.

Well, the cashier, that had the pistol to her head earlier, survived. Unfortunately-

"You fuckin' bastard! You let me live but then do this to me?" She ran for her life.

"I was just shopping at target, grabbing a few things and-,"

She was looking at a bathing suit on one of the mannequins when shit hit the fan.

"It was a cute suit. I was thinking how much Joey would drool seeing my tea cups ride in that top. Oh, he'd cum his pants over me, but then-,"

Screaming came from the front of the store.

"A green smoke drifted in the doors and everyone started running."

People fell to their knees when the gas consumed them and then they changed.

A rabid thing with a watery mouth chased the poor cashier.

"I can out run it."

No, you can't.

"I have to run faster."

You won't make it.

"Please…,"

That thing was on her.

She fell to the ground and it tore at her top, WHAM! Them titties came spilling out.

"Why?"

You said you'd do a topless scene to live. Here it is.

The mutant man with puss infected flesh smeared his face all over her chest. His Cobra Commander got all hard and hot.

"Don't let him rape me!"

Sorry, the story is, what it is.

Her clothes were torn off and she tried to escape. She didn't.

That mutant had himself the best nut.

Cum dripped from her cunt and ass.

The cashier began to thrash as the green gas spilled over her body

"This is unfair."

The silicon lips beat like chicken wings in summer.

The ship came to a stop.

"We're here," Montel said. He finished cleaning his Fleshlight in the sink and used a towel to dry the silicon kooter. "Good luck, you fine ass hoes; be careful, ya' here?

"We always are," Kelly said.

The four girls stood in the elevator basket. They each had a sweet glossy neon painted chainsaws like something from Hot Topic.

Steph held the elevator remote.

It was like an old mine shaft elevator thing. I don't know why the rest of the ship was ultra futuristic with glossy materials from another world and the elevator crap. I guess just one of those mysteries.

FLAPPY, FLAP, FLAP, FLAP! Montel blew into the Fleshlight. The silicon lips beat like chicken wings in summer. He smiled to the girls and waived. "Oh, they'll be fine. Shit, every week I put them in the most dangerous situations and they survive. One day, I'll get them killed. Shit, that is the whole game, to test them, isn't it?"

Steph hit the button.

Ginger adjusted her bikini top. "I can't get the fabric to cover my nipples." Her white supremacists were squished whales in the little top.

The four of them wore Victoria Secret bikinis.

Now, don't think me a chauvinist. Geez, anyone who fights knows clothes can get in the way. And mutants, shit this was going to be messy. Bikinis are easier to clean.

The basket lowered to the ground and the girls climbed out.

"So, the creature releasing the mutating gas is in a Trampoline world?" Liz asked

"Guess so," Kell said

Steph cupped her titties. "Looks like these piggies are going to be flyin.'"

"All of ours will," Ginger said. She still tried to get the small fabric to cover her nipples, "It just isn't wide enough." She had some amazing pepperoni nipples, except, they were a really soft pink color. But the size, HOT DAM HOTDOGS! them are good!

The camera stayed on their asses as the crossed the parking lot.

Montel watched the feed. With two lubed fingers, he got his Fleshlight ready. "Yep, lube it up, toss that bitch in the microwave a few seconds, and I's bout to have this daytime Talk Show Host himself a good 'ol time!"

The girls entered the building

"What's this shit?" Liz asked, "Ghostbuster?"

Kelly's eyes were wide; all their eyes were.

"This is something new," Steph said. Her pussy quaked. Not because she was turned on, but this was a male creature and her construction crew was called.

The terrible monster turned toward them and spit, SPLAT! Sending chewed up people out of its mouth in a pulpy mist.

It was a huge beast with swingin' nuts and a hairy gnarled package. It had pink skin like a young baby, but its body was bloated. The thing was packed in the building and some weird tentacles came from it anus.

Imagine Kermit the frog bathed in the toxic ooze from Ninja Turtles and then reimagined by Guillermo del Torro.

"ROAR!" It screamed and green gas, POOF! Came from its ass.

"Gas masks girls," Ginger said

The bikini clad girls put gas masks on.

The creature stormed forward through the thick gas.

"Move it girls," Liz shouted.

Kelly hefted the chainsaw over her shoulder and ran.

The girls split directions forcing the monster to choose who to chase.

It was a good moment to run because through the entrance door poured hundreds of the town's residents. Except these residents were fuming mutants with drippy mouths and bulbous growth that popped putrid puss.

The girls sprinted up separate stairs leading to the trampoline platform.

The giant mutant stretched the fuckin springs to extreme.

BOING! Kell took a few bounces.

SWIPE! The giant struck at her with a clawed hand.

She flipped and pulled that chainsaw to life, VROOOM!

The rabid mutants charged up the stairs behind them.

They sprang across the trampoline.

Liz jumped a line in front of two mutants, VRRRRR! The teeth of her chainsaw went through their necks.

The mutant heads toppled and bounced on the black matts.

The scene was some kind of Cirque du Soleil shit. Mutants flipped and soared in a ballet of absurdity.

Ginger bounced. Her tits went zero gravity.

VROOM! With her chainsaw she severed a mutant's body.

Gore and intestines spilled out. The body was split in two.

Steph somersaulted over the giant mutant's arm.

CUT! Her chainsaw blade opened a furrow in its bristly arm.

It roared and swiped at her with its left hand.

Steph landed. Her girls wobbled in the tiny bikini top. She tumbled across the trampoline avoiding the blow.

"I got this," Kelly said. With a direct bounce she headed towards the thing's testicles.

She held the chainsaw over her shoulder with two hands in preparation for a vicious attack.

WHOA! This is about to get gross. Montel watched on the big screen aboard the ship. The screen had several camera feeds. They were controlled by Montel's mind; he could move them and zoom-in on command.

Montel's robe was open, and his talk show meat was squeezed into the velvet soft Fleshlight.

His swollen balls were ready with cum. *Damn, that Kelly's got some hot pockets on her!*

The giant mutant's tentacles, coming from it ass, attacked.

"No! Help!" they grabbed Kelly. She dropped her chainsaw.

Here we go, Montel zoomed in.

The tentacles removed her top.

Ginger fought off mutants, CHOP! SLICE! *I need to get over there and help!*

There they are! Montel jerked it with the silicon pussy. *Damn, gotta' love mutant fights with hot chicks!*

"No, stop!" Kelly shouted.

THWAK! SWIPE! Liz fought off the mutants surrounding her. The blade cut through bone and organs. She looked over. *Shit, I better hurry.*

Ginger sailed over her head.

SLICE! Her chainsaw removed some tentacles off the giant.

Kelly dropped but the remaining tentacles caught her and wrapped her back up.

Some of the slimy things prodded between her legs.

No, don't let those things wiggle into my velvet underground.

Motel stroked his meat. *This show is amazing!*

SLURP! GOBBLE! The silicone sucked his cock.

The mutants flooded towards the giant. They started climbing its legs.

Liz chased them.

Steph came from the other side. "Takeout their legs!" she said.

"Good idea," said Liz.

They ran into the group and swung their chainsaws at the thighs and knee caps.

THWAK! The giant backhanded Ginger as she approached. BOING! She bounced off a trampoline wall and tumbled across the mats. One of her tits slipped outta' the top. *Damn, my girls just won't fit.*

Legless mutants with spirting blood writhed on the ground.

"Should we feel bad these were normal towns people?" Liz asked.

THWAK! Steph took the head off a small mutant girl with her chainsaw. The head bounced, and mouth snarled. "Nope, they are mutants now."

The giant roared. Its tongue trailed out if its mouth.

"Oh shit!" Liz tried to move but she was too late.

SWIRL! The tongue wrapped her up and pulled her towards its mouth.

Montel zoomed in on her squeezed tits. *Oh fuck!*

"Help!" Kelly shouted.

Steph bounced a path around the giant. *Where's an opening?*

Ginger got tangled in the dying mutants' bodies that were bleeding out.

The giant tried to stomp her with its foot.

"Ginger watch out," Liz yelled.

She rolled out of the way. The giant's foot came down hard, stretching the springs.

Dammit, Liz looked at the large teeth. *Fuck, its gonna' eat me!*

"LADIES!" Montel entered the park. His robe was open, and he sported a white banana hammock with a wet spot on the crotch. "Come 'n get it Big Boy," he said, a cigar hung from his black lips.

Montel held two huge sci fi guns.

"Montel!" the girls shouted, glad to see him.

"Yeah babe-eez, looks like you needed some reinforcement." That bad-ass fired those guns.

CLAKKK! CLAKK! CLAKK!

His rounds tore into the creature's legs.

The tongue released Liz. She yanked that chainsaw to life and, BRRRRRR! Open the chest cavity of the giant mutant as she fell.

SLUSH!

Its organs, blood, and stomach acid retched out.

Ginger screamed.

SPLAT!

She stood up. The gore coated her head and body. "Thank guys, geez." She shook off. Her tits wobbled wildly.

Kelly was released too and fell.

Montel kept firing, "Take that ugly bitch!" The sci fi rounds tore into the thing's face making a pulpy mess.

Steph moved around the soggy trampolines and ended the lives of the remains mutants with the teeth of her chainsaw.

Click... Click... "Outta' bullets." Montel joined them on the trampolines. "Ain't gonna' be no on left here in this town, huh?"

Steph looked at the dead mutant children and their parents, "Nope; looks like it'll be a ghost town here for a while."

"Government's comin' to clean up?" Kelly asked.

"Soon as I call 'em. Now, let's get you ladies back to the ship and cleaned you gals up."

The girls looked at one another.

Blood and chucky soup splattered their sleek bodies.

"Come on girls, "Motel said as he walked towards the door, "The shower orgy ain't gonna' start itself!"

And-

-they went back to the ship where they had a rowdy orgy.

THE END :)

CHARLES
IS
CHARGED

Bridget Chase

CHARLES
IS CHARGED
Bridget Chase

A Mere Mortal

Scott Baio was strapped down to a table.

A doctor filled a syringe.

Scott had been charged on murder and was about to find out what happens after death.

Lethal injection, shit; fuck, fuck; I'm scared; I didn't kill them; this cant' be happening.

His mind rolled in a violent tsunami.

Two armed guards stood by the door.

A two-way mirror was the main feature in the stark room.

On the other side, were unknown people watching the execution.

How can they watch me die? I'm innocent!

"I'm innocent," he said.

The two guards held stern faces. One said, "That's what they all say."

"No, Charles; you are guilty," the doctor said with a sinister grin. He was a bald man with no facial hair and smooth skin. *Ah, that about does it.* He squirted poison from the end of the syringe.

"It's best you accept your actions. You're going to see the lord today."

"Dammit, I told you my name is Scott. Fuck, Charles was just a character I played and the Pembrokes were a fictional family. None of this makes any sense."

One of the guards stormed over.

"You psychotic piece of shit! I saw what you did to those girls and her paren-,"

The other guard hurried over and placed a hand on the guard's shoulder, "Let it go. This guy is getting what he deserves. Come on, people are watching."

"You're right."

The two guards went back to the door. The upset guard sniffed and wiped a tear away.

"Any last words?" the doctor asked. He held the syringe to the bulging vein on Scott's forearm.

Last words?

His racing heart and mind fired like fireworks making any rational thought impossible.

Scott's lips moved but no sound came out.

"Fine; Charles you are hereby being put to death by lethal injection for the murder of the Pembroke family. May God have mercy upon your soul."

Scott whimpered. "I'm not Charles."

KA-BOOM!

What Friends Are For?

Scott thought that was it. The leaving of the world was like an explosion.

"Charles, It's me; Charles?"

Scott opened his eyes.

I can't see!

From the haze, emerged a face.

"Charles it's me Buddy; Buddy Lembeck."

"William Aames?"

"No, Buddy; come on. I'm getting outta' here."

The shackles on Charles' wrists were removed.

The ones on his ankles were then loosened.

Scott sat up.

Smoke from the explosion filled the room.

BEEP, BEEP, BEEP!

A sudden shower of rain was released.

"Come on," Buddy said; he helped Scott off the table.

COUGH! A guard on the ground moaned and rolled over.

The double mirror was blown out. Everyone on the other side, had fled.

"What's happening, William? Why are you here?"

Buddy helped Charles through the broken two-way mirror.

"WHOA!" Charles stopped.

A woman stood there wearing dark sleek tactical gear and held an assault rifle.

"Easy, she's with us," Buddy said.

"This way, I got a clear path," the woman said. She was devastatingly beautiful. Like a real knockout- brunette hair, a lean athletic build, and eyes that kill; but the giant assault rifle was what really kills.

"She's amazing," Scott said.

Buddy said, "I know that's Firefox."

BOOOM!

A flash and then smoke.

(COUGH) "Maybe not. Fuck, we were followed," Firefox said, "Move."

With a hand she pushed them against the wall next to the door.

CLAKK-CLAKKK!

POP, SNAP! Bullet ate the door frame.

Splintered fragments flew.

Firefox crouched and leaned her back to the wall.

A break in gunfire.

She leaned out.

KA-KA-KA-KAKKK!

The muzzle flashes lit the smoke.

The gunfire was returned.

"Here." Firefox held out an uzi for Buddy.

He took it, "What do I do?"

"Lay down fire above my head. I'm going in."

Going in, who is this chick? Scott wondered. *I nearly pissed myself and she is going in? Is any of this happening? I must be dead.*

Buddy nodded.

In a low crouch, Firefox disappeared thought he door and into the smoke.

Buddy stood and aimed high.

BRAA-KA-KA-KA-KK!

Hot rounds flew down the hall.

Firefox stayed low; she pulled a nasty knife from her leg sheath.

The popping light guided her.

There one is.

She could see an elbow sticking around the corner.

I don't know how many there are.

She was about to find out.

Firefox grabbed the exposed arm.

She tore around the corner and right as the guy was gasping, STAB! She shoved the knife up-under the soldier's helmet and under his chin.

The guy screamed in a quick pitch and then was silent. The sharp end of the knife popped out on of his eyes, POP!

Firefox spun in a ballet of practiced death.

Three other guards were startled and raised their guns.

She, STAB! Drove the blade into the first guy's groin. He howled. Still moving, SLICE! Tore the grisly blade across the next guy's neck.

Scott heard the men scream, "She's butchering them!"

"That's Firefox for ya'," Buddy said, "I was lucky to get her aboard this mission. Her services costed five million dollars."

"Holy shit, how'd you pay her?"

Buddy leaned out and peered down the hall.

A last dying scream resounded.

He slid back next to Charles. "Ah, it was this whole thing where me, and my buddies, robbed a bunch of casinos and such. I think they made a couple movies based off our heists."

Wow, is Buddy really a kick ass casino robber? Or am I in some afterlife?

"We're clear," Firefox yelled down the hall.

"Good, let's get you outta' here, buddy," Buddy said.

"Geez, and go where? I'm a convicted murderer."

The Quantum Conundrum

"Thanks," Scott said to the waitress.

"Isn't this place great?" Firefox asked. "I always come eat here after I kill people."

"Yeah, sure is," Buddy said. He popped a salty fried pickle into his eager mouth; followed by a big swig of cold beer.

The waitress set down burger and fries in front of each of them.

Scott picked up the beer. It was frothy and super cold. SWIG, "Oh that's good. Especially because like an hour ago I thought I was going to die 'n shit."

The three sat at a small table in the dive restaurant.

Scott had a beer mustache on his baby smooth upper lip. "So. what's the plan? How did I get framed for murder? And how do I know I'm really not dead and this is some strange fake reality?"

Firefox popped a delicious, salty fried pickles into her beautiful mouth. She smiled cheerfully as him, "Oh, you're not dead. This is real. If it weren't you wouldn't have flinched at the gunfire."

"Hmm."

Buddy chimed in, "I'm not sure who did this but anyone that frames my best friend should die." He took a bite of the burger. Cheese and grease dripped onto the wax wrapper. CHEW CHEW! "I do have an idea of who done it."

"Yeah, who is that?"

WIPE! Buddy smeared a napkin across his mouth. "Well, I don't know their name, but I suspect it was an one armed man."

Scott rolled his eyes, "Oh, Buddy."

"What, its true. A man missing a limb is up to no good. Science, bitch!"

Firefox butted in, "Is there someone from your past who might have done this to you?"

Scott was staring at her cleavage. Twin compact, springy mounds held tight by her combat jumpsuit. *Damn, could those tits be any prettier? Maybe this is heaven?*

Firefox, played by Amy Acker, noticed; she didn't say anything.

"Um," Scott Baio thought a moment. "No, no one comes to mind. Everyone pretty much adored me."

"Hey look," Buddy said. "That guy over at the table."

He pointed to some old man with a large grey speckled beard wearing a slicker, like a fisherman.

"Yeah," Scott said.

"He looks bad. I'm going to check him out," Buddy said. He got up from the table and went to the bartender. He said something. The bartender pulled out a long samurai sword from behind the bar. Buddy thanked him.

"What's he doing?" Scott asked Firefox.

She sipped her ice-cold beer, "Probably nothing good."

"Hey, old man," Buddy said

The fisherman turned, "Huh?"

SLICE! Buddy brought the blade down.

CHOP! SCREAM! The fisherman howled. His chopped off arm fell onto the table and then on to the floor. Blood sprayed from the severed shoulder. It sprayed the people sitting at nearby tables.

"I got him," Buddy shouted to Scott. He had a big 'ol gin on his face.

Blood and dark matter pelted the ground in rhythmic spurts like a heartbeat.

Firefox turned away from the scene and asked, "You sure you don't know who did this?"

"Nope." Scott said. He pinched a few French fires and dipped them in ketchup.

People gathered around the fisherman and applyed towels to the stop the bleeding, a few people called 911, Buddy stood smiling.

"Well, what do you think about that guy?" she asked and gestured towards the bar.

Scott looked, "HOLY SHIT!"

A man stood behind the bar. He held a bow with a flaming arrow knocked and aimed at Scott. The man was Charles.

"It's me!"

Scott dropped under the table.

Firefox kicked back her chain and stood. THWOOM! She tore a pistol outta' its holster and took aim.

The people in the dive restaurant screamed. Chairs flew, and people ran for the door.

THWAK! The arrow was released.

It missed Scott and TING! Stuck in the jukebox.

The jukebox jumped to life and Abba's 'Dancing Queen' came on.

"How is that me? I don't get it," Scott said.

Buddy huddled with him. "Yeah, and he has two arms? Mysterious...,"

Firefox aimed.

"Do it," Charles shouted, he lowered his bow.

Damn, I was framed by some copy of myself. I have to do something, Scott stood up. "Stop!" *Hopefully I can reason with him. I mean, Charles is a nice guy, I'm a nice guy, I mean were a nice guy.*

"Why did you set me up?" Scott asked.

Charles vaulted the bar's counter. "Me? What about you? You set *me* up!"

"I did no such thing; take it back!"

"Are those burgers?" Charles asked.

"Yeah."

"Think I can I have one? I mean I feel like I haven't eaten in days."

"Um.. okay."

The four sat down at the table.

They ate burgers and fries in relative silence.

The bartender had his foot up on the juke box and tried to pull the arrow out.

"Cheers," Charles said.

The group, CLINKED! Their glasses together.

The burgers were eaten, and baskets cleaned.

Firefox wiped her mouth with her napkin "So, what's happening with the two of you? How do you both exist?"

"Yeah, and I want to know which one of you is my best friend?" Buddy asked.

Charles and Scott looked at one another.

"One of you say something," Firefox said

"Well, first off I'm not Charles. My name is Scott," Charles said.

Scott looked at him perplexed. "No, I'm Scott; you're Charles."

"No, I played Charles in a tv show. My name is Scott, Scott Baio."

"Wait," Buddy said, "Scott what's all this Scott stuff? both of you are Charles and I'm your best friend."

"I'm confused," Firefox said.

"Look, Scott said, "I was framed for murdering a family that doesn't exist. I don't know how this happened; Buddy, who doesn't know he is William, saved me from death, and now I see you."

"I was framed too," Charles said.

"So, both of you are Scott?" Firefox asked.

Buddy rubbed his head. "There must be some better explanation."

"There is," Charles said, "You said you were saved from death row? I wasn't!"

Gasp! Firefox covered her mouth.

Every one looked at her

"Sorry; that was just surprising."

Scott asked, "What do you mean you weren't saved?"

"They killed me. The doctor injected me and I got really sleepy-,"

Scott, Buddy, and Firefox exchanged looks.

Charles continued, "-Yeah, they fuckin killed me. Or at least, I thought they did. I woke up in a nearby cemetery under a tree."

"Lee Park?" Buddy asked.

"Yeah, I was confused; so, I headed home. That's when I saw you guys. You came in here and I thought, shit if anyone was responsible for setting me up, it would be a twin or clone, or whatever you are-,"

"-So, I bought a bow 'n arrow, down the street, and was going to take you out. Well, not you Buddy; you're my best friend."

"Interesting," Firefox said.

"Yeah, interesting," Scott said, "So, now there are two of me?"

Charles looked at him.

"Two of us; two of *us*. And, we still don't know why I was on death row? Or, how the fuck both of us exist?"

Charles squirted ketchup over some hot fries, "Yep, guess not; it's a mystery all right."

The lights dimmed.

"What's this now?" Scott asked.

A deep Synthwave song stole the air.

BOOM! The restaurant door flew open.

The heavy beat introduced a man in rhythmic movements.

Dry ice rolled the floor and a man on roller skates entered. He did some disco dance number.

A disco ball dropped from the ceiling and lit the interior with the psychedelic flavors of the 70's.

"It can't be," Scott said.

Charles' jaw dropped open, "A third one?"

The third Scott came up to the table, "Hey guys-,"

No one said anything.

"-You guys are both here because if a rip in the 'time space' that separates parallel worlds."

"Whazza?" Buddy asked.

The new Disco Baio did some 'Stayin Alive' finger pointing and hip thrusts as he spoke. "Yeah, that's how I'm here too. You see, I was sentenced for murdering a fictional family; but unlike you guys, I was pardoned by the mayor at the final moments. He was a huge fan of Happy Days and some shit."

Scott crumpled his napkins and tossed it on his plate. "Dammit, this is all well and good, but this doesn't provide any answers to why we were all framed."

Disco Baio shook his feathered hair and skated in backward circles. "I came for more than confusion. I do have answers."

"Well?" Charles asked. *Damn, I don't look too bad in that disco white jumpsuit. Might have to hop on Amazon and buy me one. He pulled out his phone and BING! Added that shit to his cart. PRIME MEMBER BITCH!* 'Saturday Night fever jumpsuit on the way to your door.'

"Stay here," Disco Baio said, "The answers are coming." He skated over to the bartender.

The bartender was some hairy looking Ben Affleck guy.

Disco Baio leaned over the counter an the two shared a passionate kiss with an excessive amount of tongue.

"Yuck," Scott grimaced. He looked over at Charles.

Charles shrugged his shoulders.

Disco Baio wiped the saliva off his lip with his forearm.

With a cheery smile the bartender changed the tv channel.

Disco Baio came back to the table. He did some finger gun dance moves at the people he passed.

The bartender stopped on a new tv channel.

A dark electronic-rhythm wrapped the atmosphere.

"Joanie," Scott said.

"Yes, Joanie," Disco Baio said.

Her picture was on the news.

The new reporter commented with a plastic face, "Joanie from beloved show Joanie loves Chachi and spin off of Happy Days; is a wanted fugitive."

Firefox ordered up a round on shots.

"Joanie was last seen at the Seven Eleven on Clint and Bartid. She is wanted in connection to a series of grisly murders; ohhhh."

The news cut to a black bitch crying, "I just don't know what happened; that crazy ass white woman just came in and started choppin' people up. Oh, my poor Phil. Phil! Oh god Phil, go to the light honey. You here me? Go to the LIGHT!" The woman sobbed.

A blonde reported stepped and pushed the woman out of screen. "I'm here at the horrific scene. It would seem our beloved and cherished actress has been traveling on a murderous rampage."

The report cut to a picture of Joanie. They put devil horns on her head and fire as the background with a cackling laugh.

Cut back to the new anchor. "If anyone sees, or has any information 'bout her where 'bouts, please contact the police immediately. Joanie is very cranky and very dangerous. Do not approach her. Kimmy Snuggler reporting."

"This is nuts," Buddy said, "Why on earth would she kill the Pembrokes? They were the nicest family, ever!"

"And for that matter," Firefox added, "Kill them in multiple worlds?"

"I don't know," Scott said.

"Me either," Charles said.

Disco Baio smiled, "Well, for answers to that, boys; we's gotta' do a little traveling."

He turned from the table and shouted, "Waitress, we're gonna' need some to go boxes; oh, and refills all around." He pointed to their drinks.

Turning back to the group he said, "You all ready to get freaky? I know she is."

He pointed to Firefox.

Why'd he point at me? She wondered.

Freezer of Time

"Is this *really* how we'll travel to the parallel world where Joanie is hiding?" Firefox asked.

She was topless eating ice cream.

The guys were shirtless and eating ice cream too.

Charles, Scott, and Buddy tired not to drool over her great tits. They each snuck glances.

SLURP! Disco Baio took a big 'ol lick. "Well, the ice cream and being topless, no. That's just 'cause we need to lower our core body temperature. I thought this was the best way because we are traveling through an interdimensional gateway inside this Baskin Robbins' freezer."

"Co-oool!" Buddy said. "Yeah I'm certainly glad for this body cooling thing." *Will you look at them titties, VROOM! YABBA DABBA HUBBA HUBBA!*

"Oh, oops," Firefox said.

Some ice cream dripped onto her chest.

Oh my! GIMME, GIMME! 'Ol Scotty boy wants a lick.

"Silly me." Firefox wiped the drip of ice cream off her tit. "Oh, it's getting away." The drop rolled down to her nipple. "Geez making a mess here." She used a napkin and dabbed at her nipple.

Blood dripped from, Scott, Charles, and Buddy's noses.

Disco Baio, SMACK! Clapped Scott on the back. "Everyone eat up. We's gots to go!"

Scott, Charles and Buddy ate their cones. Tents were pitched in their pants.

Firefox licked her beautiful, soft lips. "That was good."

The guys nodded.

Disco Baio called to the Baskin Robbins ice cream guy. "Good sir!"

He was a young, seventeen-year-old pimple. His phone out and he recorded Firefox.

"Good man! (cough) Excuse me!"

"Huh?" The worker looked at Disco Baio.

"We will be in need of your quantum paradoxical freezer."

The boy looked confused. "Sure; uh, whatever you want." He lifted his phone back up.

"Oh, would you look at that." Several drops dripped down Firefox's tits tracing the contours. She wiped them with away her finger, put her finger in her mouth, made a tight ring with her lips, and sucked them clean.

The Baskin Robbins guy stepped aside.

Buddy tossed the last of his cone in the trash.

The group walked behind the counter and to the back.

Disco Baio skated to the freezer door. "Ready to bend space, and travel to a new universe?"

"Yeah, yep; sure guess so," they said and nodded to each other.

The teenage ice cream worked stood in the doorway recording.

I Came for Revenge

"Well, that was easy and quick," Buddy said.

They walked out of the freezer. Dry ice spilled out the door and led the way. The freezer opened to a subway station underground. Tons of people milled about. Hardly anyone noticed the random two-dimensional steel door gateway with people coming out

"You bet, and what about the outfits?" Disco Baio asked.

Everyone looked at themselves.

Scott wore-

-*Wait, I look like . . .*

-he wore brown suit like Napoleon Dynamite and had a blonde curly wig on.

Charles new outfit was, *a sweet number,* "HOT DAMN! I'm dressed as Cobra Commander!"

"Hey what's the big idea?" Buddy was dressed as Popeye the sailor-

"-Woman? Why do I have tits?"

He pulled the low-cut top away from his chest. "Hmm, okay; maybe this isn't so bad."

"Captain hook?" Firefox asked.

"And, a sexy one at that," Scott said.

Firefox extended her leg and looked at the thigh high leather boot below her short red skirt. "Who came up with these outfits anyways?" She asked

Disco Baio was dressed like Elvis "Mysteries of time travel. You get all sorts of outfits comin' out the other end."

"So, where to?" Scott asked, "Where do we find Joanie?"

"We don't," Disco Baio said. He wiped a thick curl of dark hair from his face. His sideburns looked like part of a helmet. "She... finds... us!"

"Hahaha, perfect," a woman laughed and said.

The crowds of people in the subway made a hasty exit like they were actors on a stage production.

"Good, you brought them."

A woman walked the parting wave of people.

"Joanie?" Scott asked. "Wait, brought us? No!" He turned to Disco Baio. "Traitor!"

Disco Baio walked away from the group, "Sorry guys Chachi loves Joanie."

"Why would you do this?" Charles asked Joanie.

"Well, I did it for love," She said.

Disco Biao walked and stood beside her. He threw an arm over her shoulder, "Yeah bitches, love. Love for me!"

SHINK! Joanie pulled out a wicked sharp dagger and STAB!

"Oh god, why?" Disco Baio held his stomach.

TWIST YANK! Joanie ripped it out.

"Oh man, my guts!"

Hot intestines piled on the ground like wet noodles; bloody wet thick noodles.

Disco Baio fainted, twitched, and died.

"WHOA! Are you nuts lady?" Buddy asked, "That wasn't cool at all! No way, no how. I had myself three best friends, you murdering bitch!"

"Thank ya', thank ya' very much," Disco Baio said; and then died, like for real this time.

Someone stated a slow clap. A man walked out of the shadows.

"Fonzie?" Scot asked, "I should have known."

The Fonz wore a one-zie that looked like Tigger (Winnie the Pooh).

"We have a problem," Firefox said.

Twenty men with flaming faces entered from the darkness beyond.

"Hey those are-," buddy said.

Charles picked up, "You; they're you. Well, you, if you were like a bad-ass Ghost Rider 'n shit. Damn, you look good in leather with a flamin' face; scary."

"Ya' see," Fonzie said, "You fucked up Happy Days and the chance of a spin off. Your ass is grass, man. And, you never loved Joanie enough. She's a special lady. Needs to be loved right."

"So, you're just going to kill me, and Charles? Is that it?" Scott asked.

"More than that," Joanie said. She snapped her finger.

The walls with dark tubes rolled away on wheel like a theater set being changed during a dropped curtain.

"HOLY-," Scott said.

"SHIZZ-," Charles said.

"NIT-," Buddy said.

"Murder balls," Firefox said.

With the walls moved, there was revealed a large room. It looked like that fuckin laboratory where they had that Stargate in the movie-

-stay with me here, Stargate.

"You killed thousands of me," Scott said.

Littered on the ground were thousands of murdered Scott Baios. Each, now a lifeless corpse swimming in retched blood and organs.

"Yes, and now I'm down to the last two of you." Joanie said with a very happy grin.

"Yeah, the last two's of you's," Fonzie said.

Oh, wait; I haven't said what Joanie wore. She wore; let's see-

-oh, she wore a poison ivy outfit. Like Poison Ivy if she were pin up doll. Heck, for fun let's make the green outfit painted on, and-

-yeah, Fonzie was cupping her painted tits while they explained all this shit.

Not sure you really care; so, lets turbo charge this shit and get to the battle…

Battle with the Flaming Buddies

"We can't be wiped out of existence," Charles said. "If we're killed we have no idea what the ramifications could be!"

"We won't be," Scott Baio said, "Sorry bitch, but you's about to die."

Firefox took a fighting stance. Her one hook hand gleamed.

"Let's put a stop to this and then get tacos," Buddy the Popeye the sailor woman said. He adjusted his tits and skirt, and then, put his fists up. *Shit, even my nails are painted. But, I'm bald too; this is weird.*

"Attack!" Joanie shouted.

The Ghost Rider Buddys charged.

"Oh, shit," Buddy said

A Ghost Rider whipped a flaming chain at him.

He ducked

THWAK! It cut the air above his head.

"Uh, help!"

"One minute, Buddy," Scott said. He dodged a chain and POW! Punched a Ghost Rider in the face, SIZZLE! "Ouch! Fucker." His knuckles smoked.

POW! Scott caught a fist in the jaw and staggered back. His Napoleon Dynamite glasses came off when his ass bounced off the ground.

"I can't take this guy," Charles said. He was being pummeled on the ground.

A ghost rider was fuckin' him up. Luckily, Charles had the Cobra Commander gear; so, the actual damage was minimal.

Firefox was whipping ass. SLING, POW! She kicked, flipped, STAB! And spun.

Ghost Riders were knocked to the ground "Sorry Buddy Ghost rider," STOMP! She crushed it skull with her boot.

"What's this?" Buddy felt something between his tits

"NO!" Joanie shouted; she knew the power of what was discovered.

Buddy pulled out a can of Spinach, "Ak kaka kaka!" He tore the lid off and squeezed the can. Green boiled-shit arced in the air and into his mouth.

Scott blocked attacks, "Go BUDDY! GO!"

"Well blow me down!" Buddy's forearms and tits grew huge. "I'm Popeye the sailor woman," TOOT TOOT! He blew steam outta' his pipe.

The Ghost Riders stopped; their flaming eyes grew large. SNAP CRAKC! They twirled those chains of marvel 'n magic.

SOCK, POW, WHAM! Buddy came in with big 'ol powerful fists. "Sorry parallel world buddies." SMASH! "I don't know why you helped Joanie, but-," BLAM! "Take that."

The Ghost Riders flew like roster feathers in a cock fight, BEKAH!

"I'll take Tigger," Firefox said, "You take Joanie."

Scott and Charles cracked their knuckles in unison. They charged.

Firefox ran at Tigger.

The Fonz bounced around on his orange tail and laughed. "You can't catch-,"

Firefox did a low spin kick. The camera caught a up-skirt shot of her black panties.

"WOOPS" Fonzie fell to his back.

He punched wildly.

"Bring it," Joanie said.

Scott punched.

Joanie dodged, BLOCK! She stopped Charles' attack, KICK, POW!

"ARG!" Charles held his stomach.

CLOCK! Scott caught her upside the head with his fist.

She snarled Bastard, "You'd hit me, Joanie?"

"Well yeah; shit, you've killed me thousands of times."

And then Scott had an idea. *Baio magic!*

"I summon the power of all the dead Baios from each corner of the cosmos. Come into my body!" Scott put his arms out.

A ghostly green Scott Baio face appeared above them all.

It said, "You'd call upon the universal of the Biao life force?"

"Yes," Scott said; "Me too." Charles said.

"So, shall it be," the ghostly apparition said.

Some 90's morning tv show music started playing.

The dead Baios rose off the ground. Green energy was pulled from each of their chests.

"Oh shit," Joanie said.

CRACK! Firefox rang Fonzie's head off the cement floor. She looked up, "WICKED!"

UPPER CUT! Buddy sent the last ghost rider flying.

The phantom energy funneled into a large dragon. It flew over to Scott and Charles and then descended into their bodies.

Their muscles bulged, and shirts lost their sleeved. Their outfits changed to that of the double dragons.

HIGH FIVE! Their palms smacked!

"Let's get her," Scott said.

Joanie looked over at the Fonz, "Damn." Firefox had him pinned. *My love…* She reached a hand out to him.

Joanie turned back to Scott and Charles. "I'll get you, my pretties, and your little Buddy, too," she said. "Oh, also, you'll pay; and you'll never know the love of these titties, no sir." She put her arms over her head and swung her tits around. "See them girls dance; well, never for you, no!"

"Wow," buddy said; his eyes locked on those bouncing grapefruits. *Oh, so delicious.* "Maybe I can see why the other me-s followed her."

She threw a smoke bomb, POOF! And vanished like the tv show Joanie loves Chachi.

Scott and Charles looked at their hands.

Scott said, "We have so much power, what should we do with it?"

Charles flexed a bulging bicep, "We should do something that benefits the world, suppose."

"Well," Firefox said and approached, "You guys do what you want, I got an email from the CIA, a new mish."

Buddy strolled up, "I think we should tie these guys up and leave them for the cops, like batman; and then, hop back through 'dat portal, so I'm not a woman anymore."

Scott and Charles agreed.

Buddy took a last look down his top. *Slimpy biscuits, I'll miss thee.* They are mighty pretty.

"So, that settles it," Scott said.

The group went back to the two-dimensional door.

Party at Chili's

Firefox talked to the bartender.

Scott came up behind her and tapped her on the shoulder. She turned and then wore a big grin.

The two hugged.

Scott placed an order for drinks and gestured with his finger saying, all around.

Buddy came in. He wore a real Popeye costume.

The three hugged and Firefox commented about him not having tits.

Buddy laughed.

Joanie came over and covered Scott's eyes with her hands. He guessed a few times and then she removed them. He turned and smiled. Joanie kissed him on the cheek.

Firefox placed a hand on Joanie's shoulder and made a comment, and then laughed hysterically.

Joanie shrugged her shoulder.

Charles entered Chili's and the group greeted him with a shout.

He came over and receive claps on the back from everyone.

The Ghost Rider buddies, the doctor and the guards from death row came in.

Scott handed them beers. He shook the doctors hand and they all had a laugh.

A bunch of other Scotts strolled in all casual with cheerful demeanors. They still wore the bloody makeup and special effects. Behind them came the phantom Biao head, as well as Disco Baio. He still wore his roller skates and did some disco moves over to the bar.

The last to enter was the jukebox. Charles came up to it and tired to pull the arrow out. The jukebox gave him a friendly pat on the shoulder and they walked to the bar.

Drinks were handed out and then a hot ass waitress brought an appetizer sampler tray.

They each eagerly grabbed some food.

Beers were kicked back, laughs had, and good food eaten.

Buddy tried to pick up the hot waitress but she waived him off, instead going for-

Fonzy walked in the door.

The group turned and raised their beer mugs in a cheer.

END

Bridget Chase

Eighty Fists of DEATH

EIGHTY FISTS OF DEATH
Bridget Chase

Jessica Biel

"Jessica Biel's been kidnapped! Sweet Jesus. Jean Claude! Jean Claude!"

Jean Claude climbed out from under the upstairs sink. "What you want Granny?" he shouted.

His old grandma shouted at him from downstairs. "Jessica Biel's been kidnapped. Once you're done fixin' that sink, I think we should go do something. She's such a sweet girl, don't ya' think?"

Jean Claude put down his wrench. He got up and went to the top of the stairs. His granny looked up to him from the first floor.

She was old, like eighty, with a purple sundress, big 'ol thick glasses, knobby legs, drooping cheeks and hair like Van Damme in 'Time Cop', except white. Well, really, she looked a lot like Van Damme if he were eighty, wearing a dress, and had lipstick smearing a wide ring around his lips.

"We can't do anything Granny; best to leave it to the police," he said.

"Those police won't do nothing, shee-it. Did I raise a Jean Claude, or did I raise a Van Damme?"

"Grandma, that doesn't make any sense." He gripped the banister railing. *Shit, what does she think we can do?*

Granny Damme started to cry. "It's Jessica Biel, she's beautiful, lovely, such a sweetheart, and in the hands of a madman."

"How do you know it's a madman?"

"Because of this!" Granny Damme whipped out a newspaper from behind her back.

"I can't see it," Jean Claude said, "I'm coming down." FLIP! He somersaulted the banister and fell a story to the ground "Umph!" Jean Claude took the paper from her.

The headline read: Jessica Biel, God's reason for creating the world, has been kidnapped.

There was also a picture of the suspect.

"STEVEN SEAGAL!" ROAR! Van Damme crushed the newspaper into a little ball in his hands. "That fucker!" he tossed the wad and, SPIN! THWAK! Spin kicked the crumpled paper. It went flying into the kitchen and landed in a pile of other wadded up newspapers.

"Hey, I wasn't done reading that" Granny Damme said.

"I'm done with these ridiculous stories involving Steven Seagal. Just let the police handle it."

Granny Damme sighed, "Oh, Jessica; you poor beautiful thang."

Jean Claude climbed the stairs. "I'm gonna' finish fixing your sink and then we can have a nice lunch."

"Grilled cheese?"

"Sure, grilled cheese. Now please, forget about this nonsense."

"I can never forget Jessica Biel, never. She's such a sweet girl," she said under her breath.

Granny Damme went to the coat closet. She opened the door buried herself inside and rummaged the top shelf. "There they are."

She pulled down a shoe box.

Granny Damme cradles the shoebox in her hands and went to the living room. She sat down on the plastic covered couch and placed the box in her lap.

She opened the lid.

A pair of worn out sneakers were inside.

"It's been a long time, fellas; but looks like I need my ass kicking shoes, again."

Oh That Ponytail

"Dance with me."

"This is weird," Jessica Biel said. She was tied to a chair.

Steven Seagal held her ponytail in his arms. "I thought I lost you forever, my love." He rubbed the hair against his cheek. "How did you wind up on her head of all people? Oh, it doesn't matter I'm just glad to have you back. You're so pretty... yes, you are...,"

The hair said nothing.

"Seriously, just let me go. I won't press charges," Jessica said.

"Hush, I'm trying to enjoy this reunion. It might not be important to you; but I've waited decades to find my ponytail again."

"Ouch!" Jessica's head was yanked.

Steven hugged her ponytail too his chest and swayed like it was a lover.

"Now that I found you, I'll never let you go. We can be together forever!"

Steven imagined his ponytail in a white gown. *Oh. wouldn't it be grand.*

How great it would be giving his vows to his pony tail and then slipping a ring onto the strands of hair.

Forever...

"Ouch, easy," Jessica said. "Just cut it off and let me go. It will grow back. You can have it."

Steven dropped the gathered hair. "Cut it off? Are you crazy? My ponytail is a living thing. No, we'll just have to figure out how to manage this relationship. I'm thinking I'll have you put into a medically induced coma."

"A what?" Jessica's eyes went wide. "You can't!"

Steven picked back up the hair. He petted it. "We'll see. Either way, it would be best for you to be unconscious when I take my ponytail to bed tonight. Old Steven's getting horny, baby!" He smiled cheerfully.

Jessica peered over her shoulder.

Below Steven's hefty gut was a tent pitched in his pants. It pushed out on his oriental robe thing.

Yuck!

The bloated actions star swayed. "Hey, Short Round, why don't you go ahead and buy us tickets for a cruise this week. It's time to vacation with my love-," He kissed the ponytail. "-And kill the things I hate."

Steven glared over at his captives.

Bruce Willis, Dwayne Johnson and Sinead 'O Connor were tied and gagged and lay in a pile together in the corner. They smelled of piss and shit.

Those bastards! Killers of magical ponytails. Yes, they will die at the bottom of the ocean!

"Sure tang Mr. Jones... I mean Mr. Sa'gal," Short Round said- the Asian kid from Indiana Jones and the Temple of Doom. He swiveled around in his office chair- cheap office chair- and typed on the computer. *Oh, I hope he w'ewease me after this ow'er. He not fun to work fow as Mr. Jones. Nope, Mr. Jones nevew make me scwub back or ass.*

"Soon, my life will be complete," Steven said, "Oh, and Short Round. Find out how to induce a coma with drugs, would ya?"

"Sure tang Mr. Sa'gal!

Jessica hung her head.

"No you're the cutie," Steven said to the hair, "No you are!" He tickled the hair with a fat finger.

Craigslist

Granny Damme listed an ad in the personals section on Craigslist.

Woman seeking man.

The ad stated that she was in need of a new grandson. One that would help in retrieving Jessica Biel from the arms of a madman.

Adventurous type, a must.

Granny Damme pushed her glasses up her nose and waited.

Refresh…

Refresh…

Refresh…

She was impatient to get an email response.

I hope it will be someone strong and manly.

DING DONG!

Why, who could that be?

Granny Damme got up from her pink chair.

Oh, how lovely to have a visitor.

BANG! BANG! BANG!

"Impatient assholes aren't they?" she asked her cat Kurt Wussels.

She shambled to the door.

"Oh, dear me, Justin Timberlake?"

"Yes ma'am, I'm sorry to bother you; did you by chance hear the news?"

"Oh, yes I did."

Granny Damme wiped the front of her sundress trying to make herself more presentable.

"Your wife has been kidnapped."

"Yes, ma'am." Tears built in his eyes. Justin started sobbing with a hand covering his mouth.

"Oh, there, there." She patted his back.

Justin cried hard. He was bent over with hands on his knees.

Granny Damme asked, "So, what can i do for you?"

BING! He stood up, nose and eyes dry. "Why yes, I was hoping to enlist the help of your grandson; I need Van Damme's services in ass kickery. I went by his mom's house and she said that he was here, fixing your sink."

"Oh, you met my daughter. Isn't she just a peach?"

"No, ma'am, she was a woman, but very sweet indeed. Anyways-," Justin leaned in and tried to look inside, "Is Van Damme here?"

"Oh, yes come on in." Granny Dame stepped aside.

-Long story short...

"Yep, too bad Van Damme wouldn't help but between the three of us, I think we can save Jessica," Justin said. He sat in the passenger seat.

"Oh, we'll save her. Hell, every mish I've had with Kurt Wussels turns out okay."

Granny Damme steered the vehicle. "It's pretty cool you have the Thunder Cats vehicle."

The vehicle was a steel number with a cat face, open cockpit, and huge paws coming off the front. Its tank-treads tore up the freeway and its body consumed several lanes.

Cars swerved and crashed. People screamed and swerved their vehicles. Smoke and fire littered the freeway behind them.

Granny Damme steered with one hand. Kurt Wussels rode on her shoulder. The open air whipped at his fur.

Justin shouted over the wind, "I got a hot tip that Seagal is taking Jessica on a cruise ship. I was thinking we can jump him there."

"Good idea," Granny Damme said. "I brought my bikini, so this will work out perfectly."

"So, take this puppy to the docks and get us some tickets to board?" Justin asked.

Granny Damme nodded.

The Pelican Spy

There she is. Hmm, guess she is going to try and wreck Steven's ponytail vacation murder plot.

The large pelican flew above the Thunder Cats vehicle.

Shit, that freeway is fucked!

Tobey Maguire beat his wings.

The feathers were falling off and the bird beak barley stayed on his face.

This is dumb. Why am I a pelican? Shit, I should have known better than to sign up with this movie.

But he was a pelican and his oversized humorous costume proved it.

Damn, I can barely fly. This shit isn't safe.

Either way, he broke away from the chase and headed toward the luxury cruise liner to tell Steven about the complications to his plan.

And if I'm lucky, he'll pay me in fish. Raw fish. Wigglin' hoppin' raw fish.

Tobey Maguire licked his lips.

And there is was.

I'll just go land on the railin'; see if I can't spot Steven from there.

He fell in a turbulent descent.

I would have done better if my fuckin wings worked right.

His left arm had lost half its feathers. The raw cloth of the costume showed through.

And... LAND!

Tobey landed on the railing, but his momentum made him stumble forward and trip. He rolled across the deck.

Women in tight bikinis and oiled men grimaced.

"Fuck, that bird is diseased or something." A woman said. She carried a colorful drink, SIP! JUDGE!

"Yeah, I'll get rid of it," An athletic guy said.

"No, please!"

Tobey was kicked. "ARGH!" He slid under the railing and fell to the ocean, SPLASH!

Pool in the Ocean

"Look what we found, boss," a Tiger Man said. He was half human, half tiger, but really it was just a man wearing an oversized mascot head of a tiger.

Tiger Man held Tobey up by the feathers on the back of his neck. Next to them stood Lizard Man- same motif.

Steven Seagal removed his sunglasses. He sat in a lounge chair, Jessica by his side-bound, next to the pool. He had no shirt on and his paunch was offensive to the sun's rays.

"Pearl, by god! What's happened to you?"

Tobey was dripping wet.

"Shit some guy kicked me and I fell into the ocean. I nearly fucking drown. This suit isn't made for water and the fucking scuba team, to support the stunt, never showed up. I could have fuckin' died!"

Steven looked at Tiger Man. "I can't understand a word he is saying. Get me a translator. I need to know if Van Damme is on his way or not."

The Lizard Man nodded to a waiter. Like Tiger Man he was shirtless, wore flip flops, and colorful board shorts.

The waiter came over. "How can I help you?" he asked Steven. The server wore a rubber bird beak over his nose and mouth. The elastic string was visible.

Steven said, "I need you to translate this gawd forsaken bird's gibberish."

The waiter looked at Toby. "My what a mess."

Toby shrugged.

The Waiter Bird Man cleared his throat, "BEKAH!"

Tobey looked at him.

"BEKAH! The waiter tried again.

Toby turned to Steven, "Granny Damme, Van Damme's granny is on the way. She is with Justin Timberlake and a fierce cat. So, you better be on the lookout."

Steven looked up the the Waiter Bird Man.

"It would seem that this Pelican has a damaged vocal cord or something, but from what I can put together, there are people on their way that plan to stop you from killing Bruce Willis, Dwayne the Rock Johnson and Sinead 'O Conner; as well as rescue a captive."

Steven scratched his chin.

"Mnfnf," Jessica said through the gag. She lay on her side on the lounge chair wearing a hot bikini with her arms tied behind her back and ankles bound.

"Anything else you will be needing, sir?' the Waiter Bird Man asked.

"Ah, yes," Steven said, "That gentlemen there-," he pointed. "-What drink might that be?"

"Oh, that's a 'Murder on the Cruise Ship'; one of my personal favorites," the Waiter Bird Man said, "Would you like to order one."

"Sure," Steven said, "It sounds like the perfect drink for this vacation, MWUAHAHAH.... MWUAHAHHA... MWUAHAHAH!" He laughed maniacally and then glared at his henchmen.

Tiger Man and Lizard Man joined in "MWAUAHAHAH!"

The Waiter Bird Man joined in "MWUAHAHAH!"

Toby cackled, "MWUAHAHAHA!"

Everyone stopped.

Silence.

"Well, I'll have that right over," Waiter Bird Man said.

"Thanks," Steven said; he lowered his sunglasses and leaned back.

"What do we do with the bird?" Tiger Man asked.

"Hmm. Let me see."

Steven leaned over and spoke in whispers to Jessica's ponytail.

"Really?.. no... I suppose..."

He turned back to his henchmen.

"Kill him"

"What? Wait!" Tobey said. "No, no. CUT! CUT! Where's the fuckin director? CUT! CUT!"

Tiger Man and Lizard Man drug him away.

Tobey kicked and flailed. "I'm not really a bird. This is just a movie! It's a movie!... It's a movie-,"

"-Right?"

The Bikini Wax

"Well, you ready?" Granny Damme asked.

"One minute," Justin said from the bathroom.

Kurt Wussels sat on the bed. His hulking thighs were oiled, and he wore a colorful Hawaiian bandana around his neck. He was a buffed-up body building guy wearing a furry cat head. He wore a banana hammock and both, his skin and that, were airbrushed like cat fur. Earlier thought Kurt Wussels had been an ordinary cat.

Granny Damme petted his head. "Oh, isn't it just amazing we were able to get on this cruise ship, last minute? Oh yes, we were lucky; oh yes, we were!"

Kurt Wussels purred and leaned into her.

They had gotten a room and changed into suitable attire for an attack.

The bathroom door opened.

"Um, I don't think I can wear this," Justin said.

'Sure, you can. You look great," Granny Damme said.

Justin looked down at himself.

He wore a Robin costume. Like, the one from the sixty's with little green tights, elf shoes, a tight red shirt with yellow cape, and a little wee black mask.

"Perfect," Grandma Damme said.

She wore the Batman costume from the same tv series.

"I don't know. I mean; can't we stop Steven in normal clothes?" Justin fished his balls around the small green undies.

"No sir; now, no more complaining. These outfits will keep our identities a secret." Granny Damme adjusted her saggy tits under the thin spandex. They reached her yellow utility belt. "Now, let's get Jessica before it's too late; she is such a sweet girl, ya' know?"

"Okay," Justin said, "Where's the key card? I don't want to get locked out of our room."

Kurt Wussels walked up. The cat man held the card between his teeth. He was taller and bigger than Justin.

Justin took the card, patted him on the head. "Oh, you're such a good kitty, aren't you? Okay let's go!"

He opened the door.

"JUSTIN! Oh, my god, It's JUSTIN!" The women went all crazy.

He looked over at Granny Damme.

She shrugged her shoulders.

Raptor Attack

Steven Seagal sat in the driver's seat of the automated electric SUV. Jessica was curled on her side in the seat beside him tied up and gagged. Her ponytail laid across his thigh.

Tiger Man and Lizard man, Bruce Willis, Dwayne Johnson, and Sinead 'O Connor occupied the back seat.

Yeah, there were a lot of them back there and they were jammed tight. Especially, because Tiger Man was a hulking creature.

Anyways, a lush tropical forest surrounded them.

Steven looked at the small information brochure. "I can't believe they have a Jurassic Park on a cruise ship. How awesome is that, ponytail?"

The hair said nothing.

"Yeah, I should feed my enemies to the dinosaurs," Steven said, "Hell, I might even shit myself when I see the T-Rex. Oh, no baby. I'm just making a joke. You know 'ol

Steven ain't scared 'nuffin'. I told you how I was a real police officer before n' shit."

The automated green SUV began to speak in a woman's voice. "And on your left, we'll be stopping next to the raptor habitat. Raptors are vicious creatures born only to kill. If you have small children, you may roll down your windows down and lift them up to the roof for a better view. Oh, and in the trunk we have a cooler full of meat if anyone would enjoy BBQing during the tour. You'll find the electric grill inside the glove compartment.

Tiger man licked his lips. "Boss?"

"Sure thing, good fellow, go on," Steven said. "And if you all don't mind I think I'll close this privacy curtain that separates the front cabin from the rear; 'cause I'z 'bout to get freak-ie! Up in here."

Lizard man smiled. He rubbed Bruce Willis' thigh- too high up.

What's this about? Bruce tried to slide away.

YANK!

"Ah, now some privacy," Steven said.

Jessica grimaced.

Steven hefted his gut and fished for his fly. "Oh, there you are you Kung Fu monster, you. Yes, Ponytail is back. Oh, ponytail play with my balls like you used to."

Oh god, he isn't? Jessica closed her eyes. *My fuckin hair.*

Steven had his frank and beans out. He beat his meat, and with the other hand tickled his genitals with the hair.

And in the back…

No… nO… NOOOOOOO!

Bruce's fly went down and the Lizard Man… went down.

Dwayne closed his eyes and fought to control the sobs. *This is just so disgusting!*

Tiger Man stood outside the vehicle and threw the meat on the grill, SIZZLE!

"Ah, would you look at that; how cute, Velociraptors."

Ten were lined up along the four-foot-high, three beam, wooden fence. Oh, and they were six feet tall.

They watched him grill.

"HI-YA!"

Granny Damme, with Kurt Wussels on her back, and Justin swung into the scene on thick vines.

Tiger Man looked up.

Granny Damme swung in and, TWACK! Kicked him in the Tiger face. He fell knocking over the BBQ.

The raptors looked to one another. Their leader nodded.

Justin, Granny Damme, and Kurt Wussels landed.

Tiger man rolled back and got to his feet. "Sons of bitches! You's gonna' die!"

"No, I'm not, you wife kidnapper!" Justin shouted with a little cry to his voice. He ran with his fist cocked back.

Swing and a miss.

Tiger Man dodged, got the outside of the blow and WHAM! Drove his fist into Justin's stomach.

"Umph," he doubled over.

Rage played on Granny Damme's face, "She is such a sweet girl... she is such a sweet GIRL!" She ran forward.

Tiger Man laughed, "HAHAHA!" Because the granny ran really slow.

"What's all this?" Steven asked. Hair was strangling his cock. He pulled aside the partition. "Lizard man?"

SLURP! POP! His lizard face came up from Bruce Willis' lap. "Ya' boss?" He wiped wet stuff off his lip.

"Go check outside, I think I heard something like punches and a plot being wrecked 'n stuff."

"Sure boss," Lizard Man looked down at Bruce's sausage. "I'll get back to you later," he whispered.

Thank god! Bruce sighed; well, sighed through his gag. *How would I live with myself if I had nutted in that Lizard Man's mouth?* he wondered.

Don't look at his cock, Dwayne thought, *but what if its bigger than mine? No don't look.* He snuck a glance. *Damn, its big like I thought.*

Dwayne looked over to Sinead. She smiled knowingly.

Damn, bitch saw me look. Will have to kill her when we get free.

Lizard man stepped from the vehicle.

He saw an old granny kick Tiger Man in the face. As he fell back the old bitch lunged forward and, BAM! Punched the Tiger guy in the Baskin Robbins.

Lizard Man leaned in the SUV. "Boss, we got an old lady, some dude, and a huge cat thing beating up Tiger Man."

"Shit," Seagal said.

"AHHHH!" Lizard man screamed and was torn away from the door.

Bruce, Dwayne, and Sinead shouted through their gags.

Steven opened his door and looked out.

Lizard man screamed and gurgled. Two raptors tore at his gut. A third one looked at Steven. "Sheee-it!" He shut the door.

Tiger man fell to his knees.

Granny damme, THWAK! Round-house kicked his face. It was a slow-motion-epic-thing with rain. Rain, which only appeared in this scene.

"Meow," Kurt Wussels said.

"What is it? Granny Damme asked.

Justin looked too. "Shit, Velociraptors. I had no idea there would be velociraptors here.

Steven twisted in his seat. It was challenging because of his weight. "Get out, get out, get out!"

Bruce, Dwayne, and Sinead shook their heads, no.

He grabbed Bruce and pushed towards the open door.

Jessica pulled at her wrists, *almost*. She felt the tape slide. *Pull harder dammit, I'm Jessca Biel. I have sex appeal. I can make a thousand-year-old corpses come. Pull bitch, pull!*

Sinead fell out the door.

WOOM! Raptors were on her.

Jessica got free and rolled the window down, "HELP!"

"Jessica?" Justin shouted.

Raptors, eating the meat from the grill, were between him and the vehicle.

Granny Damme straightened her Batman mask, "Lets kick some raptor ass."

Justin nodded.

Kurt Wussels danced a sort of pee pee dance out of fear.

Granny Damme and Justin ran forward- Old lady Batman and stud-ly Robin in an ill-fitting boy-toy costume.

The raptors turned.

Granny Damme soared in with a punch.

The raptor rolled back and threw her with its foot.

BAM! She slammed into the back window of the SUV.

Dwayne, and Bruce looked at her.

"Oh, hey boys," Granny said and then slid down the glass. Her tits smeared the window, coming-up next to her face.

"Damn," Steven shouted. He shoved hard.

Bruce and Dwayne fell to the ground.

Justin kicked a raptor in its neck. It hissed and swiped at him with a small arm.

He ducked and twisted coming around to its side.

Justin jumped on the raptor's back.

"Die you lizard, scum!"

A raptor jumped on Granny Damme. She grabbed its jaw and held the teeth apart. They pressed in towards her neck.

Steven tried to start the vehicle. "Damn you, start!"

WHACK! He was punched in the face. *Geez, that hurt*. He looked at Jessica.

Another one of her fists was coming.

Block, ARM-LOCK!

Jessica cried out. She brought a foot up and, KICK!

Steven's dark sunglasses flew off. "Bitch!" He tweaked her arm.

Shit, it's gonna' break; what do I do?

Sometimes Ponytails Die; and Sometimes Not

"Let me go, or the ponytail gets it!" Jessica held an electric shaver to her hair.

"No bitch! Don't, okay… okay. Don't hurt my ponytail," Steven pleaded. "Where did you even get an electric shaver, anyhow?"

"Doesn't matter," Jessica said.

"Ponytail are you okay? She's not hurting you, is she?"

The ponytail said nothing.

Jessica scooted away. She opened her door and climbed out.

Justin was on the ground on top of a raptor. SNAP! He broke its neck. "Jessica!"

"Justin? Are you wearing a Robin costume?"

"Uh, yeah, long story; but I brought Van Damme's grandma to help save you."

Jessica looked at the other fighter.

WHAM! POW!

Granny Damme dropped into the splits and punched the two raptors next to her in their nuts.

Justin got up and ran to his wife.

They hugged and then kissed.

Damn those lips are good. Justin got excited-

-because Jessica is hot as fuck; so, I have to pretend that he wouldn't get bored of her like most people do with their lovers.

Granny Damme, UPPERCUT! And knocked a raptor off its feet; and then, BLAM! Punched through the heart of another.

She tore the organ out and threw it on the ground.

Kurt Wussels pounced on it and rolled to his back where he juggled it with his paws.

The vehicle shook, and its shocks groaned as weight was relieved. Steven climbed out. "You bustards!"

Bruce Willis kicked out with his bound feet and, TRIP!

Steven face planted on the muddy ground.

Like violent worms, Bruce and Dwayne climbed on top of him. They tried to wiggle and head butt him to death.

SMACK! Bruce headbutted Steven's nuts.

CLOCK! Dwayne bounced his body and brought his skull into Steven's face.

Blood dripped from his nose.

Steven Seagal did some Win Chung attacks.

He grabbed Dwayne by the ear and twisted.

"Urgh," Dwayne cried out in pain.

Steven reached down and hooked his fingers in Bruce's nostrils and lifted. Bruce squirmed and was thrown aside.

The Kung Fu Master hopped to his feet in a surprising display of athleticism.

Justin and Jessica looked right as the attack came.

KAPOW! Steven hit Justin with an elbow to the face. Justin fell to his ass.

Steven grabbed Jessica by the arm and twirl, FLIP!

Flipped her onto her back. She hit the ground hard. He stepped on her neck.

She clawed at his sandaled foot.

"Get away from her," Granny Damme said.

"No, it my ponytail and I'm going to show you that it belongs to me."

He unzipped his pants.

Jessica would have cried don't or no, if she could breathe well.

Steven took his junk out aimed at Jessica's head and, PISS!

SPUTTER! GAGG! Droplets of piss rained down on Jessica's face.

"A golden shower? No!" Granny Damme shouted, "She's such a sweet girl! A SWEET GIRL!"

Rage hit the old lady.

Steven kicked back his head and laughed maniacally.

Dwayne starred, not able to break himself away from the scene. *It's so violent and dominating!*

Fury told Granny Damme what to do. "Eighty fists of death!"

Granny Damme stepped wide. Her batman cape rose with an unseen force. She clenched her fists and puckered her anus. Her floppy tits took flight.

Steven stopped laughing and looked over. "Oh Shit." He tried to run.

Justin grabbed him around the neck, "Get him Granny Damme; he kidnapped Jessica Biel and peed on her. She's such a sweet girl; you just don't do that!"

Granny Damme charged.

STARS! KABLAM POW! SLAM! KABLAM!

Her fists moved in a fury. They were faster than the eye could see.

Smoke, a lightning bolt, and spark came off Steven's face.

Justin ducked his head, but held on; and then-

POOF!

Justin stumbled forward. "What the-?" He looked around. "Where'd he go?"

Granny Damme's orange fists faded back to normal color. "Well, I either partical-ized him, or sent him through time."

"Is that even possible?" Justin asked.

"Oh, yeah, it's possible alright."

Granny Damme came over to Jessica. "Honey, are you oaky?"

Justin helped the old lady to help up his wife up.

Jessica's wet hair clung to her forehead. "Yeah, geez, what the fuck was all this about?"

"I don't know babe," Justin said, "But it's over."

He kissed her.

SPLIT! SPUTTER! "Yuck!" Her lips were wet with piss drops.

Granny Damme threw her arms around the two of them. "Oh, you two are such sweet girls."

VROOOM! The Thunder Cats vehicle pulled up. Kurt Wussels was driving.

"How'd he get that thing on the cruise ship?" Jessica asked.

"Eh, don't worry about it," Granny Damme said, "Let's jut go home and clean up. Clean up *real* good! MWUAHAHAHAHA!"

Justin and Jessica looked at one another.

HONK! HONK!

Another green SUV pulled up behind the mayhem. The family inside gasped.

The father of the family asked, "Is that Bruce Willis?"

Party at Jackie's Brick House

Tiger man and Lizard man played pool. Tiger man took a shot. Two raptors sat at the nearby table waiting their turn.

Bruce Willis and Dwayne Johnson played darts. TWAK! Dwayne went to the board and pulled his out. Bruce clapped him on the back for the victory. Sinead came over carrying beers for them.

They each took one.

Grandma Damme danced on the dance floor. She gyrated and moved in ill-coordinated movements.

Tobey Maguire kicked back a shot at the bar for courage and headed to the dance floor. He started grinding on Granny Damme.

Jean Claude came up and grabbed him by the collar and led him off.

Justin and Jessica were enjoying drinks at the bar with Steven Seagal. Steven mimed hugging her hair and playing with it.

Jessica slapped at him playfully, to stop joking.

He gave a no I'm serious look.

Justin smiled and pulled his wife away.

They joined Granny Damme at a table with Kurt Wussels. He still wore the body paint but not the mask. He was some buff black dude.

Justin and Jessica sat down on the bar stools.

Nachos were on the table.

They joked and laughed and ate. Granny Damme did shitty punches imitating her eighty fists of death.

Justin put his fists by his face and then opened his fingers quickly like his head exploded.

They laughed and looked over at Steven.

He turned his back to them and talked with the hot bartender. He admired her ponytail by running his fat fingers through it.

She had no idea.

The Thunder Cats Vehicle walked in the door.

The group of them cheered and raised their glasses.

The Waiter bird man waived the Vehicle over and the Vehicle sat next to him and a few other raptors.

END

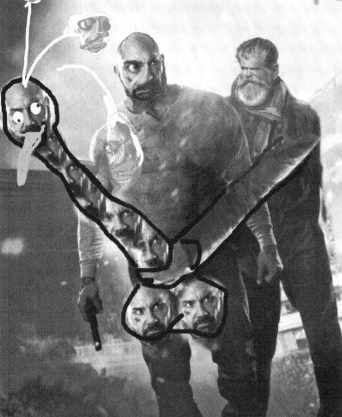

BRIDGET CHASE

FINAL
POINT

MOVIE CLIFF SERIES

FINAL POINT

Bridget Chase

A Niece Time

"Wow, this is amazing; there must be like thirty-five thousand people here. Thanks for bringing me; man do I live soccer."

"No problem; let's have a great time without any unnecessary violence or explosions," Michael said.

Michael Nuts and his niece, Alice, walked down the central isle stairs to find a seat. They were high up with a raucous crowd in Ham'samich Stadium.

Alice said, "Yeah, the violence really ruined our ice cream outing last time. Remember the poor guy who had to clean up all that blood and melted ice cream?"

"Yeah, I do; what a dope. Nope, tonight will be prefect; perfect I tell you."

"Oh, how about we sit here?" Alice asked, and sat.

"Um, no; that's someone's lap."

"OH!" Alicia looked behind her.

She sat on some dude's lap.

He smiled at her. *Don't get a boner; don't get a boner; come on man, don't think about that ass rubbin' yer crotch! She's too young. I know the weight feels good and she has tits; so, it's kinda okay; but look at that big-fuck of a guy with her. He'll kick my ass fo' sho'. Damn, my weenies waking up. Oh yeah, feels good. Uh… real good.*

"I'm sorry," Alice said and got up. "I thought you were a chair."

"How 'bout over there," Michael said.

"Perfect."

They walked over and sat.

Michael was a big fucking dude. He wore an army jacket, had a beard, and a shaved head. His eyes said, 'Where's the action,' and his jaw said, 'I can handle it'. His lips, on the other hand, said, 'I like to eat some pussy for breakfast'.

The game and shit went on. Soccer players ran; people cheered and shoved food in their mouths, and Alice looked over several times and smiled at Michael, making him know he was a good Uncle;

If you ask me kinda' old for an uncle, but shit, he was an uncle.

The Big Boy Box

The door blasted open to the VIP stadium box.

Men wearing black rushed in and grabbed the people inside.

"Perfect." A man in a suit who was rather lanky came in and cracked his knuckles.

More men came in behind him carrying utility boxes.

"Set 'em up over there, boys" Mastermind said.

He walked to the glass window overlooking the entire stadium. "Perfect."

The tough looking white guys opened the containers and removed tech equipment. They went about doing some shit until one said, "Okay, we're set up boss."

"Good, now let's kidnap us a niece."

The Impossible Plot

Alice stood in the bathroom. She was checking herself out in the mirror. "Damn, you's looking totally fine.

Did you see those guys checkin' you out? HOT DAMN! I'm a babe!"

She adjusted her tits. "Oh, you girls are really comin' in fine. Yeah baby; I'm just a love machine; baby don't work for nobody but you, YEAH BABY!"

Alice was doing a little dance number in front the mirror when, BANG! The door busted open.

She turned, "OH SHIT! I wasn't just singin' or dancin' or nothin'."

The woman aimed a gun at her.

"You're coming with me," A trashy girl, with corn rows, said. She looked like a wannabe UFC chick, but we all know they're not dangerous.

"Please, don't hurt me," Alice said.

The woman came up, gun still aimed and grabbed Alice by her hair. She drug her out of the bathroom.

Michael heard his phone ring. *Well, that's unlikely with all these screaming people.*

Even more unlikely was that he picked up an unknown number. Shit, most people let it go to voice mail; hell, if they even have that set up. Let's get real, if it's important, they'll text.

Alice has sure been in the bathroom a while? Hope it wasn't them hotdogs?

He answered, "Michael here."

"Mr. Nuts, listen carefully; we have your niece-,"

GASP! Michael stood up.

"Hey buddy, you're blockin' my view; outta the way," A soccer fan said.

"-You are going to do exactly as I say. Somewhere in this stadium is Demetri Brosnan. I want you to find him and bring him to me. If he is not found in ninety minutes; we'll detonate explosives killing everyone inside."

Michael looked around, "But, that is like thirty-five thousand people you are holding hostage."

"Correct."

"But, that is like thirty-five thousand people I really don't give a fuck about."

"We know, that is why we have your niece, Alice."

Michael looked around the stadium for anything suspicious.

Nope, nothing stuck out.

"Why don't you get Demetri yourself?" he asked. "Shit, I mean why did you randomly choose me; I've never even met the guy. Might I suggest having one of your own men go get him. Hell, here's an idea for you, put your men at all the exits, and after the game, nab him."

"No," Mastermind said, "That is nowhere near as fun, or mastermind-ful."

Michael asked, "How do I know you aren't lying?"

Mastermind turned to his crew of thugs, "Kill the power."

BLINK! The stadium lights went out.

Backup generators kicked on and emergency lights came to life.

Michael looked around, "Okay, cool trick; I'll do it. How do I find him?"

The stadium operations team and security team went crazy in the control box. People shouted orders and others scrambled about doing whatever protocol shit they were supposed to do.

"Got 'em," a nobody guy said.

The operations team sighed.

The lights came back on.

Mastermind said. "You'll find Demetri in row 47D Seat J; and I'll text you a pic."

"Cool," Michael said, "But if I do this; I *will* kill you. I'm a bad motha'-,"

"Shut ya' mouth," A woman said. "There are kids around."

"-I won't hesitate to jump a sports bike from a higher roof of the stadium to a lower part; I'll also be willing to hit someone in the face with a fire extinguisher. Oh, and when I find you, I'll shoot you like this, BANG! No problem; I won't even flinch; kill people all the time; all the time."

"Whatever," Mastermind said, "You have eighty-nine minutes." He hung up.

Michael's eagle eyes scanned the crowd. Forty-seven 'D' seat 'J'.

And, there was a man seated there. Older guy, grey beard, looked like Pierce Brosnan with a beard.

Michael's phone vibrated; he pulled it out; a text with a picture. He held it out in front of himself, comparing the two.

"Demetri Bronsan,' Michael said. "Ya' bastard!"

The two matched.

The Unimportant MacGuffin

"Yo' man, I've come to deliver you to someone."

Demetri looked up. "Do I know you?"

"No, bro," Michael said, "But, someone sent me to bring you to them. They have my niece and they have this whole place held hostage."

Demetri looked around at the crowd. "Sure doesn't look like they are held hostage."

"Oh, yeah, they are; they just don't know it yet. Anyways, you seem to be the macguffin, so, come with me."

"The what, now?" Demetri asked.

Michael put his hands on his hips, "Geez man, use your phone; look it up, MacGuffin."

MacGuffin pulled out his phone. "Ah, yes; I see you're right. Okay, I'm in; what do we do?"

Michael pulled out his phone. "I call the guy in charge." He dialed. "Yeah, it's me. I have him; let my niece go."

"Oh good," Mastermind said, "Well go on, and-,"

"-Shit, I got another call," Michael said, "Hold on." He put Mastermind on hold.

"This is the police; we heard there's a situation involving a MacGuffin and you, is that true, sir?"

"Yeah."

"Okay, well listen close; closer, there ya' go. If you bring that MacGuffin to the man in charge, he'll detonate the bomb."

"Are you sure?" Michael asked.

"Yeah... we are sure."

"Okay, I'll call you back."

Click he changed lines.

"Mastermind?"

"Yeah."

"That was the police."

"Great."

"They said you'll blow the place if I bring Demetri to you."

"Well, sure, seems like somethin' I'd do; I'm wild like that, what can I say?"

"Then I won't bring him."

"Okay, I'm sending men to hunt you, and kill you. Once I have Demetri, YOUR… NIECE… DIES… TOO!"

"Okay, deal." Michael hung up. He turned to Demetri and asked, "So, why do they want you?"

Demetri lifted his hat and scratched his head. "Do you use Head 'n Shoulders? It doesn't seem to work for me. Fuckin' dandruff. Oh… um, not sure. I'm just a dude enjoying a game."

"I doubt that," Michael said. "Let's get my niece back. She has school tomorrow; so, she has to get to bed at a reasonable hour. I'll keep you safe 'n shit, too."

"Cool."

Chaotic Game Plan

Michael pulled out his pistol.

Where he got it? No one knows, but who cares because he was in some back hallway and bad dudes with ponytails were sneaking down the hall.

"Get behind me," Michael said.

Demetri practically climbed on his back.

The fist dude sportin' a black jacket and ponytail came around the bend.

CLAK! Michael fired.

"Ah, you got me; ooh, it hurts; damn I'm 'a bleedin'. Ah, psych!" CLAK! CLAK! The man returned fired.

His buddy peaked out behind him. They both almost looked the same.

Bullets ate the hall.

Demetri covered his ears. "Does violence have to be so loud? Shit, back in my day we killed people silently."

Michael said, "Turn off your hearing aid, old man."

"Okay."

CLAK! CLAK! CLAK!

A bullet went through one guy's chest; he cried out. "DAMN, all my hopes 'n dreams of villainy, gone; goodbye world; I never made you my bitch." CROAK!

"Ya' bastard!" The other guy ran out, firing.

Michael aimed at the wall and, CLAK! Fired the bullet. BING! It cut a notch in the wall and bounced off.

SPLAT! It went through the bad, oh so bad, dude's face.

"Take that Hop Scotch," Michael said. "Okay, come on MacGuffin, let's take the elevator." He walked down the hall.

Demetri didn't move.

"Yo! Let's go!"

Demetri put a finger up. He fished around in his ear. "What? What's up?"

"We're going."

"Okay, cool; should have said so."

Mothafukaaa, Michael aimed at Demetri's head. *Naw, better not*; he put the gun down.

They got to the elevator and Michael called the Mastermind.

"Hey."

"Hey."

"So, I killed two of your men; shit, I almost killed Demetri, too."

"Well, don't do that you fool."

"Hell," Michael said, "I don't really need him. I'm coming for my niece; all he is, is extra weight."

"No, no, no, bring him along," Mastermind said. "So what floor you going to?"

"Umm," Michael looked around, "Maybe the top floor. Yeah, the top floor sounds pretty good."

"See ya' soon, sweetie."

"What?"
Mastermind hung up.

Violence goes up

Demetri cowered in the corner, "Oh, guys, watch out. Oh please, Ouch! Be careful now. Those are my toes."

BLAM! Michael punched a guy in the face.

The bad dude stumbled back and hit the wall.

THWAK! The second bad dude punched Michael in the stomach.

"URG," he grimaced. He brought an elbow to the guy's nose. CRACK!

The first guy lifted a gun.

Michael caught his wrists and struggled with him. CLAK! CLAK! The gun went off.

"Guys, watch it, will ya," Demetri said. Bullet holes appeared by his head. He pulled his knees up and cradled them to his chest. "Ouch, that's gotta hurt. Ooh, get 'em Michael. DA-YUM! Is that arm broken? Oh, so gross, so gross. No, you're not going to do that, are you?"

Michael stomped the guy's head into the floor.

CRACK! The guy's skull popped like a hot grape.

Michael slicked blood off his face. He stuck a hand out to Demetri. "Let's get my niece."

Scenic Ride

Demetri hung on Michael's back like a back pack. Michael steered the sports bike.

Demetri ssid, "Kinda' lucky finding a sports bike way up here, huh?"

"Yeah, it's perfect. But hold on tight, cause I'm pretty sure I'm gonna' do something super crazy; or my name isn't Dave Batis-,"

"-Michael Nuts."

Demetir leaned his head against Michael's big 'ol swoll back.

"You like that? Pretty comfortable right?"

"Yeah, you're like a big bear."

"Feel those traps? Been working super hard on them; doin' drop sets of shrugs 'n shit."

Demetri felt Michael's neck. "Yeah, pretty cool. Think I would look cool with traps like that?"

"Maybe."

BRRRRR-BRRRRRR! Two bikes came down the hall in front of them.

What will I do? Michael wondered. *Hmm, I'm super cool, and suave, and swoll; so, think of something super cool would ya' brain; come on now.* He flexed. *I'm forcing my steroid blood into you, brain. Think, will ya'?*

Ah ha!

"Demetri grab that fire extinguisher."

"We are going awful fast; seems impossible."

"No, grab it. Be a worthy MacGuffin."

"Okay."

Michael sped the bike near the wall and, YOINK! Demetri grabbed it.

"Hand it to me."

Michael gripped that red steel fucker. He aimed the bike right towards one of the approaching bikes.

"I'm gonna' take his head off."

BRRRR! As he passed by, Michael swung that shit.

DING! It rang off the bad guy's head.

His head kicked back he flew off the bike and back flipped.

"Damn, that was awesome," Demetri said. "It's a good thing there seem to be, like, no people around or nothin'. I thought this was a stadium 'n shit; shouldn't there be people everywhere?"

The other bike sped by and then hit the brakes, skidded, and turned around.

Okay, brain be clever. Michael thought. He pulled out his phone.

"Hey."

'Hey."

"So, I killed another guy. And now, am going to do a huge motocross kinda' jump, which I'll make but the chick on the bike here, wont."

"Stacy? No don't kill Stacy. Damn, man; she's like the only chick in my crew. You cock blocking som' of a bitch."

"After that, I'm coming for you."

"Okay."

Mastermind hung up. He turned to Alice. "Your Uncles comign."

Alice was tied to an office chair. The ropes strangled her titties.

"Fester?"

"No Nuts."

"Who?"

"Michael."

"Oh, Michael; yeah great, he kicks ass. You should have seen what he did to the guys checking me out at Dairy Queen. They had to close that store for like a month just to clean them up."

"Dang."

Michael put the phone in his pocket. "Hold on."

Demetri squeezed him. "Did you ever know, that you're my hero?"

"No."

"You're everything I wish I could be."

"Stop."

"I could fly higher than an eagle."

Michael twisted the throttle.

The chick on the bike followed.

BBBBRRRR!

The bike raced to the edge of the roof and, BOOM! Flew off.

"You are the wind beneath my wings." Demetri clamped his eyes shut.

"KABOOOOM!" The chick's bike blew up for no reason other than she wasn't cool enough to pull off the stunt.

BAD-UM! The sports bike magically managed the landing on the roof fifty feet below without so much as a flat tire.

Michael pulled the bike to a stop.

A fireball lit the sky behind him.

Wrong MacGuffin

BOOM! The door flew open

Mastermind turned.

"Give me my niece," Michael shouted. Demetri rode his back like Yoda on Luke.

"Uncle," Alice said. "Oh, and who's the dude?"

"I'm the MacGuffin," Demetri said, over Michael's shoulder.

"Really? Kinda' seems like I'm the MacGuffin."

"Hmm, there can't be two," Mastermind said.

Michael hefted Demetri into a better position on his back. "Hmm can we both have different MacGuffins?"

"I don't think so," Mastermind said.

"So, now what?" Michael asked.

"Jean," Mastermind said.

A huge hulking dude bigger than Michael came in the room; he had to duck under the door frame.

"Someone has to die." Mastermind pulled out a gun.

The Gift Exchange

Michael sat by the fireplace. He could barely see over the huge box in his lap.

Mastermind came in. He pulled a big wrapped gift on a wheel barrel. He wore a hugely-thick, obnoxious designer coat.

"Well this is really a nice place," Mastermind said.

"I know, isn't it?"

"We're going to have a great time together in Denver. Winter is so great here."

"It is," Michael said, "It really is. So, I was thinkin' we should exchange gifts first; ya' know, take the tension off. Then we can grab a good dinner. I've asked around and found a really nice place."

"Dinner for two sounds lovely. Sure, let's get this outta' the way. I sure wouldn't want to spoil all or skiing with petty mumbo jumbo."

"Cool," Michael said. "Well, here is your gift."

Mastermind clapped, "Oh you shouldn't have." He ran with high knees over to the large box.

Michael placed it on the ground.

"Oh, I can't wait to see what you got me."

Mastermind ripped that gift-wrap paper. He used a small knife and cut the packing tape along the box's edge. He opened the top flaps and looked in.

"Oh splendid."

Demetri smiled up at him. "Hey there."

Mastermind closed the lid. "Thank you, really, thank you. And, *here* is your gift."

Michael rubbed his hands together. "Oh great. Alice, I'm unwrapping you now." He pulled at the paper. "Man, my brother has been *so* pissed since I lost her. Fuck, it's all he's talked about for the last six months. Mastermind, you're a real standup guy, ya know that?'

Mastermind smiled.

Michael opened it. "Wait, where is…. Is that? NO!" He looked at Mastermind.

"Sorry chum; Alice has been dead for six months. Actually, we're all about to die. You didn't know but being a madman kinda' makes you a bit bipolar and suicidal. But thanks for showin' up with Demetri. My life is now complete."

"He *was* the MacGuffin!" Michael said.

Mastermind smiled.

"Hey, what's this about a bomb? Let me out." The box shook around. Demetri shouted.

"Ka Boom!" Mastermind said.

KA-BOOOOM! The room exploded. A fire ball blasted the windows out of the small skiing cabin. The roaring fire tumbled into the sky.

Burnt and bloody shit, in little pieces, fell to the ground. Steam rose from the roasted pieces of flesh from where they lay in the snow.

END

FULL HOUSE
ON ELM STREET

BRIDGET CHASE
ONE BADASS BITCH

FULL HOUSE ON ELM STREET
Bridget Chase

"What is this wet slippery thing?"

Stephanie screamed.

She darted out the bathroom. Her towel clung to her body.

Oh, don't be a prude. This is me, in like, season eight when I developed and started flaunting a little sexuality for all the boys who were growing up too fast and to keep them from outgrowing the show.

Her little TGIF cupcakes danced in bouncing twirls. *We are so happy and jiggly,* they sang.

"HELP!" Steph shouted again.

Before Joey even heard her shout; he sensed Steph's naked body. He could always tell when she was naked, *but this time it was different.* "I better go check this out!"

He put Mr. Woodchuck down.

His puppet was dressed as Wonder Woman, wig and all. Mr. Woodchuck's small blue panties were askew.

I wasn't doing nothin' swears-zies. I was just trying out different costumes out on Mr. Woodchuck. Nothin' sexual; no sir.

DJ got up from her bed and ran to the door. "What's the matter Steph?" she asked.

Steve was left sitting on the bed.

Damn, now I got this boner to deal with. Not that that's unusual. DJ is such a boner tease; I don't know why I'm with her sometimes. Damn the devil to hell!

His cock raged and balls were swollen. *How many seasons will it take to bang her little sofa cushion? And now, what's this with Stephanie?*

Stephanie met DJ at the bedroom door.

"The bathroom," Stephanie said, "Something was in the tub with me!" She was panting from adrenaline.

Steve looked over. *Seriously? I'm horny as fuck and have been storing a nut for 18 years and now; Stephanie is standing there soaking wet all naked except for that little towel. I mean look at her. I can see them little titties through the thread bare towel. Come on! Cut me a break here.*

"Something was in the tub?" DJ asked, "Let's go see." She turned to Steve, "Steve you coming?"

I wish I was. "Um, yeah just a moment." *Damn, why won't she ever put out with her pink Jebly? All I'm asking for is to fill her belly with a quick sticky load and have her beg for me for more; you know? What's the problem with that?*

DJ and Steph went across the hall to the bathroom. on the way DJ called out, "DAD!"

"I'm here DJ, what's the problem?"

He appeared out of nowhere along with Joey and Jesse.

Joey eyed Stephanie's biscuits.

Well, blow me down, he said like Popeye in his head, *she's all wet, and nude, and damn, I wanna' make her my sausage biscuit sand' ich number five breakfast, please, oh please, oh please! Look at the way her tittie biscuits press at that towel. VROOM! HUBBA HUBBA WHOA!*

His eyes traced her collarbone and then dropped.

Oh, they are so small and squishy. I just want to cuddle them and love on them. Oh, you're so pretty little titties. Are those her nipples? It can't be-

-Yes, it is-

-No-

-Yes; oh, strawberry gumdrops my balls hurt.

Danny noticed too, *No I didn't.* And he jerked off in the shower later thinking about it; *no, I didn't. I was thinking about Kimmy-*

-dammit;

No, I wasn't thinking about Kimmy or Steph. Hey... wait! I didn't do anything in the shower.

"What's wrong," Danny asked. *Don't look at her corn muffins.*

"In there; something grabbed me," Steph said and pointed.

Danny marched in and had himself a good fatherly look around.

The tub was filled with water.

Shut it, I wasn't thinking anything. Geez, what kind of narrator are you? I'm going back to the story.

"What? I don't see anything," he said, "Nothing seems to be the matter, honey."

"Well, there was something there," Steph said.

"So, tell us what happened," DJ said.

"Wee-hell... I was bathing; soaping up my body like I always do when I'm naked in the tub; I made sure to lather my little summer hams really good," she looked up at her dad, "Just like you taught me too."

His eyes darted around. *No one heard that!*

Steph turned to the rest of the group, "And anyways, I was running the soap along the curves of my belly thinking about-,"

She paused, looked at Steve, and then looked away quickly.

Did she just? Holy HELL! Score!

Steve wanted to shoot his fists into the air.

I can't believe it, she's been beatin' that jelly clit thinkin' about 'ol Steve, here. Way to go, champ! Way-to-go!

"-Well," she continued, "A hand came from the water and grabbed me."

"Grabbed you where, honey. Let me see," Danny said.

"Dad, I can't show you."

BING!

Joey swallowed hard. He knew where the creature had grabbed her- *By the PUSSEA! Yes sir! Damn, bet those creature fingers slipped right on in there. Lucky fucker, wish I were a damned creature.*

"I'll have a look," Jesse said, "Step aside. If there is a groping monster in there, I'll find it! My nieces shouldn't be groped unwillingly; not on my watch."

Joey's eyes shifted back and forth.

Stephanie readjusted her towel. It hugged her teen contours.

Joey shuddered with desire.

Rebecca appeared in the hall.

The hall which we never see in the show.

"Jesse!" she shouted.

"Yeah, babe?"

He was kneeling looking behind the toilet. *If I find that monster, why I outta'... Nope toilet's secure.*

"We have a problem," she said.

"Huh, what's that now?"

"A poltergeist torn my nightie."

"A poltergeist did what, now?"

The guys all turned.

BANG! Steve appeared in a cloud of smoke, "What's this? Are you okay?"

The men drooled.

Rebecca wore an ultra-slinky black nightie. It was sheer, and she wore no panties. NO PANTIES! Her battle toad was hairless and aggressive, *GRRR!* The top was ripped and one of her breasts hung out- HEAVY. Her pink Skittles nipple made the men float like cartoon characters following their nose to the scent of food.

All of her soft skin was visible. ALL OF IT!

"Uh, boys," Jesse pushed through them, "I better handle this. You guys take the bathroom."

Jesse and Rebecca left.

His dick was out before even making it to the attic. "Don't run from my fleshly poltergeist."

Michelle came down the hall. She gave Jesse a thumbs-up. "Go do her dude; in every hole!" she said.

"Michelle," Danny said, "Why don't you go down stairs; it isn't safe here."

"I'm not afraid, dude."

"We all should be," DJ said

"Why is that?" Danny asked.

"Look." She pointed to the bathroom.

The back wall and tub were gone. It was replaced with a fiery Hell dimension portal burping exploding Takis.

Things moaned, and shadows moved.

"This can't be good," Steve said. "I liked things better when everything was about tits."

"Huh? Tits?" DJ asked.

"Twix," Steve said, (cough) "Twix." He looked down, buried his hands in his pockets, and scuffed the floor with his toe.

Danny grabbed the door handle.

BARK! Comet ran past into the bathroom and, LEAP, jumped through the paranormal gateway.

"COMET!" They all shouted.

Stephanie dropped her towel. "COMET!" Her little Buddy Lembeck's were bare, wet, and spring.

Remember, this is Stephanie from season eight, just to clarify again; *not season one you pervs, hahaha.*

Joey grunted, "I gotta' go," he ran off. *Oh honey biscuits; oh honey biscuits...* His fingers curled by his mouth and his teeth chattered.

Weird clicks filled the hall. Creatures emerged from the flaming portal.

SPLAT WIMPER! Comet's body was thrown to the ground. The puppy trembled and died right there. His dark puppy blood streaked the clean title floor.

Yeah, it's clean. Well, was clean. I'm Danny Tanner and this is my house bitch; I keep my shit spotless!

Michelle cried. *Oh, Comet I loved you. You were my favorite dog.*

Danny pulled the door shut.

"What about Comet?" DJ asked.

"It's too late."

They raced down the hall and down the stairs.

"We better call the police or someone," Danny said.

They entered the kitchen.

Stephanie left her towel. *Geez, I hope no one will care. I'm totally naked and my family is here.*

Cory Matthews peered though the kitchen window. *Oh, man, TITTIES! He pulled out his camcorder and zoomed in on Steph's Sea Biscuits. Damn, I want to cream those Toby Maguires.*

Later Steve would find out about the tape and he forced Corey into making him a copy.

Steve looked at her jelly filled cupcakes. *Gimme' my chocolate milkies, bitch!*

The kitchen ceiling changed, and creatures dropped to the floor.

Steve screamed like a cheerleader and ran.

DJ will be pissed, but shit, she doesn't put out so fuck her!

He flew up the stairs and BAM! Slammed the door to DJ's room. He huffed and caught his breath. He hadn't been this frightened since that night racoons had chased him through the park on his way home. *Damn, I hate the way niggas always hangin' out in the park at night.*

The creatures landed, and dark curling bodies unfolded, standing upright.

"What do we do?" DJ asked.

Danny grabbed a mop.

"Really," Joey asked, "You're going to start cleaning?"

"No, geez, well probably not."

He held the mop like a Bo staff.

Stephanie got behind Joey.

Oh man, this is great, he thought. *She's butt ass naked and this close to me. It'd be awesome if she did a little reach a' round and skinned my melon.*

Michelle got behind her sister.

The creatures roared, and the lights flickered on the sound stage. Men in the live audience covered their crotches. *Man, Full House has never been this hot*, they all thought. *We better go back and watch earlier episodes.*

And, they would find out that earlier episodes were just as hot.

The only thing more erotic was the episode of Boy Meets World where Jennifer Love Hewitt guest stars.

Which only happened because that lucky prick (I'm not even gonna' look up his name) was dating her. Damn, what a lucky mother fucker! He dated Jennifer Love Hewitt in her prime. Like, idk, seventeen to nineteen or something. Fuckin unbelievable. Okay, back to...

One lunged with its claws.

"Dad," DJ shouted. She ducked and ran past the thing.

Two more were there and attacked. She fell to the floor and kicked at them.

THWAK! Danny came with his mop. It smashed the first one's face. "I'm coming DJ." He hurried over and used the wet mop to knock them away.

"Oh gosh; oh gosh; oh no!" Joey said. He didn't want to fight.

Monsters approached.

Steph and Michelle clung to his back.

Steve made it upstairs, went into DJ's room, and closed the door.

He should have been concerned with the Hell World meshing with this reality, but he wasn't.

No, I care about my nuts being sucked. I mean seriously I'm done with this wholesome family. DJ is just a tease; you should see her; she makes out with me for like five minutes, rubs my thigh, and gets my conveyor belt rolling. Then, nothing.

Oh, and Stephanie bounces around here with springy tits and short skirts. I'm just so done.

He laid back on the bed. SIGH! And let out a deep breath.

His dick was hard. *When is it not?*

Downstairs...

DJ was on her back. She heard grunting.

SMACK! *What's this wet slippery thing?*

She pushed the thing off her face.

"Sorry," Danny said; he held off creatures with the mop.

"NO!" Joey cried.

A dark ink creature grabbed Michelle's arm. It threw her over its shoulder and ran out of the living room.

"Stop!" Steph shouted.

Danny saw it run past.

The other creatures attacked

BLAM! A creature backhanded Joey. He fell and Steph, attached to his back, fell with him. SMACK he landed on top of her.

Steph was on her back and Joey was face down. Her legs were spread and, *I'm in between… Oh my god!* He was wearing thin shorts and his dick rubbed her thick cleft flesh.

"Get off," she said.

SMAK! A creature kicked Joey. He rolled to the side.

"NO!" Steph shouted; the thing grabbed her wrists and lifted her.

Joey looked up. *Man, she is fine.*

Steph dangled from her wrists. Her body was stretched long.

"Get away from her!" Joey did a low ninja spin kick.

SLIP! The creature's legs were taken out, and it fell.

DIVE! Joey moved quick and caught Steph breaking, her fall. She was in his arms.

This is okay; yeah, it's okay; just don't tell anyone.

Shit was going down in the living room; but, *shit , I don't care. Well I didn't until-*

Steve felt a hand on his zipper.

ZIP! Fingers opened his fly.

DJ?

"What the hell?" Steve sat up.

Michelle smiled. She was kneeling between his legs.

"Michelle what are you doi-,"

"-Do it," said a deep voice.

Creatures came from the bed and wall. Their inky hands grabbed Steve, pulled him down to the bed and held him.

He strained to lift his head and see over his stomach.

Michelle slipper her hand into his boxers and freed his robo cock.

"No, Michelle don't, well, may do; but don't!"

Michelle took his cock into her mouth. Her lips made a tight ring on his flesh.

How does she know how to suck like this?

Michele went to town and bobbed her head like she was a brain-dead bimbo back stage at a NSYNC concert.

This is okay, yeah, it's okay; just don't tell anyone.

Down stairs the fight went on.

DJ took an elbow and was knocked over the iconic couch. A dripping thing lept on her.

What's that? Oh my god! Something thick and heavy prodded at her thigh. She wore a small sexy skirt with thigh high stockings to tempt teen boys into watching the show and tuning in each week to catch her sexy new outfit.

Yeah, it tempts Steve a lot too.

"Get off of me." She wrestled with the thing.

PING! Stephanie rang a photo frame off a creature's head.

ARGH! Joey cried as infected teeth found his shoulder.

"Here I come!" Jesse lept down the stairs and tackled two creatures.

"I'm coming too," Rebecca said she ran down the stairs. Her titties hopped like spaghetti on sundae (yes, that spelling was intentional). They were perfect and one was exposed by her ripped lingerie.

Oh, titty, titty, titty!

Danny clocked one, BAM! With the end of the mop.

Dark blood matter sprayed from its Nickel nose and rained on the floor.

This is a nightmare! Not on my floor.

Untidy messes distraught our favorite dad.

RING!

Danny sat up in bed, "Holy SHIZNIT!"

"Dad," cried Steph.

"Dad," shouted DJ

"DJ," shouted Michelle.

"Jesse," shouted Rebecca.

"BARK!" barked Comet.

"Them titties," shouted Jesse.

They all met in the hall and starred at one other with knowing eyes.

"Did you all have the same nightmare?" Danny asked his wholesome family unit.

"The one with the dark creatures?" DJ asked.

"That attacked me in the tub," Steph said.

"And got blood all over the kitchen," Danny said.

"And, ripped my nightie?" Rebecca said; *Oh,* she looked down. It was ripped.

Danny licked his lips and his eyes lit up, *Peach Snapple and popcorn! Sweet and salty treat!*

"Is anyone else hurt?" Danny asked.

Michelle wiped a string white loogie from her lips.

"What about Joey?" DJ asked, "He was bitten."

"I don't know," Danny said, "Let's find out."

They all ran down the hall, down the stairs, and to the basement.

The camera caught all of Rebecca's jigglin' nibblets of soft desires.

Boom! They flew into Joey's room.

Joey was under the covers jerkin off.

"You okay?" Danny asked.

"Oh, shit," Joey looked up. "Um yeah," he then looked at Steph to see if she was naked. *I want 'dem peanut-buttery Peter Pans!*

Steph notice, "Ewe gross, stop." She cupped her hands over her little strawberry fields. She wore a very thin tank top with no bra.

Joey kept his room rather chilly.

BOING!

A tent was still pitched under his sheets.

(Cough) "Uh, he's fine; let's give him a minute," Jesse said.

Rebecca bit her lower lip, *oh boy! I didn't know he was hung that way.*

Danny covered Michelle's eyes and walked her up the stairs.

Everyone followed.

"What happened?" DJ asked.

They all stood in the iconic kitchen.

"I don't know, DJ," Danny said, "But, it definitely wasn't our typical episode. No sir. Not by a long shot."

Steph crossed her arms, "It's like three in the morning; if we go back to sleep, will the nightmare happen again?"

"I don't know," Danny said.

"Next time, we'll whip their asses," Jesse said.

Rebecca held a hand over her exposed tit bubble. "I think I'll wear something more suitable for combat to bed this time."

BOOM! The back door blew open and Steve raced in. "GUYS! Did that happen?"

They all nodded.

He looked at Michelle, *does she remember; oh god she swallowed my three seasons of Bill Cosby's.*

Michelle smiled at him and bounced her eye brows.

This isn't good, Steve thought; he looked away.

Danny seemed to have picked up on something, "What happened to you in the nightmare?" he asked.

"Nothing," Steve said, *it was the best Mulder and Scully that I ever had.* "I ran like DJ's pussy and hid. No one touched me, no one sucked my-,"

Joey came into the kitchen; he looked relaxed. He saw Steph*, damn, too bad we can't go back to that dream a while.*

"Oh Joey, your shoulder," Rebecca said, "Here, let me take a look at that."

Joey's shoulder was shredded. "Huh, hardly noticed."

She took him to the island counter and pulled out a first aid kit.

Joey watched her tit move. *Damn, gonna' have to jerk it again. Well blow me down; hak hak hak hak hak.*

"Daddy, I'm sleepy," Michelle said and pulled on his pant leg. She turned and looked back at Steve. "Real sleepy."

Did she just smile at me? Steve wonder, *what the fuck man?* "Okay, guys I got to go," he said.

"No, Steve," DJ ran up, stay with me. She rubbed the front of his shorts and turned to her dad, "It's okay if stays the night, right? Like, we can't send him home. Not after-,"

Danny nodded, "Sure DJ, I know you never put out. So, I won't have to worry any."

Steve groaned.

"So, we are going back to bed?" Steph asked.

"Yeah, we are," Jesse said; he fussed with his hair, *making sure I looked good.* "Actually, we should all sleep in the living room; so, if something does happen, we'll be together."

Joey was panting. *Oh, I get to sleep right next to Rebecca. Maybe I can put my sleeping bag beside hers. Oh would I? Could I? What if I just casually slipped my hand into her sleeping bag while she is asleep?*

Rebecca's breast was within sucking distance. Joey popped a fat woodchuck.

Rebecca noticed. She 'accidently' brushed his lap with her hand.

WHOA! Joey almost came. His balls were swollen magnets.

"So, that settles it," Danny said. "Everyone get your sleeping bags."

It was hot and sticky.

The lights were out.

Sleeping bags littered the floor.

Steve snored.

Joey couldn't sleep. Not because of the threat of another nightmare.

No, it was because*, damn, these babes in here.* He could smell Rebecca. *Did she put on perfume?*

He rolled.

Over the shoulders of his Full House family, he looked at the door.

Something moved in his sleeping bag. *What's that?*

He rolled "Rebecca?" he asked in a whisper.

"Shhh, just lay back."

Her fingers slipped under his shirt and into his boxers.

"Wait-,"

Her fingers encircled his cock. *Oh, she's gonnn'a kill that 'ol Wile E. Coyote this TIME!*

"Okay, never mind. Keep going. Oh, and if you feel the urge, you can use that pretty mouth. It's (drool) just so pretty. Watch out though, I'm fully loaded."

Rebecca stroked that fucker beggin' his ball juice out with a rhythmic tug. She pressed her jellies to his chest.

Joey cupped her tit.

Yellow light slipped in the window panel on the door cutting angles in the virgin daughters of darkness.

"What? What's happening?" Joey asked.

The yellow light turned red.

"Hehehe, cum for me Mr. Woodchuck," Rebecca said with a voice that wasn't Rebecca's.

Joey screamed

Rebecca changed into Freddy Krueger.

He tugged Joey's meat with his knife gloved hand.

SLIK-SLAK "Oops," Freddy said with a laugh.

Joey screamed. "My dick! Oh god!" Blood sprayed the inside of his sleeping bag.

"Oh, now that was a cum shot," Freddy said. "Surprise, rise and shine!" He hopped up.

The others came awake.

The girls screamed.

"Joey, my god," Danny said. He bent over his friend.

Joey gasped and then passed out. Blood soaked his sleeping bag.

"Stay away; what do you want from us?" Stephanie asked.

"He wants an ass beating," Jesse said. He stood up. He wore only blue boxers.

The audience track gave approving whoo hoos'.

He took a fighting stance and, SOCK IT TO 'EM! Threw a lousy punch.

Krueger slipped past the blow and sunk his knife fingers into Jesse's gut.

"UHG!" He was lifted to tippy toes. Blood dripped from his rock 'n roll mouth.

Rebecca screamed, "You bastard!" She got up and charged.

Freddy kicked her in the stomach. "UMPH!" She bent over holding her gut.

The camera caught a nice down blouse shot of her Barbie dolls.

OH, GOLDEN YELLER TWINKIES PLEASE!

Freddy sliced her back with his finger knives, cutting through her nightie.

It fell to the ground.

Steve starred.

"Go on, pretty boy, have a sample," Freddy said.

"No, I couldn't."

Freddy moved his hand.

"No; what's happening?" Steve was controlled.

"Go on," Freddy said.

Steve crawled on all fours. His face met Rebecca's bent over ass.

"I'm sorry Rebecca," he said.

"Take a sniff!"

No, no, NO! Steve's faces entered her asshole. Like, went inside of it.

"Hahhaha," Freddy laughed.

"Stop," DJ shouted, "Stop putting faces in my families' asses."

"Oh, butt out virgin tease, or... why don't you help your boyfriend?" Freddy moved his hand.

"No, no," DJ moved under his control. She crawled below Steve and onto her back.

I can't stop myself. She reached up and pulled his Jackie Chan from his shorts. *I'm sacred; pure; I can't do this!*

She opened her young pink lips. *It's going in my mouth?*

And in that worm went.

Oh, no; I'm blowing him. This is naughty I can't be doing this.

She vacuum sucked that motha' fucka'.

No, I don't enjoy this; I really don't. It is Freddy that is making my little pony all wet and panting. Not enjoyment.

Steve couldn't breathe.

Is someone blowing me? Michelle? Damn, I'm gonna' die in prison.

Rebecca winced, *Shit, I'm glad I like anal with a dildo but this is too much.*

Danny got up and attacked.

SMACK! Freddy back-handed him.

He flew, like, fifteen feet and bounced off the wall.

"Don't hurt my dad," Michelle said.

Freddy laughed. With a flick of his finger he made Michelle's skin melt off.

She screamed and her skin, PLOP! Fell on the floor like jelly. Skeleton Michelle looked at her gore covered bone hands.

Oh no, no, no, she tried to speak but lacked the biology.

Steph couldn't scream from the shock of seeing her sister turned into a twitchy skeleton. She scrambled away on the ground.

"Whe're you going?"

Freddy ran at her.

She tried to climb up on the couch.

"Yer mine! And your McNuggets."

He climbed on top of her.

"You don't need this."

CUT! He removed her spaghetti strap tank top.

"No, stop; please!"

"Beg, I love when they beg."

Freddy got between her legs. With a long, wet tongue, he slobbered on her PEP Boys.

Oh, they are just marvelous. So springy! Guck, I got me a huge load comin'.

"Get off her, Fuck Face," a voice said.

Freddy turned.

Kimmy Gibbler stood in the open door. CLAK, CLAK! She cocked the shotgun in her hands. "You get away from her!"

Freddy smiled; "And who are you?" He climbed off Stephanie

Thank god. Stephanie tried to cover her Sea Biscuits with a couch cushion. *His Sylvester was storming my Man at Arms! Gawd my titties are slick with drool.*

"I'm your worst nightmare, Bub," Kimmy said. She aimed the shotgun

"Ah, and what makes you think you can tell me what to do?"

Freddy grabbed Stephanie.

Kimmy fired, CLAK!

BOOM! SEVER!

"What the fuck?" Freddy fell; "My fuckin leg. YA' BITCH! This isn't possible."

Freddy held his leg; it was severed from the knee down. *How did she do this? I'm in charge of the nightmares. This can't be?*

Kimmy walked over.

Freddy looked up at her. *Damn, she is kinda fine. Hell, like season eight fine.* "What great tits you have," he said.

"The better to kill you with; and the better to collect cum on. But, the second part isn't for you."

Kimmy propped the shotgun by her leg.

Danny moaned and got to his knees; he peered over the couch.

Kimmy pulled her shirt over her head.

"Damn." Freddy's jaw dropped.

"Damn." Danny's jaw dropped

Joey lifted his head, "Damn," he said and then died.

"Damn," Stephanie said. "I mean, put your top back on."

Kimmy's tits were the most glorious thing in the universe; it gave her untold-of powers. Perfect symmetry and fatty tissue were like mutant powers.

"No, don't; stay back," Freddy warned.

Kimmy moved close; she grabbed both sides of his head and pressed his face into her tittie Gibblers, GOBBLE GOBBLE!

"No, NOOO!" Freddy's face began to melt.

"You're killing me, how could this be?"

In through the door came Mr. Miyagi. He smiled and crossed his Asian arms over his chest.

"You, you bastard!" BRRRBBBLubble!

Kimmy motor boated the bastard.

GURGLE, GURGLE, DIE!

She dropped Freddy.

He fell to the ground. "Tell my mom," CROAK!

"Whoa! Thanks," Steph said.

Danny came over. "Kimmy you were amazing." His eyes got all big and doughy. His heart went all pitter patter. Danny was now in love

Kimmy put her fists to her hips, jutted her tits out; and said, "No problem, Tannerinos."

"And, who's this?" DJ asked.

"Oh," Kimmy said, "That is my sensei, Mr. Miyagi. He's been training me to defeat all the Hollywood horror creatures, monsters, and maniacs."

"Cool," Steph said, "Think you can train me?" she asked.

The old man, though his squinted eyes, looked at her little brownies. *MMM, Asian delicacy,* "Sure."

"Great!" Steph jumped up and down; her gobblers quaked because she was topless.

"What about us?" Joey asked, "Shit, I'm all dead here."

"Me too," Jesse said.

"Oh, wax on wax off," Mr. Miyagi said. He rubbed his hands together.

"Hey, what's the big idea?" Joey protested. "Leave my corpse alone, will ya'?"

The old man put his hot hands on Joey's ass.

Hey now!

Asian power-

BING!

Joey sat up in bed. His pillow and sheets were wet with sweat and-

"Wow, was that all a dream or did it really happen?" He climbed out of bed. Adjusted his hard-on.

The bedroom door opened

"Joey?" Steph peeked her head in.

Wow-zas! "Yes, Steph?" *Is she going to climb into bed with me? Maybe I'm dreaming?*

"I'm leaving with Mr. Miyagi," she said. "See ya' later."

Mr. Miyagi's head appeared behind her.

"Okay, later," Joey said. *Shit, that didn't go how I wanted.* He laid back down. *Damn, maybe I can pull us all into another nightmare?*

"Joey," came a voice from the door.

Joey leaned up, "Yes, Michelle?"

She made her eyebrows hop and licked her lips.

END

HALF NAKED CAT BITCH

Bridget Chase

Nine to Bored Now

"What's wrong with you? Damn woman; quit bein' a woman and do some'fin' right for a change."

Mr. Cuckold shouted insults at Liza Phillips. He was a thin dude with an unhealthy lean look. A shiny gold crown sat atop his head and it was rumored there was another, smaller version, on his other head.

"I'm so sorry, Mr. Cuckold. I'll fix it, I promise."

She cowered at her messy desk.

Liza was a low-level cubicle worker and looked like shit. Like, real shit. Her hair was Kentucky Fried Chicken fucked, her clothes hid her body, *and* she wore glasses. Can you believe that shit? Glasses, which we know make people look awful, just awful. What? Am I wrong? Isn't that what Hollywood teaches us?

But, under all that mess, you could tell she was a hottie in disguise.

Liza looked kinda' like Hailey Barry; if Hailey Berry lost all her money and lived on the street for a bit.

"You better do it right; shit, that's why you women earn less than men. Incompetent, women are completely incompetent."

Mr. Cuckold's dick was pretty much in her face. As it was when you are in any cubicle and the boss comes to talk to you while you're still seated. It was offensive. Liza eyed the bulge and thought she could see the imprint of the little gold crown.

His dockers, with a flat front, showed just enough bulge to make Liza know a squirrely cock was behind that thin piece of fabric and it was angry in her face.

The other men in the office sneered, the women cowered in their cubicles and tried to stay quiet.

Mr. Cuckold turned. A green-ghost fart slipped out his butt. He walked away.

Dolores, who had been standing just behind him, barred her teeth at Liza and called her a bitch under her breath. She turned and followed Mr. Cuckold.

Damn, Liza thought, *All my life I've been powerless. And, I'm still powerless. I can't even do one pull up; ONE! Guess I'll do these reports again. Shit, gonna' take me all night. All fuckin night; but guess that's okay seeing that I have no life, no friends, no cock at home to stretch me out good 'n plenty. Prolly for the best 'cause I ain't shaved my legs since the TV show Friends ended.*

She looked at the stack of papers. It had taken her a week to do.

And now, I get to do it all again; shit!

Liza had signed all the documents in blue ink. Mr. Cuckold just reminded her that all documents require black ink. But, not just any fuckin' black ink; Merger and Stanley black ink.

I guess I'll go buy some pens.

Liza got up and went to the elevator. She worked in a skyrise 'n shit, and her employer was, if you didn't pick up on the cue earlier, Merger and Stanley.

The company had a small supply store in the lobby with unreasonably high prices, which each manager rigidly enforced using their own marked-up products. The employees had to fuckin' paid for them.

Liza sighed; *I never stand up for myself.*

But, that was about to change.

She starred at her own reflection in the elevator's mirrored doors.

Her hair was gnarly. Like, sleep outside for a week and hiked a trail, gnarly.

Robbers 'n Rivers

It was late

Damn, it's late.

The stack of papers was down to the last sheet. The pen trembled in Liza's hand.

Shit, my hands never gonna' be the same; hang in there girl, you'll go home soon.

She had sighed, I don't know a jillion papers.

The moon watched the dark world and brought with it villains and a twist of fate.

Liza signed the last one. "Finally!"

Most of the lights were out.

And, I bet I'm the only one here at this hour.

Some voices made her realize otherwise.

That's strange; the janitors already came through and left, she thought.

Liza ducked when two men walked down the hall.

"Yeah, this'll be a great score," one said.

"Sure will; damn, you and me Pettin' Pete's Strip Club tonight. We'll own the place. I'm tellin' ya' what; Bimbos all around," the other said.

"Yeah, and if they want our money, they have to please our junk."

"No question 'bout that!"

The men passed.

What's happening? I don't recognize them. And why would office workers wear ski masks?

Liza moved but bumped her head, "Ouch!"

"What was that?" a guy asked.

A scary dude came over fast, grabbed her by the hair, and drug Liza off.

"What should we do with her?" the first guy asked.

"What we do with all of them, huck, huck, huck," the second guy laughed.

Liza bounced around in the trunk of a car.

The flash of the pistol's muzzle should have been more shocking.

Liza never felt the water.

Her body sank in the river.

Cat Lives

A cat searched the sandy banks for a good meal. *Naw, that's sand. Naw, that's a heroin needle. Shit, I learned my lesson last time. What 'a fucked-up trip that was. Damn, I's thought I was Heathcliff 'n shit. Hmm, booze, tar, can, paper, condom, dead body-*

DEAD BODY? I better go investigate.

Liza's body washed up on the shore. Her eyes were open, and her black skin was pale. But, not white people pale, like black pale; from being dead, like I said a minute ago. The water lapped the bank and her body.

The cat snuck up. *I'm not used to dead people could be pretty cool. I think I'll touch this one. Hell, I've passed up the opportunity a few times, but this bitch's black.*

The cat's paw touched her forehead.

Yuck. Hmm, wonder how she tastes. I can't help it, her skin looks like rotted fish and them eyes; yeah, definitely will eat them eyes, some.

The cat licked her forehead.

BING!

The world came back to Liza.

GASP! She sat up. A, "Meow." Slipped from her lips.

The cat starred at her. *Did she just meow? I think she meow-ed. Crazy bitch. Man, that was an electric lick, though.*

What the fuck happened? Liza was soaked and sitting on the bank of the river. Her nipples were hard.

Milk

"Damn, you's guys have more milk?"

The grocery store clerk stood 'n starred.

Liza sat on the tile floor of the grocery store. Empty milk cartons surrounded her. Spilled milk was all over her *and* the floor.

"No ma'am," the clerk said. He was like eighteen 'n shit, so this job was just a place he went every day; he didn't give no fucks, NO FUCKS, YA HEAR!

"Gimme, gimme, gimme; I need more milk, MEOW!"

"Ma'am are you alright?"

"Meow, yeah, geez, I just like milk, MEOW, and Fancy Feast; which aisle is Fancy Feast on, MEOW?"

People gathered.

Her eyes were frantic.

"Here, I'm gonna' take my, MEOW, shirt off." She ripped the shirt over her head and sent those dark titties flyin'.

The clerk 'n people gawked, *damn those are delicious.* His eyes locked on them dark nipples.

Liza dumped a gallon of milk over her head. "Oh, milk you's so good, MEOW, MEOW."

The cold, white liquid ran down her black tits. Her hair and shorts were soaked, and her chocolate skin had goosebumps.

A security guard, seated at his desk in the back, licked his lips and watched the security feed. *Yep, gonna' for sure make me a copy of this.* It was a high def camera. The dude had several compilation videos at home that he jerked it too. *Hell yeah I's do, one time this chick gave her boyfriend head right on that there bread aisle, she did. The bread isle! Can you believe that? Man, that was some hot footage! I could tell when she swallered too; looked like it was a big load!*

The clerk watching Liza got a boner. Oh, and he was a white dude because them white dudes love themselves some black titties, *GIMME, GIMME, squishy Supremacy.*

Why do I love milk so much, MEOW? WHY? WHY? Damn, it's good, MEOW! GUZZLE, GUZZLE! She tipped back that gallon and her deep-throating-skills came in handy.

Old Lady Know-eth Much

"What am I, MEOW?" Liza asked.

This old bitch looked down at her. "I don't know; what are you?"

Liza licked her forearm and wiped that saliva-shit across her face. "I don't know; I think I died 'n was brought back by a feral cat, MEOW."

"Hmm-," the old lady thought on this unrealistic story. She leaned on the banister of the library's second floor balcony. AIDs-laden fabric cloaked her Raisin-Nut body. "Come up here; I'll have a closer look at 'cha."

"Great, Meow," Liza said. She dropped her yarn ball and headed for them stairs.

Liza always consulted this homeless lady at the library when she needed advice. Usually, it was 'bout what hair style to wear 'n shit. Or, what da' hell is this, when she had some weird skin blemish.

Liza went up to the second floor.

The old lady turned. She was crusty, like, she lived under a ship and grew barnacles but then lived on land a bit and let that shit dry into hardened, flaky diseased skin. You should see her fuckin hair, DAYUM! Like Albert Einstein dipped his head in a cement truck and then stood in a wind tunnel.

"So, what do you see?" Liza asked.

"Well now, I see some titties." She turned away from Liza and shouted, "Does anyone else see them titties?"

A few people in the library looked up. A teen boy raised his hand, timidly.

Liza wore a pink tube top but one them oiled biscuits had slipped out.

"Okay, he sees some tits. Now, what do I see. Hmm…," The old bitch pulled at a renegade chin hair. It was kinked and gnarled. "Somebody was killed and brought back to life by the most powerful magic in all this land; and, I think that bitch was you!"

"Magic? MEOW?"

"Yes, a cat's kiss, the most powerful magic you'll find. Shit, I's once a millionaire living in Beverly Hills because of a cat's kiss." The old lady smiled with lawn mower teeth.

"Yeah? You don't look like you ever had no million dollars?"

"Well honey, I's spent that shit. Damn, I had me this cabana boy. Used to make my kooter churn butter he did. And, all my fingers were covered in, BA-BLING!"

Spit flew from the old hag's mouth and landed on Liza's lip.

She grimaced and wiped it away. "So, what does this mean, MEOW, for me?"

"This," the old lady said 'n, SHOVE! Sent Liza over the second story railing.

"MEOW!" Liza fell but was able to spin and land on all fours like a cat. She looked up and hissed. "Whoa! I'm a cat, but I look like a sexy woman as well."

"Exactly, use this power ONLY for good. Oh, and for fucking some men. It should be real nice for ya'. You's extra flexible 'n shit, now."

Liza pulled a leg over her head. "Yeah, damn, I am." She licked her thigh.

The teen boy, sitting at the nearby table, gawked and dropped his pencil.

Kwik-Mart Karate

I was just buyin' a box o' Twinkies. Hell, a girls gotta' live. So, I took that damn box of sponge cakes to the register but-

"Empty the drawer Bee-OTCH!" A robber stuck a gun in the cashier's face. The cashier was some Indian guy with a droopy thin mustache and thick saggy lips.

"Yes, yes, do not rush me; I will give you da' money. Please be patient armed robber man of great impatience."

Liza hugged the snacks to her chest. *Oh, maybe I should test my powers. Hmm, this looks like just the way to do it. But what about a costume? Hell, can't be stopping crimes in jeans and a loose black shirt. I EVEN have a bra on. Naw, that's not superhero like at all. You's gotz to show off dem' titties!*

"Motherfucker; the money, NOW!" the robber shouted.

The cashier pushed his glasses up his nose. His oily hair was plastered to his head and curry beaded on his forehead. He hit some buttons and, DING! That register came open.

Liza ran. *I'm going to stop this! I'm a superhero cat bitch woman thang!*

"Hey, watch it," the robber said.

Liza blew past, BAM! And out the door, across the street, and into a jewelry store.

Good thing I saw the robbery in progress here from across the street in that convenient store.

She ran inside.

Two men with guns wearing panty hose on their heads turned and faced her. The panty hose made their noses all squished like little angry pigmies.

"What the-?"

"Who's this black chick?" the other said. "Hey, on the ground, yous black bitch!"

Liza smiled. "Oh boys, boys, boys, MEOW. I think *YOU* should all get on the ground. Damn, that was a bad comeback, wasn't it? Yeah, will have to work on my, MEOW, comebacks in the future. Maybe, you guys have some suggestions for me, MEOW, huh?"

A chick, in a pressed blazer and tight skirt, had her hands up. Panic rode her face like a high school jock taking advantage of the retarded girl with great knockers and no sense.

"Waster her!"

The robbers both wore masks, but one guy was in all black the other wore a navy-blue under-armor shirt, he was sporty, just so we could tell them apart.

"Meow," Liza purred. She ripped her shirt off.

"Damn, we got some chocolate titties in here," the guy in black said.

"Sweet; jewelry and tits. This heist is goin' mighty fine; mighty fine indeed," the other guy said.

Liza pounced; she jumped like seven feet right on top of the guy in all black. He screamed and pulled the pistol's trigger. Bullet ate the ceiling.

His buddy aimed. "Damn, I don't want to hit you."

SLASH! SLASH! Liza raked the dude's face with her nails and, BAM! Drove her knee into his nuts.

The robber dropped his pistol.

Liza rolled off 'em in a ridiculously fast move and, SPIRING! Lept onto the other guy.

A boy, walking his dog down the sidewalk, heard a noise and peered in the jewelry store's window.

He stopped dead in his fuckin' tracks.

Oh, man titties. Oh man, oh man, oh man! He pulled out his phone.

Some black, half naked chick was kicking two dudes on the ground.

The boy wanted that black action girl. Like, wanted her really bad. Oh, and the dog watched too.

Damn, look at her go.

The black chick knelt on one guy, grabbed hold of her titties and beat the dude's face bloody with 'em knockers.

Costume Me

Hmm, that's close, MEOW, but doesn't quite say, 'sexy cat bitch.'

Liza sat at her little craft desk in her tiny dank apartment.

She drew women on a sheet of paper and created different outfits for them.

Nope, tits are too covered up. Hmm, have to show more leg, MEOW; maybe my Tom Hanks too, if I keep it shaved-up right.

She drew a mask with big 'ol eyes. *Kinda' looks like Spiderman, hmm, MEOW, no.*

Then she decided, fuck it.

I'm a super hero, MEOW. I'll wing that shit. I bet it's part of my special powers 'n shit, MEOW. Hell, never head of no super hero that couldn't make their own damn costume, MEOW, no matter their financial sit-iation' or socio-economic level, MEOW.

She scribbled the drawing;

And, decided, *I'm definitely fighting with my titties hangin' out, MEOW, MEOW.*

I Po' Po'

"You seen this shit?" Nickels came up to lieutenant Chins' desk. "Look."

Chins took the phone. He read the headline. "Yeah, read a few things 'bout her. She's pretty hot, for a vigilante."

"So, what do you think about her nickname?"

"Half Naked Cat Bitch? Seems right by me."

Nickels had his hand in the pocket of his pleated pants. He fudged with the tip of his dick like he does when he talks to most everyone. "So, you think that cat-shit is hot, or what? Oh yeah, you do, don't you? I can see it in your eyes. I know you do, don't hide it. That shit is SO hot! SO HOT! Right?"

"Yeah, she is sexy," Chins said, "And the meow-thing, sure; you're right, pretty hot."

"I knew it; motherfucker. I knew you had a thing for her. Hey Phil!" Nickels shouted out the door and across the precinct's office. "You owe me five bucks, man; Chins just admitted it. He loves the bitch!"

"Naw, naw, I didn't say that." Chins handed the phone back. "Besides, I got a date tonight."

"Yeah, she hot? Tell me she's hot. Oh, I can tell she is. You're not saying anything, but I can tell she must be hot."

"She's black."

"OH MAN! Oh MAN! Damn, you're a lucky fuckin' wetback. Okay, well, if you play with 'em titties, you's gotta' get a pics for me."

Chins smiled. "We are just going out for dinner."

Nickels looked at his phone. "Man, wish I could get this Half Naked Cat Bitch on a date. Shee-it! I'd rub her in corn and butter, and gobble that snatch; Hubba, Hubba, Vroom!"

Chins' Tang

I know what he's thinking. He's thinking, 'holy fuck she's hot as fuu-uck ME! I'm gonna' slap that sexy ass with my raging cock.'

Liza stood in the apartment doorway.

Chins starred at her with his mouth open. He hadn't said nothin' yet.

"Do you like?" she asked.

"Um, yeah, god, yeah; you look amazing." He closed his mouth.

"Good," Liza said, she brushed past him and entered the apartment. "I was going for amazing, MEOW."

Chins closed the door. "Can I get you anything to drink? A glass of wine, beer, water?"

Liza turned. "Milk?"

"Coming right up."

He went to the fridge. *Damn, she is finer than I remember.*

He had bumped into Liza outside the crime scene of a jewelry robbery gone wrong. Chins thought she was hot; but seein' her, now, in that tight black dress and the way her ass looked like, HOT DAYUM*!*

I'm a lucky fella. And that meow she did earlier; what the fuck? That shit was hot! Okay man relax; I can feel myself getting a boner; calm down, play it cool. Play-it-cool…

He took the gallon out of the fridge, grabbed a glass, and poured some milk.

Chins turned around.

Liza jumped with surprise. She pulled her panties up and fixed her dress over her legs.

He noticed the wet spot on the wall.

"Did you just piss my wall?" Chins asked.

"No, no; geez, why would I do that, MEOW? Pee on yer' wall, ha, no, no, definitely not. Wouldn't do that; nope."

Chins walked over and handed her the glass. "You sure? I think you just marked my wall like a cat."

Liza blushed. *I hope my oiled cleavage distracts him. How embarrassing, MEOW, why did I pee his wall?* "No really, um… um, I'm embarrassed I thought I felt a spider in my panties and was just fishin' for it, is all."

Chins walked to the wall. He crouched and peered at the wet spot.

Drops dripped down the wall to the carpet.

Liza wanted to change the subject. "So, MEOW, what are the plans tonight?"

"You sure you didn't do this?" he asked again.

"I'm sure, MEOW, must be a leak behind the wall or som'fin'."

"Too bad," Chins said and stood, "I think it's pretty fuckin' sexy!"

Liza's kooter walls spasmed. She bit her lower lips. "Um, well than, maybe I did piss yer wall, MEOW."

"Say meow, again."

"MEOW."

Chins pulled her to him and kissed her passionately.

Liza felt the press of his hot cock on her stomach. There was very little fabric between his body and hers.

Finally! Get that fuckin' cock inside me!

Strange Turn

CLAK!

Mr. Cuckold fell to the ground with a bullet hole in his head. His crown tumbled across the ground. The sheen of fate sparkled on across its surface.

Delores laughed, "Mwuahahaha." She was 'n older bitch, hot titties, but a sour face. She'd always been second in command, but had put together a sinister plot for complete control.

The door opened to the office.

"I have those-," Liza stopped in the doorway. Her jaw dropped. "WHOA! You killed Mr. Cuckold, MEOW."

"No," Delores said, "You did."

"No, MEOW, pretty sure you did."

Delores tossed the gun.

It tumbled in the air.

Liza dropped her stack of papers and caught it.

"No, you did." The old sour faced bitch smiled.

Damn, MEOW. Liza was fucked.

Shouts 'n shit came from outside.

People piled in the door.

"Liza, how could you do this?" Delores asked. "We are *ALL* so ashamed of your behavior; killing dear Mr. Cuckold with no remorse like that." Tears brimmed in her eyes. She had practiced this cry, but could never make it convincing enough. Until, she figured out, that, by placing a tacks in the bottom of her shoes she could step on them and cry real tears of pain. Both the sharp points were deep in her heels.

The people in the doorway gasped.

"I, I ,I-," Liza dropped the gun. "MEOW," She ran for the window.

"Hey, stop her," some guy who wore a sensible pea green colored dress shirt, said. "She's a murderer and must be stopped!"

CRASH! Liza jumped out the thirty-second floor window.

"Whoa," a lady office worker said, "We just witnessed a murder suicide!"

They ran to the window and each jumped over Mr. Cuckold's dead body in the process.

"There she is," a guy with no hair said.

Liza ran across the rooftops and did somersaults 'n flips that were entirely impossible. Well, at least for humans; but, she was some other kind of cat bitch thing, so, who's to say what she can and can't do?

John Locke stood on a rooftop. With his scarred eye, he watched. "Don't let 'em tell you what you can't do. Not ever!"

The Whip and Delores

Liza strutted down the sidewalk in her overtly sexy S&M sexy, black cat costume. *Yeah, I worked hard on this shit, MEOW.*

Revenge was going to be hers.

I mean, MEOW, I'm not mad about her killing Mr. Cuckold, he was an asshole, MEOW; but she's such a bitch for framin' me. Shit, that's too far, MEOW, MEOW, too far.

She snapped her long whip.

"YIKES!" A coupled jumped outta' the way.

"Hey baby," a guy said to her. He was a sleezy mouse.

Liza snarled, "HISS!"

"Eek!" The guy jumped and kept walking.

Yep, soon I'll have revenge, MEOW, and then I'll take over that building. Yep, I can see it now. Me, MEOW, MEOW, in the big office. All the men scared of me and cowering when they talk to me. Oh, MEOW, I'll have boardroom meetings and sit on the workers' backs, MEOW, instead of chairs. This will be great, MEOW, just gre-

Headlights blinded her.

RRRR! A car pulled up fast.

What's this now, MEOW? Liza shielded her eyes.

"Hey, don't move," a man said. He was just a dark shadow.

"Stay back, mister, MEOW," she said. "You don't want, MEOW, my kind of trouble."

"You'd be right about that, Pussy Cat," the man said. "Easy Pussy, pussy; just relax; everything's gonna' be just fine, just fine."

Liza squinted. *Is that, MEOW, a gun?*

THAW!

She looked down.

Is that, MEOW, a dart in my titty?

The word spun like soggy dough on an Italian man's greasy finger in a pizza parlor.

Hmm, MOEW I think I'm going to faint, MEOW, MEOW.

As Liza fell to the cement, the man said, "Now there's a good kitty. I'll get you a good home. A real good home."

Family Pet

"Oh mom, I want that one," the boy said.

"Honey, no; that one's ugly."

The boy looked at the naked woman in the cage. "No, she's not."

The mom sighed. "Honey, that is a terrible looking cat. How about this one?" She pointed to a small stripped kitten.

It played with a wadded piece of paper.

The boy's eyes were locked on the naked black lady. *Oh man, oh man, she is so hot. GIMME, GIMME, I've never seen tits in real life. Oh boy, would ya' look at them- all squishy, soft, and round. If I can just get her home.* "I want that one, mom. She is the perfect house cat."

The mother looked at the large dark feline. "But, it's such a weird looking cat. Are you sure?"

Liza hissed, "Leave me alone, HISS! MEOW." She lifted her leg and flashed her hairy kooter at them. Liza had been locked-up in the animal shelter for months and hadn't shaved a lick of her body.

The boy gawked at that hairy orifice. The gnarled hair ran from her belly button to her ass.

It's so dark and hairy. "I want that cat!"

The mother sighed. "Fine, let me see if she's been fixed."

The mom walked off.

The boy went up to the plexiglass window. He crouched. "Hi, I'm gonna' take you home. You're gonna' be my new cat. You'll be a good kitty. You'll sleep in bed with me, and play with yarn, ad touch my-,"

(cough)

"-And, oh, if you're *real good*, I'll give you milk."

Liza perked up. "MILK!" She rushed over and put her hands on the glass. "Oh, yes; yes, MEOW, milk please. What do I have to do for milk, MEOW, MEOW?"

The boy smiled. "Oh, I can think of lots of things, Pretty Kitty."

END

BRIDGET CHASE

MILE 23

TALE 23
Bridget Chase

Mock 'A Markee

"Yeah, you like this shit? I own it all."

James Silver leaned back in his chair and grinned like a bitch.

Alicia shrugged her shoulders. "Sure, it's nice, but I could really go for a beach or something remote and relaxing."

"A beach? Shit bitch, this is my beach," he said. "And, see this hair? All mine."

James ran his fingers through his dark hair.

"That's cool," Alicia said, I've had many haircuts for movie roles, too."

"Okay, okay; I don't want to get into any zombie bullshit. But, let's get on with why I'm here. Oh, and I think I'm gonna fuck you. Like real Super-Star smooth 'n shit; but prolly wait till the end or some shit, cause I'm a gentleman and Mark fuckin Walh-,"

(Cough) "-I mean, James fuckin' Silver."

Alicia leaned onto the table.

She was a hot piece of ass with some good boy knockers that she didn't show off enough; but hopefully will in other movie roles. She was also a bad bitch working for the CIA and shit. A real beauty. Man, what a beauty. Lips like, HOT DAMN! And eyes like, YER KILLIN' ME HERE BITCH! Oh, and her ass. Fuck, go on and kill yer'self now. To think there's a man out there fucking that killer babe nightly while the rest of us can't, shee-it.

She said, with her fantastic, I want to suck your cock lips, "I brought you here because your country is missing nine pounds of radioactive isotopes."

James frowned, "You sure, bitch?"

"Yeah, I'm sure."

"That doesn't sound like the America I know. Hell, hold on; James can't just be believing any 'ol shit. Hold the phone, I'm callin' headquarters." He looked down to his crotch and said, "Yo' think while yer down there you can hand me my phone?"

The Thai bitch, suckin' his nob, fished in that movie star's pocket.

Alicia rolled her eyes. "Men."

SLUPR, POP! "Here, sir; yous phone, sir"

James took the phone.

The Thai bitch went back to gobblin' and milkin' white man jizz for a paycheck.

He held the phone by his face. "Base, Bitch!"

"Dialing, Base Bitch," the phone said.

"Colonel Malkovich Mayhem, here."

"Colonel, it's me, James."

"Hey James. You with that hot-ass CIA lady, Alicia?"

"Yes, yes I am. So, I heard we's missing nine pounds of radioactive isotopes; is that true?"

The Colonel stood in front of a board meeting. Other officials sat around him. *Damn, here goes. I'm gonna' be fired.* "Yes, James we lost enough radioactive isotopes to destroy, completely destroy, six major U.S. cities."

The other military men and political people, gasped. "Well, that is way too much," one said.

"Okay, boss. Well, I'm gonna fix that, cause I'm a badass and here at the Thai U.S. Embassy," James said.

"Okay, thanks; that would be super helpful. And, if you get a chance, nail that Alicia ass for me; will ya?"

"Will do... UHHHGRRR- ARG!"

"What was that?" Colonel Malkovich Mayhem asked.

"I just came."

"You came?"

"Yeah, got me this Thai bitch scarffin' my nob. She just swallered."

"Cool," the Cornel said, "I got a black bitch on mine, but my nuts take a little while, old pipes and such. Ya know what I'm sayin'?"

Colonel Malkovich Mayhem stood in front of the room with his wang sneakin' out his fly. A naked black woman was on her need giving the military man a Scully.

"Yeah, I do," James said, "Talk later."

"Okay, UHGGGRRR-UHG, OH GOD, YES! ERRR... ERRR..." (Cough) "Well, old pipes still workin'."

"Nice!" James hung up.

He said to Alicia, "Okay, I'm in; let's do this."

"Great," she said. Alicia sucked a popsicle. She slid that cold shaft in and out of 'er lips. "Let's go to the embassy." POP! Her lips smacked.

Private Places

"Oh, here comes my guy," Alicia said. She leaned out the open window of the sixth floor American Embassy.

James starred at her ass. *Damn, wanna' lift that little skirt and mutate that oyster; NIO-CE!*

"You say something?"

"Naw; so, what's this about an informant?"

Alicia walked over. "As I told you when I was butt ass naked doing yoga- what you didn't listen?"

"Naw."

"Well, this Kung Fu master, special forces guy said that he has info 'bout the missing radioactive isotopes."

The door opened.

"Hey, guys."

"Hey," James said.

Alicia asked, "Are you our informant?"

"Yep."

James crossed his arms, "Cool, but we have to know you are who you say you are. Alicia let's send him to the doctors. You do have a doctor's office in this Embassy, right?"

Alicia unbuttoned a few top buttons of her blouse. "There, show a little cleavage. Um, yeah, there's a doctor here."

"I don't this that's a good idea," Informant said. "I'm Thai, and my government want me dead. Oh, you should have seen guys I killed 't get here. I's like-,"

Informant did some punches and kicks.

"-And, oh yeah; I knee this one guy, but his friend came charging, so, I like, flipped over head 'n shit. WHAM! POW!" he punched.

James put his hand up. "Sure thing Pencil Dick; you're some bad-ass action star, I'm sure. But, you're going to the doctors so they can verify you by... I don't know; some shit way."

Informant shook his head, "Okay but I warn you."

"Don't worry 'bout warnings Thai mothafucka', I'm part of an elite Special Opts team, part the CIA called, Overwatch; and, on my watch, you'll be safe. Oh, and Alicia, those are great ta-tas."

She smiled. "Thanks."

Alicia was leaned on a desk and squeezing them hams together with her arms.

Government Street

"Who's this asshole?" James asked.

Alicia, two American fellows, and some Thai guy were in a room, inside the Embassy.

Alicia said, "This is some Thai official, and he's here to threaten us."

The Thai guy looked like a bad-dude, but a bad-dude with money and connections. He sat in a chair.

"Oh, threaten me huh?" James swaggered over.

"Yes, I was just telling this gorgeous lady, with tits that I want to cum on and an ass like a Thai goddess, that I want the informant back. If you don't give him to me. I'll take him."

James folded his arms over his chest. *Does this make my arms look big? It does, right? Yeah, those are big boy guns right there!* "Id like to see you try. Shit he's with our doctor where there is no real security. Oh, and check this out-," He pointed to his hair. "This is real, mothafucka'."

The Thai man nodded. "I'm just sayin', watch your back."

NO! YOU WATCH YOUR BACK!" James shouted. He shed a tear. "Asshole, tellin' me to watch my back," he said under his breath.

Alicia wrapped him in her arms. "It's okay, it's okay."

James cried, "Dude's just so mean ya' know; and that come back was awful."

The Thai man stood, "Well, I'll be off. By the way, do you have a floor plan to this building?"

Alicia said to Dukey, "Dukey, give this man the floor plans."

"Sure thing."

Dukey dug in a desk drawer and came out with a rolled sheet of paper. "Here ya' go."

"Thanks." The Thai man took it. "Do you think you could highlight where the doctors are at?"

Dukey nodded. He fished around for a highlighter and then marked the page. "There ya' go."

"Thanks."

The Thia official turned to James and said, "Remember, watch your back."

"NO! YOU WATCH! YOUR BACK!" James shouted. Then he buried his face in Alicia's tits, and cried.

She hugged him. *Well, I prefer my tits getting wet from cum, but tears are okay, I guess.*

SNIFF! James smeared his wet nose in her cleavage.

Turn Head, Cough

Informant sat on the paper lined table. He only wore boxers so that everyone could see his physique.

Two doctors were in the room.

One came up. He pulled a syringe from his pocket.

They are spies! THWAK! Informant kicked the doctor in the head- a concussion, if I ever saw one.

The doctor fell to the ground.

The other doctor grabbed him around the neck from behind.

Informant clawed at the forearm around his throat. *This wont work.* He yanked hard and hip throw, CRASH! Threw the doctor through a partition of glass.

Two men with guns rushed in.

Informant turned. He, BAM! Kicked the first one's knee backwards.

The guy fell and screamed.

Informant rolled over the table and palm-STRIKE! Drove the other guy's nose into his brain like Nicholas Cage in Con air.

23 Miles

"What do we do Colonel Malkovich Mayhem?"

"Relax James, all you have to do is escort Informant twenty-three miles to the rendezvous point. There is a plane waiting for you."

James held the phone to his ear. "I don't know man. Twenty-three miles is far. The government is after this dude."

SCREECH!

James ran to the window. "I mean, as we speak four SUVs are pulling up and armed men are climbing out. They're going to storm the building!"

Colonel Malkovich Mayhem said, "Good God man; you're Overwatch, the most elite Special Opts the CIA has, and if you do this thing right, I bet Alicia will let you fuck her."

"What are you talkin' bout. She'd let me fuck her right now; right now, ya' hear."

Alicia stood next to Informant. He looked at her.

She shrugged and smiled.

James wiped his sweaty forehead. "Your right. I'll get him the twenty three miles, or I'm not Mark Wa- I mean James Silver!"

Stair Climber

Alicia's tits flew everywhere. She had taken off her top and was only in a bra. *Hey, a girl's got to try and out-do the main character anyway she can.*

James was in front of her and Informant behind.

'Damn, so many stairs," James said.

He and Alicia carried assault rifles.

"Shh, shh," James hushed them. "Someone's coming."

Footsteps came from a lower level in the stairwell.

"Sounds like four or five of them," Alicia said.

The Informant was unarmed. "Give me a gun."

"Naw, we can't do that," James said, "You have to show off your Kung Fu skills; a gun would be too easy for ya."

"I have an idea," Alicia said.

"Whoa what are you doing," James asked.

She removed her black bra. "What do you think?"

DROOL! Both men's mouth hung open.

"I'll distract these guys with my sparkling tits of magic, you lean over the rail and shoot them."

DROOL! The men's eyes were fixed on them pretty 'ol pink nipples.

Wow, what lucky man gets to suck on those? Damn, James, you need a woman with Slimers like that.

James didn't have anyone. He was single because work was hard and isolating, which is why he wanted Alicia. They had the same sort of job. Men's logic on those kinds of matters is always rock solid.

Alicia went down the stairs. She looked back. "You got the plan? Shit, lift your gun up… well, do something."

DROOL! The men starred

"Psst, whatever." She went down the stairs.

James leaned over the railing.

"Hey boys!"

"WOWZAAZ! HUBBA HUBBA GIMME GIMME! Number five sausage biscuit egg san'mich!" The men hooted and hollered flattering barks.

James fired CLAK CLKA CLAKKKKKKKKK!

Men screamed death and the stairwell got a new paint job- color- bloodshed.

"Okay, you got them James. Come on down."

James and the Informant ran super-fast. Like POOF! Cloud of smoke and they were there.

"Damn." James was let down and panting. Alicia had her bra back on. "Okay let's get to the vehicle transport. We have nineteen minutes," he said.

Anti-Hollywood

"Well, it was a good fuckin' try," James said. His arms were tied over head and he hung suspended in a dingy wet room.

Alicia hung, as well as the Informant. Oh, and Colonel Malkovich Mayhem was there too for some reason.

The Colonel said, "You tried and failed. Come on man, you were supposed to be the best?"

"Yeah, yeah," James said, "But, have you seen this?" He shook his head around making his hair whip. "It's all real *and* all mine baby."

Sweat beaded on the Colonel's forehead. "Well at least tell me there was awesome explosions, an epic car chase, gun fire, maybe an airstrike, and lots and lots of action."

Alicia grunted. Her wrists hurt from hanging. She said, "Nope, we basically got into the SUV and our caravan pulled out. Two blocks away we were surrounded and captured."

"Did you shoot at least once? Like, one single bullet?" Colonel asked.

James shook his head, and shook it excessively making his hair waive around. "No, they got us fair and square."

"Damn," Colonel Malkovich Mayhem said. He hung his head. "We're going to die."

"Yes, we are," Informant said. "On the bright side, before we go, we get to look at her titties. I mean, I guess there 'r worse way to go."

The colonel looked up. "Alicia, think you can swing my way a bit? Might make me feel a bit better seein' them Gravy Platters. 'Ol Grandpa's hankerin' for some springy cupcakes.

Alicia swung her legs for momentum. Her tits warbled. She turned towards the Colonel. "So," she asked, "How would our lives have turned out if we had made it? James?"

James had a boner. "Well, I imagine we would have had an epic car chase, made it just in the nick of time; like maybe the plane was just taking off the ground and we had to either drive aboard or jump aboard. Anyways, safe; you and I would have fucked, maybe dated. Hell, I might even 'v been with you a few months. We would have gone to that beach ya' wanted to go to, and I would have let my hair fly in the breeze."

Sounds nice Alicia said. "Think maybe we could get that fuck in, since we're going to die and all?"

"Sure."

"Let me try." Alicia squirmed with her legs trying to get her skirt off.

James kicked and shook, "Damn pants." He whipped his spine like a fish outta' water.

"So, Informant," Colonel asked. "How would your life have turned out?"

The Thai Kung Fu master thought. "Well, I'd go to America, tell your government all they wanted 't know. They would pay me like I's Eminem back in the day, and I'd start a new career with less violence; like maybe, open that bakery I always want open. Oh, and one day, a fine, like ultra-fine woman, way outta' my league, would come in, and she fall in love with me; all romantic and happy ever-after kind of t'ing."

The Colonel nodded. "Sounds nice."

Alicia gave up tryin' to get naked. James didn't he curled his body up and tried to get at his zipper with his teeth. He wasn't close, not close at all.

"And you, Colonel?" Alicia asked. "How would your life have turned out?"

"Well-," the Colonel imaged many possibilities, "-First I'd-,"

The door sung open. A man came in and raised a gun. CLAK! CLAK! CLAK! CLAK!

The guy with the gun walked out of the room.

A Thai guy, at a control panel with monitors, asked. "You kill those gabby fucks?"

"Yep," the guy with the gun said, "One round through each of their heads."

"Even the bitch with the tits?"

"Yep, but I's still gonna fuck 'er."

The control panel guy said, "Cool, me too, let me know when you're done."

END

OPRACALYPSE
Bridget Chase

Dat Hunger

That stomach of Oprah's was hungry. Bitch had been on a super-cleanse as prescribed by Julia Roberts, queen of nutrition and queen of culture, for nearly a month.

"I's fuckin hungry! So Gawd damn, hungry!"

Oprah stood in front an elaborate mirror. Her thick flesh was hanging like grocery bags on that body of hers.

"Feed me!" her stomach said. "You got big 'ol lips, use 'em to feed me!"

She put her sausage hand on her belly. "I can't; this is the diet that'll make me skinny and loved; but not loved like being rich and having a show- loved. Naw, real, raw love; the love that people give when you're thin 'n beautiful- God's love. I bet it will be great and worth it. That love is coming for me; no-way that people would treat me the same as they did when I'm fat. Nope, I'll be able to love myself and have everyone love me, finally. Because thin is perfection!"

"Fuckin' feed me!" That stomach shouted.

"No stomach; only a few more months of eating toilet paper and I'll be skinny and as loved as they come. You listen to me, stomach, and you listen good; I decide what you need, and if I say you need toilet paper, then you is gettin' toilet paper!"

"NO! YOU LISTEN BITCH!"

"Eek! Oh, no!" Oprah stumbled back and sat on that pristine toilet. No one should be witness to what happened next.

Kunis Divin'

"Oh, how lovely this ocean is," (BUBBLE! BUBBLE!) Mila Kunis said.

She swam next to Ashton Kutcher beneath that blue sea made by God for them Hollywood Celebs.

The two had some microphones in those helmets 'n shit, so as they could talk a bit while diving.

That hot bitch Mila wore a tiny blue bikini. And, the scuba tank 'n vest was cinched up tight under them tits making Ashton go, 'WHOA! DEM GATORS BE ANGRY!' Her ass was tight too, when she kicked them thin legs.

So, they went on down to those depths of the ocean.

Mila was wanting to see them Dolphins. "You know where they live and such?" she asked.

"Sure, Baby Cakes, I know where Atlantis and shit is. That's where all dolphins be. But, be careful, you're a hot bitch and dolphins like themselves some hot bitches," Ashton said.

Tom Sweat

"And a one, and a two…" Richard Simmons showed Tom Cruise them moves to get fit.

Richard was guiding Tom to get pumped for his new Mission Impossible movie.

Tom was sweatin' hard like a canned cat.

"Are we almost through?" He asked because he was outta breath, and Tom needs breath, despite what some think about celebrities.

"Through?" Richard asked, "We've only just begun. Now, shake that gawd damn Shake Weight like yer jerkin' off them Back Street Boys, back stage after a concert.

Tom went to it and shook it like that was his life's purpose.

"So," Richard said, "What be going on with you, other than that new Mission Impossible movie number twelve, Da' Mustard Clause?"

Tom gritted his teeth. He followed Richard's pose and bent over, 'n shook that weight between his legs.

"Well, not be much. I'm divorced now, and those Scientology bastards give me everything I want. I have new and different girls each night; all having just turned eighteen and shit on that day they're brought to me; I fuck 'em on their birthdays!"

"I never heard nothing about that," Richard said.

"Yeah, nondisclosed 'n shit. I got babies all over this word."

"Cool."

"Yeah, so I'm thinking I'll get into doing superhero shit. I mean, I seem to be some god of Hollywood and the world, you know. And that is like religion these days, so I'm pretty gawd damn special. I'm thinking I'd start fighting crime, save the world 'n shit."

"Cool," Richard said, "You need a side kick?"

"Maybe, we'll see."

Great White Oprah Whale

"Feed me, Bitch!"

"Okay, okay." Oprah hopped in her SUV, BRRRR! She took off down that fucking street. She had already eaten everything in her fuckin' mansion house, even the laundry detergent. "Outta' the way sons bitches!" HONK! HONK!

Damn, she took them turns likes they were lit. SCREECH! She peeled around the corner.

"What do you want?"

Her black belly gurgled. "I's want Dolphins bitch! You starved me too long. Head on out to dat beach. I's gotta' eat."

Oprah lifted her shirt. Her stomach had grown and spilled over the waistband of her pants.

BOOM! That sand blew up when the SUV hit the beach. She pulled a donut. At the same time, the Queen of Day Time TV opened her door and went flying out.

She didn't even stop that car none. Nope, just let that shit keep hauling ass with no driver. People screamed, it plowed through a sand castle, ran over a couple chicks sun bathin, and eventually stopped when it hit parked cars.

"Oh no! What's happening?" Oprah began to change. PLOP! Her body swelled and that flesh sagged. FLOP! She fell to the sand and clawed for that water.

"Feed me! I want dos dolphins! Feed me!"

"EEEAAAAHHKAAA!" Oprah roared like a beast. Her flesh ripped outta' her clothes. In a tan bra 'n granny panties, she wiggled into that water.

"I MUST EAT!"

Dolphin Meat

"Atlantis is destroyed," Ashton said, "Damn, how could this be?"

Mila gasped, her nipples went all hard. "It's a disaster!"

"Let's investigate," Ashton said, "Maybe we can use our Hollywood super powers to do detective shit, and fix this."

She nodded.

They swam into the rubble of that city.

"There," Mila said.

Two dolphins were all twisted up in metal and shit. Some of the pieces went through them.

"Naw, that was Oprah, alright," a dolphin was saying to his friend when Mila and Ashton approached.

"Whoa! Who be this?" the other asked.

BUBBLE! BUBBLE! "Hey, are you guys okay?" Mila asked because she was sensitive like that 'n shit.

"No. That Oprah bitch came 'n destroyed our city, and ate everyone. SHE ATE EVRYONE!" The dolphin was played by Jack Nicholson and had his face CGI-mapped over the dolphin's. He began to weep.

"Well, he thinks it be her. Can't be certain though, because the thing that did this was a blubber monster," the other dolphin said. This one was played by Adam Sandler.

Mila was shocked, as people are when they hear something they didn't expect. "Oprah? No way! I heard she's on some new-crazy diet, anyhow."

"Nope; she ate us," Jack Dolphin Nicholas said.

"Yep, she ate all of us," Adam Dolphin Sandler said. "Our precious city and way of life is no more and will never be again. I'm so sad, this fish boy is sad, he is."

"I can't be having this," Mila said, "Not in *my* world. Not on *my* planet!"

Oh, and she spoke dolphin language in case you were wondering how this communication was happening for those out there who need everything explained to them.

Jack Dolphin Nicholas said, "Hey, since I'm pretty much dead here with this barb through my stomach, you think I could see them titties? I mean, I saw 'em in 'Forgetting Sarah Marshall', but kinda felt that picture of you flashin' in that movie was photoshopped, and it'd be super dolphin cool to see them in person before I go to heaven."

"Yeah, me too; hashtag metoo," Adam Dolphin Sandler said, "Let's see them bitty titties!"

Ashton was accommodating and hitched his shoulder like, 'whatever, let 'em see. What do I care? I'm gay anyways.'

"Okay," she said, "Here-." Mila pulled them bikini cups away and let them cupcakes out.

"Oh, wow," Jack Dolphin Nicholas said, "They're everything I ever dreamed."

"Yeah," Adam Dolphin Sandler said, "They are the Pearly Gates 'n shit."

"Thanks!" Mila kneaded them little pancakes together some like she does when she wants a dude to jizz on 'em.

CROAK! The two dolphins perished.

"This won't stand." Mila put them boobies back in her top. "I will take revenge; I just need an action hero partner."

"Me?" Ashton asked.

"No, a real action star!"

Fate Delivery

"Oh, hi Mila," Tom said after opening the door.

"Hi Tom," she said.

He noted that she wore a sexy tight black top, some corset artillery thing with guns on her hips, and yoga pants that make ya go, BOING! THATS A HOT ASS! GIMME GIMME! TATERS!

"What's up?"

"Well, I came to your house because I have a superhero mish in need of a super hero."

"Me?"

"Yeah, so comb that hair of yours, and let's go."

"Cool."

Richard Simmons ran up in his gay spandex. "A Mish? Can I come? Tom, can I? Huh? Tom? Mila? Tom? What do ya say?"

"Sure," Mila said.

"I don't have to comb my hair, do I?" Richard asked. His hair was a bird's nest of curls and frizz.

"Naw, guess not."

"Here," Tom Cruise said, he pointed to his utility belt. "Hop in. When there's trouble I'll get'cha out."

"Cool!" Richard Simmons dove into that small utility belt of Tom's.

"Let me get my diamond and gold comb."

Mila waited.

Dat Duo

"Where are we gonna' find her?" Tom Cruise asked.

"The only place left with any dolphins- Sea World," Mila said.

The two drove down that LA freeway, stopping every five feet because of the heavy traffic.

"This won't due," that hot bitch Mila said, "Take to the sky, Tom."

"Sure thing." He hit some buttons on the dash board. He was driving some gnarly GI Joe vehicle and with a couple clicks on the dashboard that thing converted to a bad ass helichopper.

CHOP! CHOP! CHOP! Them blades ate the air and that vehicle floated off that hot summer cement.

As they rose to da sky- "Would ya' look at that." Mila pointed.

"Whoa!" Tom said.

A wide trench came from the beach and ran across the city. Buildings were destroyed, cars crushed, and smoke rose from that shit.

"Do you think that was Oprah?" Mila asked.

"Could be," Tom said, "But she's a big-bitch, now. How big ya think she has to be to make a cater in the earth like that?"

"I don't know. She must be like forty-feet wide and a thousand tons."

"Cool," Tom said, "I like fightin' big bitches; let's follow those tracts."

Roll Cameras

The audience was in a delight. All them housewife-ladies were super excited to be on set for that gawd damn Oprah show. They were all hoping to get a car or some shit and see their guru in action.

The ladies' nasty-nesting panties were in a wicked twist of excitement, but then came that Oprah, but not the Oprah they were expecting, no.

"BLAH!" That worm meat bitch was some kind a killer whale but with rolled fat, squat legs, 'n arms. Them lips were thick and squirrely with teeth that wanted lunch. Oprah licked them lips looking at them delicious calories 'a people.

Oh man, she rolled into that live studio set and roared. Them people went all, "AHHHH!' Man, but did she gobble 'em up. Oprah licked them chops and swallered people.

Bones crushed, heads popped like grapes, and intestines spilled down her throat.

"Feed me," she said, "Feed me!"

People were vaultin' shit and runnin' like Gump for their lives 'n such.

She's a big old bitch and rolled around like a thick 'ol whale, smushin' shit, 'n breaking shit.

Them cameras eventually cut and that network ran a technical difficulties screen card.

Oprah was still hungry even after that carboard set was destroyed, like maybe three people survived and crawled their way to safety.

"I needz food! I's a fat bitch who starved for too long. Time ta let da Oprah out!"

She squirmed her way out that building on her Mufflin Man stomach.

Da Cruise Report

"Looks like the bitch hit up Sea World," Tom Cruise said.

"Why you think she did that?"

"Shit, she's some monster-thang, must need herself a big meal."

"Shamu?"

"You bet!"

"Damn, that bitch better not eat that whale; I love that guy," Richard Simmons said from within the utility belt. "He sure is nice. I once threw him a fish 'n that whale smiled he did and said, 'Thank you, kind sir, you are most gracious.' Can you believe that shit?"

They ignored the exercise guru.

"So, what's the plan?" Mila asked, she rubbed her cunt through the crotch of them yoga pants with the muzzle of that pistol 'a hers. Action got that chick off hard!

"I guess we'll do a fly over 'n then we see what's happening."

"Oh, looks like it isn't good!"

Below them, Oprah was in that big pool a water with Shamu. A shit ton people were clappin' and laughing thinking they found themselves a good 'ol show.

"Damn, she's big," Tom said.

Oprah looked like Jaba da Hut; I know she always kinda does, but now she was a bloated Jaba, and that water wasn't helping none. Her skin was wrinkling like a raisin.

Shamu raced around that pool splashin' the people. Oprah gave chase.

"I'm bringer 'er in," Tom said, "Come on!"

He moved that chopper over the scene.

The two got out of them chairs and perched in the bay doors.

Mila said, "Hold on a sec. If we're goin' in water, best I get naked."

Tom agreed even though he wore a thick 'ol leather jacket, jeans, 'n other trendy shit.

Mila stripped them clothes and her little boobies danced; she dropped them pant- rascal was shaved. She wore just the tactical vest around her waist with them guns.

"Let me gear up," Tom said, "Richard!"

"Yeah?"

"I need you to become big 'ol bruiser gloves; like, I need to wear you so when I punch, shit, it goes kaboom."

"Roger," Richard said, "Hold on."

That exercise dude was capable of magics of kinetics. He reshaped his body. "Ready."

Tom reached in that belt and pulled out them Rock 'Em Sock 'Em gloves. They were golden and had Richard's face CGI-ed on em. He slipped them on, and POW! Punched them knuckles together.

"Now I'm ready."

"We better hurry. Looks like Oprah's gonna have dinner.

That dark Opraba (Oprah 'n Jaba) had that killer whale pinned below her heavy flesh. Them dish rag tits were all heavy 'n laid oved that poor theme park attraction creature.

"Let's go."

The two lept outta' the helichopper.

FREE-FALL!

They twirled in cool acrobatics and with no chutes.

KA BOOM! That helicopter ran straight smack into a skyrise off in the distance. Like, hundreds died and tons a money done in damages, especially in them streets. A kid was smushed, too.

Tom didn't care; he cared about his hair, though.

Mila pulled out her guns and let that bitch have it.

Side Dishes

CLAKKK KKKKK! Mila bullet rounds popped on that pepperoni flesh of Oprah's.

ARGH! That bitch turned her head 'n hissed.

"Dive formation," Tom said.

Mila and him somersaulted mid-air 'n, PIKE! Speared their bodies; SPLASH! Perfect dives into that deep pool.

They both swam to the surface.

Oprah lurched her body and came at them.

Tom charged them Simmons Power Gloves. Them things turned all glow-y yeller. And SLAK! He hit Oprah in that big face.

Her cheek fat took ta' swishing across her face and drool wretched from her lips.

CLAAKK-KK! Mila fired those guns. The hot rounds dimpled that nasty flesh.

"Iz kill you, Iz kill ya! Iz just wanna eat dis whale. Its flesh will feed my flesh, MINIONS! I needs ya' MINIONS!

People cheered, "HOORAY! What a show!"

'N outta that stadium stands came three Oprah minions.

That fat bitch said, "Let me introduce you to my team. We's got Dr. Phil."

Dude jumped and flew over that water wearing a cape, no shirt, but them black slacks.

"And, Ellen."

Skinny bitch rode a magic carpet and had a bazooka.

"And, da lady of psychic powers Miss Cleo!"

Black, round bitch laughed and her eyes glowed red, she floated too with a couple balloons and a nasty tarot card whip.

Tom and Mila hopped up to that fish feeding platform. "You, Oprah minions, you better leave. This bitch is paying for what she did. What did she do again?" he asked Mila.

"She ate those dolphins and destroyed Atlantis with that big ass."

"Right, she ate dolphins and destroyed that great under water city 'n shit."

Dr. Phil had a large staff. "We will do no such thing. We are controllers of daytime minds. We will protect Oprah with our lives."

"So be it," Tom said.

Dr. Phil's staff glowed at its jeweled-end and, ZAPA-RASCAL! A green energy fired off.

Tom and Mila rolled out the way of that blast like sleepy puppies.

Mila fired back, CLAKK-KA-KA!

Dr. Phil dodged the rounds.

Tom jumped high in the air and cocked back that fist of his.

"You're toast; like, breakfast toast," that Simmons Left Power Glove said.

"Yeah times for you to die," Richard Right Power Gloves said.

Dr. Phil, just like when he went bald, didn't see it comin' and Tom, SOCK-A-TOOI! Punched 'em good.

"Gimme' a kiss," Richard Right Power Glove said, and, SMOOCHIES! Kissed Dr. Phil's cheek.

KA-BLAM! It was lights out and our Dr. Phil; he fell into that water, KA-PLUNK!

Opraba roared. "We's hungry! We's hungry!"

That Shamu was still pinned beneath her and growin' weak.

"I must eat!" Opraba was a famished feast 'a flesh.

Mila said, "Tom, you get Oprah. I'll get the two others."

"Roger, good thinkin'. Who knew ya' had a brain, and damn, you's hot, butt-ass-naked with them guns."

Ellen and Miss Cleo, hearing the plan rushed Mila.

Tom soared in the air and landed on that platform by Oprah. She was a stinky bitch, too.

"Let that fish go," he said. "Sea World needs it, 'n I need Sea World."

"We'll do no such thing. Hunger, we's a hungry black bitch. Our fat needs meat. Our fat needs Shamu."

Opraba roared and opened that mouth, showing teeth. She went in for a big bite.

Tom did a street fighter upper cut

"Here we come, bitch," Simmons Left Power Glove said.

KA-BLAM! Tom power-punched that whale jaba under her triple chin.

Opraba's eyes rolled back. FART! A bubblin' intestine-gas rolled out that bloated belly n out that asshole.

The audience screamed in terror as the green smog rolled out like morning fog over a grass prairie.

"Mila," Tom called, "We has gotta' move."

SLIK-SLAK! Mila elbowed Miss Cleo in that face a hers.

DODGE! Mila ducked a punch by the weak armed Ellen and, WHAM! Came back hard, clocking that lesbo bitch in that sharp nose of hers.

Richard Right Power Glove said, "You guys go. I'll finish Oprah."

He lept off Tom's hand and transformed back inta' his Jazzercise body. That hairy chest fluttered in the wind. He lept all the way up to Opraba and grabbed her neck. The two fell into that deep water, GURGLE! GURLE! "Drown bitch!"

"Everyone run!" Tom shouted to that audience.

People panicked and ran, but many stopped 'n snapped some pictures for their Instagram.

Tourist Trap

"I can't believe they made us pay the full ticket price," Mila said. She wore a tank top, no bra- hard nipples, and some tight ass-huggin' jeans.

"Yeah, you'd think having me, Tom Cruise visit would be a greater reward than money. Besides, you're right, Mila, we were the ones who took down Oprah; so, we should get in for free."

The two walked down the tight corridor and-

"-WOW!" Mila said. "I still can't believe that they stuffed Oprah and put her as an attraction at this Side Show.

Tom let out a long breath. That taxidermized Oprah filled the room. Her leathery skin was hardened to near plastic, and the sight was still one that was hard to describe.

A nearby kiosk played some narrated recording about Oprah's diet, mutation, and subsequent defeat.

"Look," Tom said, he pointed to the small monitor.

It showed parts of the Sea World battle as captured with phones.

"Yeah, she's a dumb bitch," a voice said.

Mila and Tom turned.

Adam Dolphin Sandler and Jack Dolphin Nicholas stood on their tails next to them.

"You're alive," Mila said with much excitement. She lunged forward and hugged the two dolphins.

Adam Dolphin Sandler cupped a feel of her boob with his flipper. *Oh, they are very nice! Softer than I expected.*

Mila didn't notice.

After the hug Jack Dolphin Nicholas said, "Yes, and we have you to thank, Ms. Mila. Your boobies saved us. Following your visit, we were overcome with titty power and not only did my friend, here, and I, instantly heal, but we were able to rebuild Atlantis in just a few hours."

"That is wonderful," Mila said.

"Yes, it is; but there is one more matter that we could use your help on, if you are so inclined."

"Yes?"

Adam Dolphin Sandler said, "You see all the women folk dolphins were killed. Um, (Blush) we need to repopulate our world and we were wondering if...?"

Tom stepped forward. "I'm a super hero. Let me help!"

END

ROBO
KONG

Bridget Chase

ROBO KONG

Bridget Chase

Give 'em the Steel, ROBO Ape thing, uh; YEAH!

"I see you there, bad guy. In the dark shadows, bending that 'Uptown Girl' over. You are under arrest. Please pull your assaulting cock from that poor woman's vag."

ROBO Kong held his awesome sci-fi pistol leveled at the perp.

The guy, with his pants around his ankles, stopped fucking the bent over chick. "Stay outta' this Tin Can. This chick wants it, and I haven't got my nut off yet."

"Please help," the woman said. She was gorgeous. Like, this guy really found himself a good one. She looked like Pamela Anderson. She had a short dress on and it was hiked up over her ass. Her tits were wrecking balls swingin' all over.

"You're a fool, "Robo Kong said.

CLAKKKK-KKKK!

The dude screamed and fell over. "My nads, my fuckin nads. Oh, shit what did you do?"

"Protecting and serving," Robo Kong said.

The woman ran up. Her tits flapped all over, "Thank you, so much. Here, let me repay you." She got down on her knees.

Robo Kong put the end of his gun to the top of her head. "Do it good bitch; it's the law!"

She wrapped her lips around his pneumatic piston and pumped that shit like oil from the earth.

Robo Kong did his job and sprayed those titties with gorilla grease.

∞

"It's nice serving the city," Robo Kong said.

He sat at his kitchen table and spooned that baby food soft-stuff down his ape gullet. He'd taken off his Robo helmet and the ape's bald robot face was a nightmare.

The hot bitch he'd saved knelt under the table and was workin' a wad outta' our hero's junk.

It was a thick sucka'; so, she had her work cut out for her.

Yeah, I kept her around. It's not every day you meet a gal as staked as that. Oh, here we go; Le'Go my Ego!

SLOOGE!

"Swaller it-up bitch!"

GULP GULP! She did a nice job drawin' that nut out.

Billy climbed from under the table. She wiped her lips smearing that Jungle Jizz away with the back of her hand.

"How was that?" she asked with a smile, because I'm writing her super slutty.

"Just fine, Billy; here, have some dinner," Robo Kong said. He slid a Happy Meal across the table.

Billy slipped her chicken McNuggets back inside her bikini top.

Oh, yeah; she was wearing a bikini to dinner, because, well, why not? This is fiction after all. I mean what is the point of writing if you aren't going to take liberties? And, I think every female in this story will all be wearing bikinis, so there.

She opened the Golden Arches and pulled those flava' nuggets out. "Dipping sauce?" she asked.

Robo Kong slid his bowl of baby food towards her. "Hot 'n spicy flavor."

Billy dipped and then, MUNCH devoured it. It tasted good mixed with the ape's nut.

"So, what should we do tonight, now that you're my baby mama bitch?" Robo Kong asked.

Billy shrugged, "Netflix?"

"I only have HULU."

Billy scowled.

ZING! The lights flashed in the small kitchen of Robo Kong's rented apartment.

My apartment is small but very affordable, plus the location is great, right next to a hardware store and mechanic.

He lied, Kong got the apartment because of the pool view. After signing the lease, a receipt for a video camera sat on his coffee table for a week.

Hey, stop telling them shit! How I spend my summer's is my business buddy.

A figure emerged from the colorful vortex.

"Hey!" Robo Kong shouted, "Cut-it-out (Joey Gladstone) with the tearing of space and time, shit; I just cleaned that kitchen."

"Oh, sorry," the figure said. He approached the table

"Uncle Franklin?" Robo Kong asked.

"Yes, son; it's your Uncle."

Uncle Franklin was a great ape like Kong, but he looked like Benjamin Franklin with the balding head, white hair, spectacles, and gut.

Uncle Franklin pulled out a quill pen and held it in the air. "Kong, I've come because the great forest needs you." The Uncle then noticed Billy. *Damn, those titties be callin' me, BEA-KAH!* "Oh, hey I'm Uncle Franklin. He hurried to her side, took her hand, and kissed it.

"Nice to meet you; I'm Billy."

"What's this about the forest old man? I can't go back there. I'm metal; see."

Kong opened his robe and showed his metal body.

"I'll rust like a motha' fucka'!"

"Ah, yes, I see," Uncle franklin said, "We'll have to figure that out as we go, but, go we must!" He still held the quill up in the air.

The AC made the long feather dance.

"What's with the quill?" Robo Kong asked.

"For this!" Uncle Franklin walked to the wall and drew a large square.

Within the outline, the wall changed to pink, pretty as pussy folds.

"Whoa!" Kong said, "You just fucked up my wall!"

∞

"Hey, you can't do that," Robo Kong said. He was laying on his bed.

Uncle Franklin knelt over him and worked a screw driver. "Nonsense let's just get this junk off of ya."

Billy helped by handing Uncle Franklin tools and laying the pieces of steel atop the towel on the floor.

"This isn't a good idea. I was an ape; but, after I was shot fifty bazzillion times, science made me into this living robot. There is nothing left of me underneath."

Uncle Franklin bit his tongue as he worked. "We'll see about that."

A few moments later...

"Done!" The Uncle got up.

"Oh, this isn't good," Billy said.

"W-?" Kong asked.

"Well..." Uncle Franklin grimaced; he turned to Billy and the two talked quietly.

"What is it?" Kong asked again.

Billy grabbed a mirror and brought it to the bed. She held it over him

"EEK! I'm nothing but a brain, a pair 'o eyes, and; well what's that?"

"Those are your balls," Billy said.

"They really are attached to my brain!"

Uncle Franklin pulled out a small sketchbook. "I'll works something out; don't cha' worry none."

Billy smiled sheepishly

Kong would have trembled if he had a body. "You'll do something? This was a state of the art, cutting-edge, million-dollar technolog-,"

Uncle franklin showed him the sketch.

"Oh, okay; That'll work," Robo Kong said

The Uncle showed Billy.

She nodded

Uncle Franklin stuck his quill high into the air. "Let's get to work!"

∞

"This is great," Robo Kong said. He was strapped to Billy's chest. His brain, eyes and balls swam in fluid.

Kong's brain spun around. The glass case made Billy's cleavage extremely super-awesome!

Whoa! I can t wait to get back in my body and fuck them pumpkins.

"Here we are," Uncle Franklin said, "The great forest."

"This is Central Park," Kong said, "The portal you opened only took us down the block."

"Hell," Uncle Franklin said, "In New York, this *is* the forest!"

"It's pretty; I'm glad we are going for a walk," Billy said. The harness and Kong's Brain Case sat comfortably on her chest.

Men and women walking in the park grimaced seeing the bloody brain in fluid.

"So, what is the problem here?" Kong asked, "I want to do this mission, that only I can do, and get my body back because Billy and I need to fuck!"

"Yes, lets hurry, please," Billy said.

"This way." Uncle Franklin guided them. "There." He pointed to the Statue of Liberty.

"Yeah, and," Kong said, "I've seen that shit, just a big 'ol lady."

"Not just a big 'ol lady. She is guardian of all forests. You might not know, but she is the central figure in keeping the earth alive."

Billy asked, "And what about before she was created?"

"Hush woman! Don't start with any nonsense. This way," he said.

They arrived at the monument's base.

"Now, what is the mission?" Kong asked.

Uncle Franklin tipped his glasses down his nose. "*That* is our mission."

"Hotdogs; get yer' hotdogs, here!" A hotdog vendor shouted. He was a greasy guy but nothing special

"What? The hotdog guy?" Kong asked.

"Yes," Uncle Franklin said.

"Does this mean we are having lunch?" Billy asked, "I love lunches shaped like dicks."

"No," Uncle Franklin said, "We are here because this villain is using regular mustard on his wieners and not using Grey Poupon Mustard!"

"No! This guy? This evil villain of most evil villains? Damn him, damn him to hell!" Kong's blood boiled n rage.

Didn't this fucker ever see the commercials? You can't use ordinary mustard. No way, no how; that motha' fucka'!

"Easy," Billy said, "You're making the water hot on my chest, and you might cook yourself."

"Let's get this bastard," Kong said, "And get me my fucking Robo body back!"

∞

Uncle Franklin returned pulling a Radio Flyer Wagon. Metal shit was piled on top.

SCREECH, DRILL, HAMMER, SQUEEK, CRASH!

"Ah, good to have my body back," Kong said.

"Do you wanna' fuck first?" Billy asked. She was horny after seeing his metal body reassembled around his squishy brain.

"No, we better deal with this crime first."

"I'd like to fuck," Uncle Franklin said.

Billy thought about it. "Sure, okay, but there are too many people around."

"How bout a handy down trou?"

"Sure."

Robo Kong stomped off on geared legs.

Billy slipped a hand down the old gorilla's trousers.

She found the sleepy puppy and made its tail wag. She yanked and yanked.

The two stood close together and looked around to see if anyone noticed.

A fat guy behind a tree noticed. He was getting a trouser handy from his fat Miss Piggy girlfriend.

The two men *could have* been good friends. In parallel universe they weren't both getting handies, and met over frisbee, instead.

The two became besties and regularly went to the Massage Parlor together, to get handies.

But, not in this world.

The gorilla's nut grew anxious. A pressure built

"I's gonna' nut-juice."

Billy smiled. Warm wet loogies squirted out and coated her hand.

Robo Kong returned. "The situation has been neutralized." He tossed the hotdog vendor's head.

It hit the ground and rolled. Bullet holes were all in his face.

"Yikes," Uncle Franklin reacted. "You could've just talked to him and asked him to use *this* instead."

He reached into his pants and pulled out a squeeze bottle. It was full. Stringy marshmallow dripped down the side. He screwed the cap back on.

"Grey Poupon!" The three cheered and jumped into the air, kicking their feet up to their asses.

∞

The hotdog vendor laughed. He sat next to Uncle Franklin at the table.

Kong waived a waitress over.

Billy sat next to him and gave him a trouser handy under the table. The others didn't know.

Kong spoke to the waitress; she smiled, nodded, and left.

The four clinked together glasses, in a toast.

Kong tipped his glass back and drank of the beer.

Uncle Franklin was telling a story to the group; he mimed using tools and unscrewing something.

Kong pointed to Billy's tits, and they were visible because she was in a string bikini- remember, he gestured removing his brain and placing it on her chest.

The hotdog guy laughed.

The Chili's waitress came back with an appetizer sampler plate and set it on the table; because our cast knows how to fucking have a good time out.

The waitress turned to leave.

Uncle Franklin slapped her ass. #metoo

The waitress huffed displeasure and left.

Uncle Franklin smiled.

Oh, and all the waitresses at Chili's were in tiny bikinis. And each was super-hot and single!

END

SPACE MUPPETS 2525
Bridget Chase

If Humans Are Still Alive

"Damn Netflix, yer killin' dis old bastard."

Grover sat in da' entertainment unit. "Fuckin' algorithms don't know shit. Damn, how I miss a good movie. Fuckin AI; fucked it all up."

Four hundred years ago, amidst the fall of man, Netflix algorithms had reached their zenith. The programs only regarded views and ratings without care as to the relevance of content. With the fall of man near, and every human compelled by the government to procreate as much as possible; it was all those little new ones who ended the legacy of movies. Too many children watched just one movie and over time all other selections were deleted until there was only a single one left.

"Fuck, I can't be watchin' that shit again. I just can't-Hook, Hook, Hook; the only fuckin' movie there is. I'm in Hell; this is definitely Hell. I mean, I don't see no fire, but this must be it." Grover was driven to tears. With his long white beard, he dried them eyes a bit.

"What? You always liked the 'Roofio! Roofio! Roo-fi-ooooo!' part. Maybe you should nap till the idea of watchin' 'Hook' again, sounds great." Count Chocula came up beside his distraught friend.

"No, I'm not tired. I've just given up hope. This mission is a failure. I'm gonna die here, alone in space."

"Alone? Geez, thanks."

"You know what I mean, Count Chocula; you're a vampire, you won't taste death. I've been eatin' it for five hundred years."

"You should be thankin' me 'n shit, for showing you how to stay alive."

Grover shut that damn video box. He got up and walked over the sub-atom cryo freeze chamber. He placed his furry blue hands on its surface. *Is that me?* His reflection eluded his sense of self. A gray-haired old Muppet stared back.

Below dat acrylic glass 'n shit floated Chris Hemsworth in bio chronic sub artic fluid.

Tri-Sarah HOLY SHIT!

"Hey Grover, dear; are ya' ready for dinner?"

"Course he's ready for dinner, bitch! Yous do this every gawd damn day. Fuckin' robot never learns."

"Hey," Grover said, "What'd I say 'bout talkin' to my robot wife, Sarah, like dat?"

"Sorry, sorry brotha'; yous knows how I is just tired of yous keepin' her as Sarah and all. Shit, mean she's a robot sex woman who can shape shift. Gawd damn man, make her Elizabeth Berkley, Natalie Portman, Emmy Rossum- HOT DAYUM! And let me have 'er a night."

"Never happen," Grover said. He sat down at the steel table. It was mostly empty.

"Yeah, I'm Grover's, forever 'n ever!" Sarah said. She wore a sexy sundress.

Count Chocula mumbled. He turned 'n rode outta' dat rom on his hover-craft wheel chair.

"Here honeys, eat up."

Grover looked that mess 'a plate put before him. He picked up his spoon. "Poor paralyzed Vampire. Not sure who has it worse here."

BLARRRE BLARRRRRE! The ship's alarm sounded.

Grover shot up, "Oh shit! We are bein' docked!"

"Really? And during dinner; how awful. Will I still be able to give you yer after dinner blowjob?"

"I don't know." Grover ran outta' that room and to the control deck. "Shit, this ain't happen none in, I don't know, two hundred years. I thought we were completely alone."

Sarah followed. "Should I make them a plate of food?"

Grover flew inta' dat control deck.

Count Chocula was already there. "This can't be good none," he said.

"Naw it can't. Hit dem visuals."

SCREECH! The large ninety inch 8k curved screen flickered 'n a face appeared.

It was a giant toad with S&M black leather with steel studs n shit on its outfit. "We're da Battle Toads, RIBBIT! We're boarding dat ship 'a yers, RIBBIT! By da' way you's a piece of shit and we's takin' yer supplies."

"Fuck off," Grover said, "We aren't just gonna' sit back and let yous rob us. I might be old 'n shit but I ain't no pussy."

"No? Really? Well fuck! Dat's what most do. Why go 'n fight us? Makes it so hard, RIBBIT," The toad said "Well, if yous don't cooperate, I'll kill someone yous love."

"Ain't nobody alive dat I love," Grover said.

The toad reached off screen and then pulled a woman into view by her hair.

"Sarah!" Grover shouted. "How?"

"Huh? This be nuts 'n shit," Count Chocula said.

Robot Sarah said, "Oh, she's pretty. Wow, wish I's as prettyas her."

"Yes, yer beloved, Sarah is ours," the toad said. "We have a super awesome machine that can create human life from the smallest of DNA strands. One of my crew is a huge Buffy fan and we made this little treat here, from a small strand of Sarah Michelle Gellar's DNA."

"Sarah!"

"Grover, help me!" She struggled against the thick fist grippin' dat golden hair 'a hers.

"Let 'er go or you'll be-."

BRRINK! All the ship's lights went out.

SIZZLE! Emergency bulbs turned on. They were a pale orange and sparse.

"What just happened?" Count Chocula asked. "Did theyz take out our power? Shit, now my milk 'll spoil 'n yous know how I hate eatin' my Count Chocula cereal without milk."

"I don't think it was dem. Somefin' else is happenin'," Grover said.

Hemsworth Fate

SHHH-K!

The cryo lid slid open. Crystalized dry ice floated in a vapor fit for a sci fi introduction.

"Whoa!" Chris Hemsworth opened his eyes. Them Hollywood pupils went in search of information. "Where am I?"

The metal infused interior told him little, except that shit had gotten' a 'lil crazy.

Man, last I remember, Is makin' out with Chris Evans. Damn, he was opening my fly 'n such 'bout to give me a wet Scully.

Our boy was a wet soggy celebrity in an unknown world.

He climbed out. *What is this? Disney world? Did I get drunk again and try to ride Space Mountain? Shit, Marvel told me if Is do that again, they'll have me star in dat Catwoman reboot, as Catwoman.*

Chris walked up ta' a set of monitors. A pad of legal paper was on the desk.

Perfect. With his acting skills, he folded that paper into origami boxers 'n matching sailor hat.

Weird noises and groans made this metal beast around him seem alive.

I'll just explore here more. Hope I find somewhere to eat. Shit can't miss one of my eight meals of skinless chicken 'n broccoli. Shit, these biceps got them a hunger goin'.

A snaking tunnel led him through a bowel of dark twisted machinery.

HISS! A door opened, and a silhouette appeared
"Hey who be that?"

The figure was big and menacing.

"Hey, back up! I played Thor 'n shit- God of lightnin', long hair, and protein shakes. I had to take me martial arts 'n shit. I'll kick yer ass!"

The dark figure lifted a chainsaw and yanked it to life.
"Oh shit!"

Chris ran like the slutty first victim in a horror movie. "Who is this guy? What does he want?"

The chainsaw man gave chase. His movements were accompanied by robotic whirrs and gear sounds.

Chris came to a dead end. "No! Help!" He banged the wall. "No please…"

The chainsaw guy came fast.

"Oh shit! That dude's Leatherface expect. Oh man, what's wrong with him?"

Chris saw a panel with a touch screen 'n shit. He started pressin' shit.

Suddenly, a door opened and, SUCK! Chris was sucked inta' outer space. The door closed.

No, this not be good. His body swelled. *Oh no! Shit, I know what's about to happen. Same thing that happened when I stuffed that one chick in my microwave 'a few years back*, POP!

His body exploded into floating pieces of Jello.

Leather face watched out the port hole.

I Toad

"Let's board dis bitch," Croak said.

"Get the guns," Fist said, to de' three other foot soldiers.

"Roger."

The toad mutants put on sci fi amphibian tactical shit. They were big old bruisers, nearly twice the size of a regular human.

SLICK! The ship's door opened. The dockin' tube snaked ahead.

"This ship is nearly empty," Fist said after some exploration. "I don't think we'll find much shit here to steal; damn shame 'cause we ain't come across another ship in centuries. Hell, been so long we might 'a lost our edge."

"Hey boys," Sarah bot stepped out from a sliding door.

"Kill her!" Croak said, but then seeing her outfit thought better. "Get 'er!"

Sarah bot wore some silky translucent nightie. Her toads were croaking and bouncy in artificial gravity. Her ass was like, CHOO CHOOO! All ABOURD! DAYUM!

Them toads became horny.

"No! The mutation," Croak said.

Fist screamed.

The toads grew these sharp barbs and their muscles went all, 'lets grow 'n shit'. Their green skin turned dark; like nearin' black 'cause that makes them bad 'n more menacing.

"Uh oh," Sarah Bot said.

Powerful, Full-Power

When the power kicked on dem monitors were showin' somefin' all to terrifyin'.

Grover starred. "Those Battle Toads 'r becoming horny toads. Shit, they is armed 'n such. How'd we get ourselves so unlucky as to getz tangled with these 8-bit creatures?"

"What do we do?" Count Choclua asked.

"I dun know, but they gotz both Sarahs. Boff of 'em. That be two, too many Sarah's, by my book. Hell, ain't no man allowed to have more than one. NO MAN OR TOAD!"

"I have an idea," a new voice said.

"Wheeer-t?" The Muppet turned.

A drippy brain floated in the room.

"Who are you?" Grover asked.

"Chris Hemsworth."

"You look like shit," Count Chocula said.

"Don't I always; anyway, I have a plan how to get you Sarah back, AND! Get outta' here."

"How's that?" Grover asked.

"Well," the Chris Brain said, "When I was a young boy a PE coach showed me great powers hidden...,"

"-Nope, stop right there," Count Chocula said, "We don't need the story after all. Just tell us Muppets what to do."

"You don't have to do nothin'; he's already here!"

Grover said, "Let's hope he ain't talkin' bout that PE Coach."

Hot Dog Vixen

"What do you think?"

"Destroy them," Ariana Grande said.

Harvey Weinstein steered dat huge space craft within combat range. "Arming the laser destroyer, aiming, putting my finger on the switch-,"

"-Just fire already."

"… And… fire!"

KA_BLOOOOMIN' ONIONS AT OUTBACK! OH, THEY IS SO TASTY!

"Oh, wow!" She cupped dem hands over her parakeet mouth.

"Yes, tis something, huh?" Harvey asked. "Never get tired seein' dat. In space explosions are super awesome 'n shit. So, what now?"

Ariana adjusted them Mickey Mouse titties in her top. "You knowz, Iz thinkin' we should visit Disney World. Would be great ta leave the dark abyss of space for a bit. Can't be healthy for us flyin around all da' time. I mean, the adventures are fun; but yous can't write song lyrics bout space none. Wait, let me try. Oh's space yous so dark and infinite like those nights wheres Iz alone because I rich 'n you be infinite like my mansion 'n shit. No, see, don't work."

"Ya' know travelin' in time and parallel worlds is dangerous; Is told you n' shit."

"Please? I'll slurp yer Mr. Belvedere on the way with my Donald Duck lips."

"You know light travel only takes but a moment."

"Okay," she said, "Here, stop at that gas station; I'll blow you then interdimensional travel to Disney world."

"Okay fine." He looked at dat pretty mouth on her. *How could I not? And, damn the devil if she ain't some hot demon 'n shit, look at dat outfit.*

Ariana wore a small tube top; dem cupcakes were all perky and ready for a fist fight, theyz was. She wore a short skirt 'n hell like Egypt.

She put on them Donald Duck bill lips.

"Oh yeah."

She strangled his Skeletor and, GOBBLE! GOBBLE! Ariana bobbed her head. Her lips peeled that dick skin way back and her tongue stimulated that head in ways only Pop Star learns from their managers, record exects, agents, and dead-beat boyfriends.

"Oh, slurpy that wirpy." Harvey's feet twitched, 'There's no place like home'.

Ariana gargled and swallered.

"Oh, here we are, Disney world."

Harvey landed dat space craft.

People pointed and gawked.

"Ah hell, ya'll get away faggots," he said to da people. "Now, what should we ride first?"

"I don't know; but let me put this bikini top on. Here," Ariana said, "Can ya' cup my little teacup titties so they don't get cold while I find that top? It be chilly in here from the intergalactic travel."

"Sure, bitch." Harvey reached over and held them sock puppets. Those nipples tickled his palms. She had some big un nipples, too.

Everyone went ape shit when Ariana Grande climbed outta' dat space craft.

Dem people said, "It's Ariana. We love you; you're our god and our hope for life and love. You're our world. You're our existence. Please we'll work menial jobs for forty years if you'll just allows us to buy over priced tickets to your concerts."

"What's the deal?" she asked Harvey. "I know I am worshipped everywhere we go but this seems; well, really good but over da top."

"I don't know myself. Must have to do with this parallel world. Ya' must be important here or some shit."

"Cool, dis is a weird version of Disney World too, because everyone be black; hell, da world I come from the park kept ticket prices high 'nuff so dem blacks couldn't afford get in."

Harvey said, "Yeah, let's go. We'll find another Disney World 'n shit; I ain't liked black people since that one nigga' in da movie 'Show Girls' got to touch dem Elizabeth Berkley titties. Man, world be unfair place ta' live when dat dude gets to fondle 'er 'n such."

"Well, if yer butt hurt you can keep playin' with mine. Later we can go back to outer space where dey float how you like, 'cause when your down here with me Eddie you'll float too!"

Today's Word

Pee Wee Herman couldn't let dem damn toads take that pretty sex bot.

No, I couldn't, shit. Maybe if Iz saves her 'n such, I can take her home; a sex bot would be mighty nice since getting a chick is really hard, seein' that I made a tv show where Iz talked to couch cushions 'n shit. Yep, mama always told me, keep yer weirdness to yerself. Now, look at me. In outter space five hundred years in the future and about to fight some toads. Moma's always right.

"Who be that?" Croak asked, "Damn, that's a skinny ass dude; is that a human? Naw, can't be they's don't come that skinny and weird."

"Let her go," Pee Wee said.

Sarah bot was stuck in a toad's arm. "Help me, please; they are touchin' my titties and this one's dick is proddin' my ass USB port. She still wore that pink nightie and them tits were all kinds of wild 'n bouncy. She was hot. Like Sarah in Buffy the Vampire Slayer season- is it five? Maybe five, no six; yeah, season six, she was super-hot if Iz remember.

I'll save them tits and ass for sure. "HIYA!" He took himself a karate stance he learned at the YMCA.

"Get this fucker," Croak said.

SLING! ZAP! Laser rounds flew down the corridor.

ZING! *Nope, can't hit me. I'm Pee Wee, toad bitches!* He bent like Gumby, rollin', flipping, and doing jumpin' splitz over the laser rounds.

ROAR! Dem horny toads Croaked. "Lets bash 'em."

The one holding Sarah let go.

The five charged him.

Pee Wee ran straight for dem like he were an awesome anime dude or somfin'. He did some crazy parkour front flip kick thang and, BAM! Kicked one toad off its amphibian feet.

Whoa! Croak couldn't believe it. *Maybe we are in for a good fight.*

Pee Wee back flipped ten feet and took another Matrix stance.

Brain Gang

"I also need my body," Chris Hemsworth said.

Count frowned. "Ain't no nigga' goin' into outer space to get yer Campell's Chunky Soup body."

"Oh, please; oh please, oh please," the floatin' brain said. "I have an awesome athletic body that'll help us on this mish."

"How about I turn into Super Grover?" Grover asked.

Chris looked at the Muppet. His back was rounded ribs 'n could be seen, and his face had gone all white 'n shit.

"I don't think so," Chris said.

Count Chocula said, "We can put you in the mutator."

Chris asked, "Why does this ship have a mutator?"

"Idk," Grover said, "Shit, never know when mutantin' somefi'n might be fun. Yes, mutate me; mutate me inta' a big blue animal, or a creature who can destroy these toads."

"And destroy Leatherface," Chris said.

"Leatherface?" The Muppet's jaws dropped.

Better Disney World

Harvey steered that ship into another cosmos and landed in at Disney World in Epcot. "We're here. Looks like Disney World."

Ariana Grande smashed her face up to the cockpit's acrylic windshield like a puppy. "Oh, wow, this looks right whites 'n Asians; yep, we're here, let's go!"

"Hold on."

"What?"

"Ya' gotta' wear panties."

"Why?"

"Cause its indecent."

"Shit, Iz don't wear panties for nothin' and I ain't startin' now."

"Okay, well at least wear shorts or a skirt."

She was bottomless.

"Okay." She put on shorts.

The two hopped out of dat space craft with a big leap from the cabin dat was forty foot high.

People gasped and gathered.

A zit covered teen drooled.

Ariana asked him, "Hey, which way be the People Mover Ride 'n shit? I really like that thing."

The blushing teen boy pointed.

"Let's go."

Harvey followed that sexy ass.

The line was a huge beast but the wait was minimal due to very good designers who knew how best to optimize the number of riders per hour.

"This is dull," Harvey said, because it was. If ya's has been on it before, you know that thing pretty much only does as the title says, it moves you about a bit and shows ya a few things.

Ariana smiled like a Down Sydrome dalmatian. "Naw, it be great! See we's moving, but not usin' our legs none. How awesome is that? Moving, but not with our legs."

Harvey looked at the scenery, "I guess it's cool. I mean, we are goin' like twenty miles an hour maybe, and we get to see some shit with our eyes. Well played Imagineers, well played. Oh, and look there, there's a hot chick, there's one too, oh and there, and there. Well, I do like this ride. Wonder how many of 'em would liken to be an actress?"

Ariana slapped his arm, "Quit looking; yas know I'm yer queen. Yer queen FOREVER!" Her eyes sparkled mysticism and anti-MGTOW magics.

The ride ended. "Now where too?"

Ariana thought. She looked around Epcot with Pop Star Eagle Eyes. "Oh, let's do Spaceship Earth. Ya' know that was the first place I got fingered. This very nice manager with cold hands took me on this ride before signin' me with a music contract. Hell, I's lucky too. He only made me give him an over trou handy!"

"Okay," Harvey said, "Spaceship Earth it is."

Lundgren Monster

"Would ya' look at me," Grover said; he was now played by a young Dolph Lundgren in a furry blue suit. Kinda like the outfits that Jeff Goldblum, Jim Carrey, Damon Wayans wore in dat movie 'Earth Girls Are Easy', which had some super hot scenes of Geena Davis in a thin bikini if ya haven't seen it; YouTube that shit.

Grover's muscle were huge 'n shit. "Look, I'm a bad ass. Man, I like this. What am I? A werewolf or some shit?"

"No, yer Grover," the director said.

"Who's Grover?" Dolph asked. "He doesn't sound Russian."

"A Muppet."

"He sounds bad ass. Well, he must be if I's playin him."

"No, typically he's cuddly."

"Oh; but look at my muscles."

"Yeah, in this scene he mutated to save his cloned wife."

"Ah; been there, sure have. Cloned wives are the best. You can mess with dem 'n shit. Be like, 'Yeah, the real you loved makin' me steaks every night. You wanna' be yerself right?'"

"Fuck!" Count Chocula proclaimed in a manner that made Grover know something was up by using a tone that said, 'Hey, something is up.'

"What?" Grover looked to his friend. "Oh no; this shit is super rad!"

Count Chocula and Chris Brain had mutated inta 'a Super 80's Saturday Morning Cartoon Action Hero Muscle Man Thang. "Guess the mutator wasn't contained." His head was Chris Brain with a mouth and fangs. He wore the brown vampire outfit, but his muscles were so swoll that the sleeves ripped and so did his pants. Kinda, like the Hulk where they just ripped to be shorts, when I reality the entire pants woulda' ripped off.

Grover punched his fist into his hand. "Let's get dem horny toads!"

The two ran like Batman and Robin after da' Commish.

They entered the battle arena.

Lava 'n dark rocks 'n shit was all around. It looked like the mouth of a somewhat active volcano.

"Where are we?" Chris Count Brain asked.

"I don't know," Dolph Grover said, "Thought wes in the ship, but hell looks like another planet."

Five horny toads stood ahead of them. They had the Sarah bot and the real Sarah clone.

Pee Wee Herman was with them but now his suit was black and his hair was combed forward and covered one eye like an Emo Anime Villian.

Chris Count Brain said, "Oh dear, lordy what happened to Pee Wee. Oh wellz guess we lost that skinny dude to da' dark side. Shits, if 'n we save yer Sarah, think I can have the sex bot?"

"Sure," Dolph Gorver said.

"Great! I'm gonna' make her look like Lucy Liu, yes sir. You won't see me fer no days 'n day. Man, we still got dat whipped cream in da fridge?"

"Yeah, 'bouts the only food we have left."

"Cool, Iz gonna' lick that off her pale titties for sure. Make them nipples little frosted towers and attack them rubber coins with my teef."

"You should bath her first; sorry Is been busy."

Count grimaced. "Yeah, I'll prolly put her in the sanitation station fer a day or so; get her good 'n clean."

"Help me," Sarah clone said.

"Yeah, enough," Pee Wee said. "I can't take anymore of this talk. De sexbot is mine. De toads promised her to me. Anyways, I'll show you she's mine by reprogramming her looks."

"No don't," Dolph Grover said.

Pee Wee went up to the captive Sarah bot. He worked them controls on her neck.

"Whoa, here we go." Sarah bot started to convulse. Her body sparkled, and she changed.

"Gross," Dulph Gover said.

"You're sick," Chris Count Brain said.

The Sarah bot had transformed into Dorothy from the Golden Girls.

Pee Wee smiled, "Yeah, I love dem old chicks, I do."

Chris Count Brain frowned. "Okay, I don't want her no mores."

Fumigation

"What's da problem?" Harvey asked.

A security guard was turnin' people away at da' entrance to Spaceship Earth.

Ariana crossed her arm and was displeased. She squeezed dem Sausage 'n Egg McBiscuits together hopin' to sway the dude with dem titty powers. "I wanted to ride this thing. What's da problem? I'm Ariana fuckin' Grande, gimme what I want!"

"Well," the officer said, he glanced quickly at her cleavage, which later he committed suicide over. "Looks like we have a fight happenin' inside. Can't let no people in. Seems there 'r these Battle Toads or some shit that took over. We think some Muppets are involved, too. We're waiting for the army to show up. Sorry folks, ride is closed till we can solve this."

"What? A fight? Shit, Iz got tear gas back at my ship want me to get it?" Harvey asked. "We'll have 'em outta' der in no time."

"Sorry sir, the army is coming shortly."

"I want to ride it," Ariana said. "Let me, now! I know Mickey Mouse and he'll come kill ya' in yer sleep; if I ask him to."

Harvey said, "You heard da lady, she wants to ride this."

"I can't let you do that."

"But I want to."

"She wants to."

"It's closed; Battle Toads are very dangerous."

"I don't care. I'm very dangerous."

"She is."

"You should care."

"She doesn't."

"I don't."

"I can't let you in."

"You will."

"He'll make you."

POW! Harvey punched da guy.

"Ouch, geez," the security guard said, "That hurt."

WHACK! Ariana soccer punted his nuts.

VOMIT! (green face) The guard fell over.

"So, what do we do about the toads?" she asked.

Harvey pondered and then an idea came. "We could release Magic Johnson in there."

"Good idea," she said, "But, then we might not be able to get him back. It took years to capture him."

"Yes, but he'll take care dem toads 'n such."

"Well, he was a huge bounty for us, but this ride is cool; okay, let him go. We'll find another way to pay for that hot tub."

Harvey nodded, "Wait here. I'll be back."

"Say that again, baby."

"I'll be back."

Ariana popped up and kissed him.

After a few minutes of bein' gone, Harvey returned driving a fork lift which carried a large cage with steel bars.

BEEKAH! BEEKAH! Magic Johnson chirped and fluttered his wings.

"He sure is wound up," Ariana said. Big 'ol feathers flew outta the cage.

"Yeah," Harvey said, "Don't think this guy's seen the sun for a long time."

The cage rattled as the giant yellow bird went ape shit.

Harvey drove the fork lift to the entrance. He lowered it. "Ready?"

"Ready."

He popped the lock.

BEKAH! Magic Johnson bolted inside dat Disney Ride. "Poor toads," Harvey said.

In moments cries and screams of agony escaped through the door.

END

SPEED MUPPETS 3

Bridget Chase

SPEED MUPPETS 3
Bridget Chase

I Got A Boat Bitches!

"I got me a speed boat, GAWD DAMN, I'M HOT!" Kermit da' Frog was at the wheel screamin' meth-ed out euphoric shit.

Dat speed boat hopped 'em waves of da' oceanic landscape at an outrageously fun speed, BRRRRRR!

Babs Bunny, Miss Piggy, and Sarah Michelle Gellar stood at the back of the boat 'n hung on to 'whatever that things called' beam. Their tits hop scotched around in them tight bikini tops they 'as wearin'.

Miss Piggy was oiled up and dripped like hot bacon grease on a Fleshlight. Sarah wore a tiny string bikini and she had no shame letting them sweet pickles dance about in da' sunshine. Babs' soft tits, with downy fur, spun zero gravity twirls all over her chest.

Oscar the grouch was inside his trashcan 'n rolled around the boat's deck, BING! *Damn, geez, I hate water and boats; why'd I come here,* BANG!

Dr. Twerk, the Pimp Muppet, rode that wakeboard behind them. He held on with one hand and puffed a joint with da other. He wore his full-on pimp outfit uncaring of the water, cause dat's how pimps do.

Grover sat on a bench seat and popped a blue monster in his swim trunks watchin' them girls bounce about all lathered up 'n bein' as tasty as nipples dipped in Dr. Pepper and Scotch.

"Yo' Kermit! Ya' gotz a text," Grover said. He fished dat fog's phone outta' a fanny pack. "Want me ta' read it?"

Kermit laid on da' speed. "Not now! I'm tryin' see how fast this baby will go!"

This whole thang was a much needed vacay for all of them furry friends. The stress of bein' a Muppet can wear anyone down.

"Cool man," Grove said.

BRRRRRR! Another speed boat with flashin' lights approached.

Kermit looked over his shoulder, "What do these motha' fuckas want?"

The hot bitches looked back. Their gumball butts winked at the coming boat.

Miss Piggy smacked her oiled ass. "Come 'n get it coppers!"

Kermit slowed the boat.

A megaphone shouted, "This is the police, do not; I repeat, do not slow down your boat. There is a bomb on your boat!"

"A Bomb?" they all asked, and panic ran through them like midnight Taco Bell.

"Hurry pull me in!" Dr. Twerk said.

Grover hopped up. The girls joined him at the back of the boat.

"Pull me in fuckers!"

They tugged the line.

"What's this about some bomb?" Dr. Twerk asked as he climbed aboard.

Grover and the girls helped him to the safety of the deck. Well, relative safety as there was a motherfuckin bomb on this motherfuckin plane; I mean BOAT!

"I don't know," Grove said because he didn't fuckin know.

The police boat pulled up along side them, and Keanu Reeves shouted, "We got an email 'bout a boat with a bomb strapped to it. It's your boat ya' poor Muppets. If you drop below three hundred 'n fifty miles 'n hour, shit's gonna' blow like Pamela Anderson's face after forty-nine."

Then he saw them three hot chicks aboard. *Sarah Michelle Gellar? Hot Dayum! There be some fine ladies here. Would ya' look at them McCraigy's Sea Biscuits skip. Mmm, hmm… daddy wants. Oh, daddy really wants!*

The two boats roared across the water, BRRRRRRR-ROAR! Like boats do; except at over three hundred and fifty miles an hour!

"So, what do we do?" Kermit asked.

"I'll help; watch out now!" Keanu did a huge Hollywood leap, with a flip, over into their boat.

The police boat slowed down and fell back behind them. The other police officers were glad to have Keanu on the force; their jobs were much easier because of it.

Dat Text

"Oh, gawd, what us bitches suppose ta' do? "We's so scared," Miss Piggy said. She climbed Keanu's back like Agent Smith in the Matrix. Her oiled tits smeared against his arms-up 'n down like it were a stiff, drippy cock.

"Yes, I think I's gonna' faint here," Babs said and fell.

Keanu caught her. "Everything is fine; I've done this shit before. Once as me, and another time, um… not as me. Anyways, I just need to take a look at the bomb and disarm it."

Grover said, "Kermit, your phones ringin' again."

"Damn." His green eyes became slits. "I can't let this thing slow down; Babs come over 'n drive this shit."

"Okay." She got outta' Keanu's arms and went to the wheel.

"Keep it above three hundred and fifty."

"Okay, no problem."

The boat flew over the water like a boat goin' fast over water.

"Here ya' go," Grover said, and handed Kermit his phone.

Kermit answered "Yo! What's happenin'?"

"Did youz see the text I sent?"

"Who dis?"

"Did you see my text?"

"No; who is this?"

"Look at da' text."

"Okay, but who be this?"

"Hang-up and look a yer text."

"I will, but I don't know you why you's bothering me on vacay?"

"Just read the text." (click) The phone hung-up.

"Damn-diggidy-dog-poop, what was that about?" Kermit asked himself.

"Who was it?" Grover asked.

"I don't know. This mysterious person with a Dorito crunch voice said to check my text messages."

Keanu came over. "Was it the bomber? It could have been the bomber. If it was the bomber you should prolly check the text."

"Oh, shit," Kermit said when he opened the message. He almost dropped the phone.

"What?" Grover asked.

"What? Was it the bomber?" Sarah Michelle Gellar asked.

"It's bad; right? It's bad," Miss Piggy said.

"It's Leatherface," Kermit said.

Dr. Twerk and Miss Piggy, gasped.

Dr. Twerk said, "Naw man, it can't be that shit; he's fuckin' crazy; been killing Muppets all across this here globe. Huntin' them down like lost socks in the hamper."

Grover trembled; he wanted to vomit.

Sarah hugged him. "It's okay, it's okay. Here snuggle my boobs. There ya' go; there ya' go."

"No," Grover said, "He's back to get me. I got away, but he is back- FOR ME!"

Keanu asked, "What does the text say?"

"It doesn't say. It's a picture."

Kermit turned his phone and showed them.

They all gasped.

The picture showed Leatherface standing in front of a Fighter Jet, fully loaded with missiles; and holding a lease slip- signed today. Leatherface grinned with his peeled face of human skin.

"Nope, never mind," Keanu said, "Never done shit like this before. Damn, I don't like me no horror movies; 'specially ones where there's jets with missiles 'n shit."

VROOOOOM! An angry jet cut the air above them.

"No!" Grover said in fear.

Parachute Point

"Oh god, watch out!" Miss Piggy cried.

The jet flew past the boat.

Kermit saw Leatherface; he was grinning in the cockpit.

"Did you see him tryin' to swing that chainsaw in that little cockpit?" Sarah asked.

Dat small cockpit didn't stop Leatherface from tryin' to do his chainsaw dance.

Grover hugged up to Sarah's body with his head squished between them titties 'o gold 'n magics. *Shit, if I's gonna' die, I's gonna' die buried in cleavage. They are so soft and warm. You got no idea how great her titties are. Man love 'em lots I do!*

Keanu said, "I have to find at the bomb. Maybe I can stop it by disarming the thing; so, it won't go boom, boom and hurt people, like 'Ouchy!'"

Babs looked back, "Please, do it. Shit, we can't keep goin' this fast; we have a quarter of a tank of gas left."

"Gimme' yer bikini top, girl," Dr. Twerk said.

"Why?"

"Don't question me bitch! Didn'tcha' learn nothin' from last time? I'm gonna' put it in the gas tank, I am; trust me. It'll raise them levels; trust 'a nigga'."

"Okay," Babs said, "Take the wheel."

He did.

Babs unfasted the booby strap behind her back and, HOT YIPPIDY-SKIPPIDY, DAYUM! Them hot, soft 'n furry titties made themselves a guest appearance, they'z did.

The boat hopped dem waves like Mexicans over fences 'n shit. Which was real fast!

Keanu couldn't help but look at them round critters. *Man, gonna' have to sample me a bit of that; just like I did with Sandra Bullock, 'cause ya' know the fear of death makes people horny; and man, Sandra, she was super horny. She sucked my dick 'n nearly pulled my dick skin clean off. I can't believe how much nut she got outta' me, and swallered it all; then begged me for more!*

Dr. Twerk took hold of dat top, opened the gas tank, and stuffed that sucka' in.

VROOM! The engine kicked to life.

Da' jet fired a missile. It took a hard turn in the sky and came at dem.

Babs took the wheel back.

"Hurry Babs," Grover said. He licked Sarah's chest.

"I need to see the bomb," Keanu said.

"What do we do?" Miss Piggy asked, "Do we get naked 'n ride you? My pig pillows are oiled 'n ready to be drilled."

"Naw," Keanu said, "Can you guys just hold onto my pants while I lean over the side?"

"Sure nuff," Dr. Twerk said, "Grove get yer blue balls outta' them titties and help here."

"But I'm so frightened; you don't know what happened last time Leatherface came around- everyone died!" He moved away from his girl's breasts.

"They did," Sarah said, "They certainly did." She adjusted the top so them celebrity nipples stayed hidden- for now.

The two grabbed Keanu and held him by his pants.

He leaned over the side. *Where is it? Where is it? Where's the bomb. It should be easily visible. Oh there!*

A huge crazy garage-sale home invention thing with blinking lights was caulked to the side of the boat with bloated white adhesive foam. It had a single antenna sticking out with a bulbous tip.

"I see it," Keanu said.

"Can you disarm it?" Dr. Twerk asked.

"Maybe; Oh, shit! Pull me up! Pull me up!"

They did and all looked to dat big 'ol sky and da' incoming missile.

KA-BOOOM! The missile impacted the water and exploded next to da' boat.

WHOANOW! The speed boat was launched in the air. They all flew up inta' da' air too.

The speed boat did and entire flip below them. They kicked their legs and pinwheeled them arms in a fierce panic and freefall.

The boat landed in the water right side up.

The Muppets, Sarah, and Keanu landed back on the boat's deck.

Oscar's trashcan, DING! Landed and then banged around like a pinball machine.

"Holy cow! That was amazing!" Kermit said. He grinned like a wild frog who was thrown from a boat while it flipped below him and then landed safely.

Babs checked her body. "Am I still alive. Oh gawd, how did we survive?"

In a shaky voice that sounded like Pinky (Pinky and the Brain) Keanu said. "I don't thing I can disarm it, NARF. Our best shot is to get this speed boat going so fast that I can pry the bomb off, drop it on the water, and outrun the explosion, NARF!"

"Sounds like a pimped-out plan," Dr. Twerk said.

"I don't think this thing goes fast enough," Kermit said, "We're already goin' three hundred sixty…. nine, yep three hundred sixty-nine miles an hour."

Keanu looked at the three girls. *They are skinny, but shit, weight is weight.* "We have to lose the chicks; they are dead weight."

"What?" Sarah asked.

"You can't be serious?" Miss Piggy said.

"They wouldn't," Babs said, "We are way too sexy and nearly naked. They wouldn't. Men can't do anything without hot women."

"No, no," Grover said, "Sarah's my wife. I can't throw her overboard."

Keanu came up and put his hand on Grover's shoulder. "MGTOW," he said, "MGTOW. Marriage is a trap; bitches be lame 'n shit. You fucked her, now let 'er go. Besides, in a few years she'll be old as fudge in Florida."

MGTOW? Grover looked at Sarah. *Can I?*

"No; here, look at my cupcake tits don't listen to him. See they are vanilla and oh so sweet 'n tasty," Sarah said.

The jet circled back and fired another missile.

Sarah jiggled them tits around. She squeezed dem and tweaked her nipples. "Grover, please; I'll gobbe yer monster; I'll let you cum them, please."

The blue monster looked at Keanu.

Keanu, that Hollywood Star of universal wisdom, said, "We're running out time."

"Come on man, ditch the chicks," Dr. Twerk said, "We's can get ourselves new hoes; ain't that hard 'n shit. Hoes be just 'bout everywhere. Dr. Twerk 'll get us brand spankin' new ones; ones that liked to be spanked. Hoes be like pennys; I'z find us more."

Miss Piggy crossed her arms and Babs frowned- her ears hung low.

"Fine," Grover said, "Lose da' bitches."

"What?" The girls were shocked.

"Great; grab em," Keanu said.

They each picked up a chick and wadded her into a ball. They raised them chick balls overhead.

"Let's throw 'em at the missile," Keanu said, "After it detonates, I'll knock the bomb off the boat and Kermit, you hit that throttle."

"Ready," Kermit said at the wheel.

"Kermit please," Miss Piggy whined.

The missile came at them.

"Now!" Keanu shouted.

They tossed them three girls high into the air.

KA-BOOOM! They impacted the missile; which became a huge-ass fire ball 'n shit.

Pieces of legs 'n arms 'n shit fell into the water.

SMACK! "Yuck!" Grover wiped his face, SPLAT! A thick piece of jelly flesh fell to the floor.

It was a severed tit.

Keanu rushed to the side of the boat. "Hit the gas!"

"Will do." Kermit pushed the throttle.

Keanu grabbed the bomb. *Come on Hollywood muscles, come on; there is no spoon; THERE IS NO SPOOOOOOOOON!* POP!

"Yikes!" He threw that explosive sucka'.

Damn, if that speed boat wasn't going like four hundred miles an hour 'n shit.

Keanu tossed dat dar bomb into dat blue ocean.

SHIC-KA-BLEWIE!

Water blasted into the sky.

Kermit, Grover, Dr. Twerk, and Keanu all looked back at the explosion.

"We never did find out if it was Leatherface who put the bomb on the boat," Dr. Twerk said.

Grover said, "We can call Leatherface; see if it was him."

"Gimme," Keanu said.

Grover handed him Kermit's phone.

Keanu dialed.

"Hello?" Leatherface answered.

"Hey, it's Keanu Reeves. We were a… wonderin' if youz put that bomb on the boat?"

"No; my plan was this jet 'n missiles," Leatheface said, "Bombs are too Looney Tunes for the likes of me."

"Who did it then?"

"No idea. Oh, wait; what's this?"

"What's happening?" Keanu asked. "Something's happening," he said to the Muppets. They looked to the sky.

"What's that headed towards the jet?" asked Grover.

Dr. Twerk said, "It's a bird; no a plane; no-."

Leatherface said over the phone, "Shit, it's John Travolta!"

John Travolta flew the sky like superman. "SCIENTOLOGY RULES MOTHA'FUCKAS!" His fist was craned out and, WHAM! He punched the jet.

"Gotta' go," Leatherface said and hung up. He grabbed them controls but the plane was already in a death spiral. *Gotta' bail*, EJECT!

Travolta saw the boat speeding away. "No, you don't! Damn, foiling my bomb plan. I gotcha' now. I gotcha' *real*, now!"

He soared to Mach One.

"Something broke the sound barrier," Kermit said. They all looked back and, BAM!

The boat nearly flipped when John Travolta landed on its deck.

"What do we do?" Dr. Twerk asked.

Keanu, master of diffusion, thought, *I could Matrix fight him. I could bail and jump in the water. Hmm I got it.* "Pelvic thrusts!"

"What?" Grover asked.

Keanu started doing himself some pelvic thrusts.

"What is this? What kind of magical move is that? My eyes... what have you done to my EYES?" Travolta asked. He found the homoeroticism mesmerizing.

"Um-." Grover joining in. He thrusted his pelvis.

Dr. Twerk followed and Kermit while steering the boat thrusted his, too.

Travolta was perplexed. "By Zues' sweet-sixteen-party, I can't help myself. What is happening? My skeleton... its, its-."

Travolta started thrustin' his pelvic with them. "Oh, it feels good! Wow, my pelvic feels so free. I'm sexy. Will y'all look at me? I'm sexy! Hey, where are the chicks? Where'd de go? We needz 'em now."

Grover pointed to the bloody piece of booby meat and didn't break from the thrustin'.

"Oh, what a shame; why'd y'all go and do that?"

The four of them continued doin' wild pelvic thrusts and Kermit steered the boat back towards shore while doin' his.

Oscar peeked outta' that trashcan. *What der fuck? No way, no; uh uh- no way.* He went back in the can. It was going to be a long winter. *Oh, no, those thrusts... they are in my mind. THEY ARE IN MY-MIND!*

Leather face parachuted in the distance. "I'll get those Muppets sooner or later, I'll get 'em!"

He parachuted over a double rainbow in the sky.

END

YOU CAN'T ESCAPE

SWAMP

BRIDGET CHASE

SWAMP
Bridget Chase

A Clean Camp

Danny swept the tent with a broom for the tenth time.

Just can't get this gawd forsaken thing clean enough.

"Kimmy," he called to his beautiful girlfriend, "Can you bring me the Clorox wipes?"

"Sure thing, Mr. T," she said.

Kimmy went to the station wagon and dug around the organized junk.

Danny walked out of the tent and went about setting up the folding chairs.

Ah, yes, will be nice to get away for a while. Besides Kimmy and I needed some alone time, if ya' know what I'm sayin' (elbow nudge). *I'm not sure about this swamp camping-thing though; seems unnecessarily dirty.*

Oh well, he resigned to enjoy it the best he could. *With my dick in her ass*!

Kimmy came over with the small container of Clorox wipes.

Damn, she is fine. I didn't always see it; but now, I can't get enough of her. The sight of a gorgeous woman carrying cleaning products made his girlish knees weak.

"Here you are, sweetie," she said. Kimmy leaned up on her toes and kissed him.

Her lips were soft and tits pointy. Those birthday cakes pressed against his chest.

Danny broke from the kiss. "Let me get the tent clean, and then, we can make it dirty again." He smiled like a villain.

Kimmy smiled and bit her lower lip.

"Oh, but not like *real* dirty. I mean, like, fuck- dirty; but still keep it tidy inside."

"I knew what you meant, silly. Why you clean up, I think I'll take a little dip."

Danny looked around. "It's a swamp. I don't think people swim in swamps."

"I do," Kimmy said, "And, I swim in swamps topless."

She grabbed the tail of her shirt and tore off.

Hello Grandma! Danny's eyes fixed on her pink bikini top. Her tits were mighty-fine: perky and ball busting.

Kimmy reached behind he back and undid the ties.

Now, there's Christmas! Danny got stiff in his pants.

"If you get done cleaning," Kimmy said, "You can join me."

Danny was torn. *I must clean. Are you a fool? Go fuck this chick. Shit! No, a clean tent is a happy weekend.*

Dammit! A satisfied cock is a happy weekend!

"I'll be there in a minute," he said.

Kimmy smiled cheerfully and walked off. She swayed her hips extra seductively as she walked away.

He knew those bouncing Gotham Knights would make him splooge hard during this camping trip.

How did I ever get so lucky? He wondered.

The Goatman Cometh

How did this ever happen? I can't believe it.
Kill;
Kill;
KILL!

I must get back to the lab. Someone will be able to fix me; for the love of god, I hope someone can fix me.

Fix what? You're a new creature. Be the monster; be the monster.

I'm close. This will all be over soon.

I'll be back at home; normal again, and things will be fine.

No, they won't. I want to kill, kill, kill. Do you smell that? I do; Oh, yes! There's a woman out here.

Can you smell her?

Well, can you?

…

I can.

Pringles Snack

"Well, the wildest place I ever fucked, hmm." Kimberly thought. "I guess in a church parking lot."

"That's not wild," Billy said. "I fucked a girl under the bleachers during a football game. Shee-it, just bent 'er over and drilled that bitch while people cheered."

"No, you didn't," Jason said.

"Did so!"

"Then who was it?" Jason asked.

Trini said, "I bet it was Rita." She smiled smugly.

Billy hit his fist against his thigh. "No way, I'd never bang that bitch, geez, who am I, Tommy?"

Zack laughed, "No man, ain't nobody as free with his meat as Tommy."

CRUNCH!

Kimberly turned to the dark woods. "Did you guys hear that?"

Billy twisted in his camping chair.

The fire made monsters of every shadow.

"What? Is something out there? Hello? Hey, whoever you are, you better leave, ya' here?"

Jason searched his back pack. "I got bear spray in here; give me a minute, I'll get it out."

"I don't like this," Trini said. She crossed her arms over her chest, snuggling them little Asian tits together tight.

Something large exploded out of the darkness.

∞

Mr. Goatman sat atop the dead bodies.

SLURP! He pulled the raw meat from the bone with his thick lips.

Legs, arms, and organs littered the ground. Hardened blood stained his fingers.

Yum! What a meal!

Shit, I'm a monster. I just ate these teens.

Yes, you are. Go on, eat another tit.

Mr. Goatman looked at the pile next to him. Only one left.

Shit, I ate three tits already, what is the harm in a fourth?

He snagged up a bloody flesh-sac off the filthy earth.

He flicked the ants away. A pink, puckered nipple starred at him.

GOBBLE!

His diseased tongue swirled his mouth cleaning away the dark matter.

You should piss on the pile of dicks.

Why would I do that?

Shit, you made a fuckin pile of torn off dicks and you want to question pissing on them? Just piss on them!

Mr. Goatman stood. His large belly was descended by human flesh. He grabbed his meat with sticky fingers.

SPLASH! Yellow stank urine sprayed the three mutilated genitals.

I'm not a monster. Its okay, I'll just go back to the lab and get this sorted out.

He shook the remaining drops off his cock.

They flung off the head of his dick and joined the dark matter which wet the earth.

Mutant Meet 'N Greet

Splish, splash, Danny was takin' a bath-

Well, not really, this is more gross than I want to think about.

Danny joined Kimmy in the swamp water. It was almost neck deep.

He had his hands on her tits underneath the water.

She looked him in the eyes.

Wow, these are great, so soft and slippery; Oh, there's that nipple. Like a pencil eraser; so rubbery. Bet they could erase wrong answers on Scantron. Oh, did I make a mistake? Here let me use these gorgeous nipples…

He lifted the weight of her tits and moaned with satisfaction.

Danny hoped a gator didn't swim up and chomp his erect junk off.

Don't think about it.

"I love you," Kimmy said.

"Love ya' too babe."

She moved against his body and they kissed.

His cock pressed her stomach.

Damn can't wait for her pussy to strangle my Mr. Clean!

Neither saw it coming.

Heavy, frantic splashing drew both their attentions.

It happened too fast.

Danny had no chance to stop it.

I didn't even see it.

THWAK! Something hit Danny in the face. He flew off his feet and then, SPLASH Went underwater.

I nearly drown.

He surfaced, but his eyes didn't agree on a direction.

"Kimmy, Kimmy?"

What the hell was that?

Focus resumed.

A distant cry, "Help!"

"Kimmy!"

Danny spun a circle.

"Help!"

That way!

He trudged his way through the swamp.

A gator's scaly back slipped through the water and away from our frantic hero.

Toxic Gatorade

Danny sludged through miles of wretched terrain.

I must save her. She's my little Kimmy poodle.

Mosquitoes were a nightmare; he had welts all over his skin. *Damn, wish I didn't take off my shirt.*

But he had.

I wonder how Kimmy is doing?

What the fuck grabbed her?

Danny's face was swollen.

Luckily, whatever it was left tracks.

It must be large.

Broken limbs and cleared Lillie pads led a clear path.

But, he wasn't expecting to come across this.

What the fuck?

A building stood in the middle of the swamp.

It was some weird blend of construction. Some parts shanty and others well-constructed.

No windows.

The broken vegetation led around the side of the structure.

Hmm, better go have a closer look. I hope you're okay, Kimmy.

Danny, with stealth, went to the door.

CREAK!

Damn, when was the last time someone came in here?

The overgrowth of vegetation said, a long time.

He didn't hear anything

I'll go around the side.

He crept through the hot humid underbrush.

Geez, I'm thirsty as fuck. Would be nice to find some water or some shit.

And, there it was, a green potion inside a plastic bottle.

Dibs!

Danny ran for the tree.

The bottle floated in a pool of marsh water infected by every putrid disease known to man at its base.

The sun was setting.

I have to drink something. Besides, looks like the caps never been opened.

It was a Gatorade bottle- fruit punch flavor.

Isn't fruit punch normally red?

It was neon green.

Oh well.

Danny twisted the cap and chugged the fluid.

His adam's apple bounce with each gulp.

AHH, refreshing! Now to find my Fuck Bunny!
"ARGH!" Danny doubled over and held his stomach.
What's happening?

Just Touch It

Kimmy was carried up a tree.

The thing that held her smelled like garbage 'n shit.

Her ribs hurt from being carried over its shoulder.

The thing's dark skin had sharp growth almost like barbs.

"UMPH!" She was thrown to the ground.

Kimmy scrambled and sat up.

What is this place?

It looked like a really shitty tree house that a person would make if they planned nothing ahead of time.

Kill her, fuck her, eat her.

Mr. Goatman looked at the pretty young thing. *What do I do?*

Kimmy let out a shaky breath. *Fuck is this thing gonna' rape me?*

Mr. Goatman paced back and forth. *Eat her? Let her free? I'm not a monster-*

You sure are.

Kimmy looked at her hands, *gross;* the wooden surface was coated in some dripping slime. It was smeared on her ass and legs.

What is this?

Then she saw.

The conflicted creature wore a tight fitted, white lab coat. He was naked other than that. The thing's large cock, SMACK! Flapped between its thighs. Its cock expelled a string tar. It dripped down the creature's legs.

Gross. Fuck, I have to get outta' here!
She looked for an exit.
She wants to escape. Look at her. Get her. Eat her springy nuggets.
Mr. Goatman looked. "Don'th moo'th!" He said in words that sounded like bubbles.
Kimmy froze.
Mr. Goatman lumbered over. His knees were knobby ulcers of fluid.
Kimmy scooted away.
Her tits hopped and heaved with her panicked breaths. She wore only pink bikini bottoms.
Take her, fuck her, and eat her.
I couldn't.
Mr. Goatman bit on his nails.
Kimmy noticed an axe that lay amongst the garbage pile next to her.
Fuck, better to die trying to live, then be killed cowering.
She bolted up and grabbed the ax. In a quick motion she hefted it over head and, CHOP! Brought it straight down.
BLOCK! Mr. Goatman raised a thick bio waste forearm.
THWAK! The blade went in deep.
Yellow ooze spilled from the wound.
Mr. Goatman snarled and grabbed her wrists. He lifted her off her feet.
Oh shit!
The axe stayed wedged in his arm.
"Stop, let me go!" She kicked at him feebly.
The creature rushed towards the back of the structure.
Kimmy looked. "NO!"

Some half hazard clothes and blankets were spread out.

The creature grinned.

"I'th gonna buck you'th,"

Kimmy's stomach rose to her throat as if she just stepped off a cliff.

She was thrown down, BAM! Onto the putrid blanket. Bugs and little things scurried away. Her head hit the floor and almost knocked her out.

The thing climbed on top of her. It pinned her wrists

"NO!"

A sloppy tongue explored her chest and curled around the soft tissue.

I'm a monster. Yes, you are. I'm a MONSTER!

A thick piece of meat pressed between her legs.

"NO!"

It prodded at the delicate fabric covering her pussy.

Cool, I'm a Mutant

What am I?

Danny looked at his reflection in the water.

What the fuck is this? Am I Swamp Thing or something?

Well, he was something close.

He looked at his arms.

He was a muscular fuck, made out of roots and swamp plants.

Well, guess if I'm going to be mutated, at least I'm buff. Shit, I've never been buff in my life. Could be worse too; I could be mutated like that dipshit older brother in Weird Science. Now that's a nightmare!

With his new mutated senses, he could feel the swamp.

Danny raised his hands and then swung them down.

The marsh water rose and then, SPLASH! Came down in a powerful rolling wave. Electric yellow bolts raced with the crest.

Okay, cool, so I control shit and am super awesome; now it's time to get Kimmy back! And dude, wait till I stretch her with my new thick root. I got a fuckin' canoe between my legs!

He could feel right where she was.

Yeah, those tits are like an ice cream shop next to a Jenny Craigs.

He marched through the marsh in a direct path.

It didn't take much time before he saw the shambled structure in the tree.

"NO!" she cried out from inside.

"Kimmy!"

Danny ran to the trunk. *Rise!* With clawed hands he made roots come alive and climb the tree.

SNAP, CRACKLE! Nope, not going to; okay, POP!

The roots tore the walls always.

What's this now? Mr. Goatman stopped.

"Bastard!" Danny said. A creature was on top of Kimmy. She was small compared to its puss filled, wet fish body.

"Get away from my Pussy Palace!"

"Danny?" Kimmy asked. She was under the creature, but was able to lean up on an elbow.

"Yeah babe."

"What the fuck happened to you?"

"Well, I'm a mutant, now."

"Hmm, I can see that. You look kinda' hot!"

"Thanks babe. Now you-,"

"-Get off my bitch! Only my meat goes in her Forever 21."

Mr. Goatman stood up. SLOP! His wet cock slipped down Kimmy's greased thigh.

Another mutant? Remarkable.

Not remarkable; fuck this guy up!

"ROAR!" Mr. Goatman howled and, LEAP! Jumped from the tree.

CRASH! The creature plowed into Danny. He fell to his back.

BLAM! He clocked the thing in its face.

It came back with a sludge hammer punch.

Danny moved his face.

The creature's knuckles crushed the earth beside his head, TWACK! In a heavy impact.

Danny brought his knee up.

"URG!" Mr. Goatman was knocked off. He rolled on the ground and got to his feet. He extended his arms and hissed heavy breaths.

Danny charged forwards and, POW! Punched the fuck out a 'em.

Mr. Goatman stumbled back. *Kill him, kill him!* He locked his feet and then bolted, BLAM! He rammed his shoulder into Danny.

Danny was taken off his feet.

"Danny, my love! My mutant!" Kimmy cried. Her pussy yearned for him.

SMACK! The muddy ground was torn up when his back hit the earth.

POW, BAM, SLAM!

Mr. Goatman beat on Danny's face.

Danny pulled his forearms up to shield the attacks.

"Stop!" Kimmy shouted, "Don't hurt my man!" She climbed down the tree and ran over. With clenched fists she hammered the thing's back. Her tits wobbled in dancing unsynchronized twirls.

Danny saw his girl tryin' to help.

So sweet, damn, and she is mighty hot!

Her brunette hair was wet and plastered to her head and her mascara ran on her cheeks.

Kimmy's dancing pink nipples made him roar with sexual power.

The marsh water rose. A tide swept together and rolled-in like a brick wall.

SMASH! Mr. Goatman was knocked over. The swell of water consumed him and then, he was dumped onto the wet earth.

Danny stood. He summoned the nearby gators and snakes.

Gators climbed from under roots and out of thick brush.

Snaked slithered out from their holes.

Mr. Goatman got to his knees. Creatures surrounded him.

A small frog croaked angrily, RIBBIT!

Danny suddenly felt sympathy for the poor putrid blob of a man.

Kimmy came up beside him and pressed her near naked body to his side. She clung on his arm like an epic sci if poster in a young boy's bedroom-

-Or a grown man's; but, then it would probably be in storage, because wives don't let men hang posters they love; at least not in the house.

Counseling

"My name is Mr. Goatman; and I'm a monster."

"Hello, Mr. Goatman," the group said.

People sitting in chairs were arranged in a circle.

"I… I'm a monster and I like to eat women. Oh, and men, sometimes, too; ya' know, when I'm hungry 'n stuff."

The people in the counseling meeting clapped.

The organization leader came over and stood behind Mr. Goatman.

He placed a hand on the mutant's shoulder.

"It's okay; You're in a safe place."

Mr. Goatman fought back tears. "I fight with the urge every day."

People nodded.

"Being a monster has ruined my life. It was only an accident, coming in contact with Chemical-Letter. But since that day, my life has spiraled out of control."

A few people wiped tears away from their eyes.

The door to the YMC meeting hall was kicked open, BAM!

Everyone turned.

CLAK-KKKK-KKKK!

Hot bullets tore through the room.

BLAM-BLAM-BLAM! The rounds popped in people's chests and faces. One round tore out a guy's eye.

The people screamed.

Blood sprayed.

Chairs were turned over.

Mr. Goatman watched the man with the machine gun enter; "Dillon?"

"Yeah, Boss-," CLAK!

A screaming woman running for the door was dropped.

"-Glad I found you. We need to get you back to the lab, pronto! I know how to change you back."

Mr. Goatman smiled. "Great-,"

CLAKKK-KKKk-KKKk!

"-Just great-,"

CLAKKKKk-KKKKk!

"-Uh, you mind if I eat a few of these dead chicks first? I mean, they've been lookin' so tasty ever since I came in here. Besides, if I'm changing back; what's the harm in satisfying my appetite?"

CLAK! Dillon blew the brains out of a guy on the ground.

J-E-L-L-O sprayed the floor.

"Do what you like, Boss. I'll be waiting in the van."

Mr. Goatman licked his lips.

∞

Danny made her come.

He was on top of Kimmy.

Her spread thighs trembled and Danny thrusted.

Just thought I'd add that.

Chili's Party

Swamp Thing Danny wore a pressed suit. He sat at a booth by the bar.

Kimmy sat next to him. She leaned her head on his shoulder.

Mr. Goatman sat across the table. He still wore the face make-up but had removed the prosthetic costume. He made a joke and the three laughed.

Dillon came over from the bar. He held a tray with beers.

Everyone was eager and grabbed a mug.

Danny kicked back a swig of the cold fluid.

Kimmy told some story and gestured to her tits.

Mr. Goatman laughed with a hand on his stomach.

Kimberly, Billy, Jason, Zack, and Trini entered the restaurant.

Mr. Goatman got partly up and gestured to them.

Kimberly smiled and pointed.

The group came over to the table.

A hot ass waitress, with giant knockers, came up and got drink orders.

Kimmy peered behind her and saw a jukebox in the corner. She nudged Swamp Thing Danny.

He nodded.

The two scooted out of the booth.

Kimberly and Trini slipped in. Jason, Billy, and Zack pulled up chairs. Dillion slid in next to Mr. Goatman.

Mr. Goatman gave him a patted on the back and nearly knocked his glassed off.

Drinks arrived, and they had lively conversation.

Kimmy dropped a quarter into the machine. She grabbed Danny's tie and let him to an open space to dance.

Kimmy did a very seductive routine.

Danny shimmied to the beat. He looked around wondering if anyone else was seeing how sexy she was being.

Kimmy ran her hands up her stomach and over her tits while gyrating her hips.

Her hands went up her neck, over her cheeks, and then pulled her hair together on top of her head.

The bartender watched with an open mouth.

Mr. Goatmen peered over the shoulder of Trini and watched as well.

Trini noticed and asked Jason to dance.

They got up from the table
They all joined Kimmy and Danny on the Chili's dance
floor
END

The
Meg Ryan
Shark

Bridget Chase

THE MEG RYAN SHARK
Bridget Chase

Helicopter Stunt Show

"So, what'cha doin' at M.A.M.A. One Research Station?" the helicopter pilot asked.

The wind played with the last two strands of hair left on Jason Statham's head; he played the character Johnny Taylor.

"They brought me in 'cause there is a big fuckin' shark creature thing, which happened to appear just in time for the tail end of summer blockbuster season."

"Cool man, how big's the thing?"

"Big," Johnny said, "Enormous. Bigger than big; bigger than we ever thought possible. As big as it has to be to make people go, whoa!"

"Man; so, sounds like it's pretty big 'n shit."

"Oh, yeah, real big!"

"So, what's a white boy like yerself gonna' do 'bout a shark creature in the ocean 'n all?" The pilot asked. "Couldn't ya'll just leave 'em be?"

Johnny's eyes became slits. "First off, you're a white dude, too. Second, no, not something that big, not while I'm still an American 'n shit. It needs to die; and it needs to die epic-ly."

"Hmm, okay man, well we are almost to the ship." The pilot steered the chopper. Its blades went chop, chop, chop!

Johnny looked over the vast sea of blue. *I'm comin' for you mothafucka'!*

"HOLY SHIT!" The pilot shouted over the intercom.

Jonny hopped up from his chair and perched himself in the helicopter's bay door. "No, it can't be! Not yet; the movies just begun! AAAAAAHHHHHHH!" He screamed with his hands on his head.

A huge shark emerged in the water below. *And*, it was fuckin' HUGE! Like, whatever image is floatin' 'round that head of yers, multiply that shit by ten; no twelve; yeah, twelve. Do da' math mothafucka'- that's BIG!

It was coming straight to the surface with its mouth wide open, boy-yee.

The pilot, seeing his role end in this adventure, began reciting the Lord's prayer. "Our Father, who art in heaven, hallowed by thy name, thy kingdom come-,"

BOOM! The huge hundred-foot monster shark shot outta' that water. Its mouth came straight for the small chopper, which is weird because metal and gas weren't a typical meal for sharks.

"I'm a badass and the hero. I can't die; so, guess I'm gonna' jump 'n shit. Here I go!"

Johnny jumped out of the chopper.

"WHOA!" His blueberry nuts rose in his belly. He went into an action star free fall.

The shark rocketed past into the air and, CHOMP! It ate the fucking chopper.

Johnny aimed his feet towards the deck of the Navy's boat below. He fell like sixty feet or something unbelievable. SMACK! He hit its surface and rolled.

SPLASH! The shark fell back to the water.

Rolling waves rocked the boat.

"My god, are you okay? You're a lucky motherfucker, or my name ain't, Bob" A navy guy said, he ran up to Johnny's side.

Johnny stuck out his hero's hand. "Nice to meet you, Bob."

"Oh, my name ain't Bob, guess that just didn't make no sense what I said; I'm-,"

"-It don't matter," Johnny said and turned away from him. "You only have a small part anyways; yer name ain't needed." He looked out to the vast ocean.

The navy guy hung his head. *Dang, thought this movie role was a break-through for me; my ma' was right, she was. Better call my boss and tell him I'll be back waiting tables tomorrow.*

Most of the men on the sprawling deck looked over the side of that ship at the huge fuckin' shark- bigger than dat ship. It swam below the surface. Helicopter metal shit floated up and rode the undulating current.

Johnny brushed off his fashionable yet functional jacket. *It still looks good right? Yeah, unharmed.* "So, take me to whatever hot bitch is in this movie. I just did a gnarly stunt, so I deserve to see her now."

"Okay," the navy deck hand said with sadness in his voice, "She's a real hottie. Ya' won't be disappointed. Oh, and she's Chinese 'n shit ya' lucky dog." He elbowed Johnny Taylor in the arm.

"Chinese, huh? I've always had myself a bit of the oriental hunger. Let's go!"

The shark disappeared into the dark depths were sharks go because they live in the ocean below the surface where their world exists, and humans don't normally go.

CGI TOM

"Here hop on in," the navy pilot said. He was a fat dude with a tight-fitting white navy suit.

A deep-sea diving vessel stood before Johnny.

"Umm, that's Tom Hanks," Johnny said.

The Navy Pilot put his hand on the metal frame. "Sure is. Pretty cool, right? CGI 'n shit."

"Hey, Johnny," Tom Hanks said. His face was digitally morphed onto the side of the bubbled steel vessel.

"Hey Tom; so, you're taking us to the bottom of the ocean to the research lab?"

"Sure am, hop inside me." An airlock door opened. "This way."

Tom's flattened steel face smiled.

Johnny climbed aboard.

"So, what's the deal with being a vehicle and such? I mean, this metal-face-vehicle-thang is freakin' me out a little. Just askin', cause, to *this* star, it seems a little odd, no offense."

"Oh, none taken," Tom Deep Sea Hanks Vessel said. "So, it began only a week ago. You see, me and my friend- shit, what's his name? Um, well my pale, quirky friend with a red mullet and I went to an outdoor carnival. Stop me if ya' heard this one. Well, I come across this Zoltar machine; it's a machine that grants you a wish. Well, I had a quarter in my pocket; so, I threw that sucka' in. That machine jumped ta' life and asked for a wish. My first thought was to be, BIG; like, big, meaning adult; then, I decided, nope I want to be a vehicle, like a real cool one; like, a transformer kina' cool one. Well, I woke up the next day and; here I am."

"Cool," Johnny said, "That was a stupidly long story. Let's just go underwater, now."

"You got it, boss." The vessel Hanks smiled and PLOP! Released into the frigid waters of a narrative that's gone outta' control.

Oriental Titty Fuck

"Ah, Johnny Taylor; good to have you aboard. I'm Jack Morris. Pleased to meet you. My, what a handshake you have; I wouldn't have expected any less from you Mr. Statham… I mean, Taylor. Now, if you look here."

Jack gestured toward the huge glass wall. It towered above them. Sharp teeth marks in a circular design marred its surface.

Jack was a scientist guy; not super interesting, just a normal looking guy with some medium length blonde hair.

Jonny had just arrived and was bein' briefed.

Jack continued, "As you can see this shark has a mouth like Hanna Montana. Which is something we never thought we'd see. We didn't think something this big could EVER exist-,"

"-But, it does," A black man said, and walked up. He guided a little Chinese girl with him. "I'm Joint, and this little fortune cookie is Shoe Shu."

"Nice to meet you," Johnny said.

The little girl, Shoe Shu, spoke up, "Yes, great monster scare me much. I's so small and walk by, then, CHOMP! I frightened; berry, berry frighten much."

Johnny put his hands on his hips, "Who the hell is this little girl? There can't be no little girls in my movie, get her outta' here, would ya'."

Two lizard-alien men came charging down the hall; they grabbed her.

"Hey stop!" The girl kicked.

They carried her off.

Johnny said, "This is all well and good, but what does this have to do with me meeting the hot Asian bitch in this movie? I's got me an oriental hunger 'n Jason ain't got no time for all this plot-movie-bullshit."

"I suppose, you would be talking about me?" A woman's voice drew their attention down the hall.

The hall was dark with invisible walls that allowed the ocean's depths to be seen. Shimmering nonsense of technological artistry made the hall almost magical.

"Now we're talking," Johnny said.

A hot Asian bitch walked up to them. She wore a flowing translucent robe. Her Asian Skittle nipples danced perceivably under the fabric.

"Shaved, too. Would ya' look at that kooter. Man, glad I came after this shark. Gonna' eat me some King Na Hwah!" Johnny said, well said pretty much to himself.

"This is Sungi," Jack said. "Sungi, this is the hero, Johnny."

"Nice to meet you," Johnny said. "Very nice; like, so nice. So, you's Asian 'n shit. I can tell cause of yer eyes; but them tits look like white girls. Again, nice to meet you."

"You as well."

Joint licked his lips. "Damn, that ass got me like, KA-BLAM!"

"So, Johnny as you can see-," She gestured to the teeth marks. "-We have a real problem; we have a crazy ass shark to hunt."

Johnny sucked his teeth. "Hmm, I see; think we can go fuck first, though; I mean, there is time, right? Yeah there is time. I think it will give the shark a chance to ambush a beach and eat lots of people; ya' know really tick people off and get the audience on our side."

"Sure," Sungi said. She took his hand. "This way to the fuck room. This research station features state of the art rooms to do most any kind of research." She looked back and winked at our boy Johnny.

Johnny grinned at the other guys. "Err, Err Err." He did pelvic thrusts.

Sungi pulled his hand and the two walked off.

Joint looked at Jack. "What are we supposed to do now?"

"I don't know," Jack said, "We kinda' don't have any lines."

"Hmm, cool. Guess we'll just stand here and wait till the story comes back to us."

"Guess so," Jack said.

Joint scuffed his boot on the ground. "Must be nice being the star. I'm bored as fuck."

The two stood in the hall and waited quietly.

Shark Things

The Shark swam to some beach and ate people. The water turned red and there were many scenes of gore and torn apart bodies. Also mixed in were alluring shots of hot girls in bikinis.

Idk, the scene was halfway sexy; as movies do, where they confuse violence with sex by blending that shit together.

But this was too much you see; *now*, the public knew about the shark and this was a problem as we fall into the conference room inside the research station.

"The public knows about the shark; this is a problem. Chinese officials want this thing dead," Jack said. He hammered a fist on the table.

Televisions, with people on them, over looked the conference table. All of the faces looked old and bitter.

This was obviously an important meeting.

"I'm hungry," Shoe Shu said.

No one listened; she had *too small* a role in this.

"Hey, how big be that thang?" Joint asked.

Sungi stood. She wore a tight black dress that made the men go, YUMMY! YUMMY! Them tits bounced around- no bra, YUMMY! YUMMY! "This shark was thought, by the brightest minds around, to be extinct for two million years-,"

"-Wrong," Joint said. "That shit is alive 'n hungry." (Static)

"He guys, chopper is outfitted with a machine gun," Johnny said. His face appeared on one of the TVs. "Why don't you guys stop with this board room meeting 'n shit and join me in the cargo hold. I got fuck-me underwater vehicles with missiles 'n other hot shit. Oh, and is that Shoe Shu? How'd she get back in there? Get her out!"

Two lizard-alien men entered and grabbed the girl. She kicked frantically.

Sungi reached behind her back, unzipped the dress, and pulled it off.

Jack's jaw dropped.

Joint popped a boner.

The screen, Johnny's face was on, went static-y.

Sungi kneaded her breast together. "Let's go kill us a Megalodon!"

Hanks' Many Roles

Sungi, Jack, and Joint walked into the cargo hanger.

"What do ya think?" Johnny walked up with arms outstretched and a shitty grin spread on his face.

"Pretty cool," Jack said, "Is that a Ninja Turtle shell?"

"Sure is; I converted your underwater deep-sea vehicle to be more badass; and let me say, Sungi, having them titties out for us is pretty badass, too."

"Thanks," she cupped them cakes together and jiggled the Asian delights, like all oriental chicks do for American men.

"So," Johnny said, "Jack, Joint, you'll take this awesome speed boat with full-on missiles 'n shit. Sungi, you get this Turtle Shell deep sea vessel thang.

Sungi walked up.

"Does this work?" She asked.

"Sure-nuff! AND! I'm the badass who is gonna' shoot this fuckin' shark from a helicopter. Ever heard of someone doin' that shit? I bet not! I added a badass machine gun to that chopper and will be all, BRRRAAAH! BRRRAAAHHH!"

He mimed shooting a turret gun.

"Oh, and these two dudes are the Bruiser Bros."

The team looked at the two men.

They look like wrestlers and were kinda' fat, kinda' muscular, with shaved heads, black pants, and wrestling boots. They looked exactly the same.

Johnny said, "That big dude there, is Bruiser, and next to him, his brother, Bruiser."

Sungi asked, "They're both named Bruiser? Isn't that confusing for a book?"

"Naw, naw," Johnny said, "It'll work just fine. The plan is, they'll jump from the helicopter and ass-kick the shark, while I fire."

Bruiser and Bruiser nodded agreement, Oh, and they each couldn't put their arms down. Both Bruisers constantly moved their arms in flexing action poses.

"Wow, this sounds super bad ass," Tom Hanks said.

"Who's that now?" Johnny turned. "Tom Hanks, ya' bastard; you're back again? Whatcha' doing on the face plate of that machine gun?"

"Oh, I don't know; figured gettin' payed for several roles was better than just one. So, we're ready for some violence."

The team asked "We," and turned to the turtle shell vehicle.

Tom Hank's face was CGI-ed onto the side.

Joint put a hand to the dew rag on his head. "This be some weird tripped out shit, if I's ever seen some weird tripped out shit."

"I think it's cool," Shoe Shu said.

Johnny turned, "Damn, little bitch is back again. What are ya', that chick from the Ring 'n shit? Lizard men!"

Two lizardmen in blue uni-tards hurried in and carried her off.

"I'll be back," she said. "I'll be part of this damn movie; you'll see, you'll see."

"Did that chic look kinda' evil? Okay," Johnny said and smeared his hand together in a fashion of having a plan. "Let's go get us a Megalodon and for the dumber fucks, I'm talking a big fuck-me shark."

Joint asked "Where's the Koolaid?"

Jack slapped his shoulder, "Dude, wrong script we're filmin' the go get us a shark, part."

"Oh, cool," he said, "So, what's my line?"

Johnny cleared his throat and said under his breath, "Damn, them is some titties."

Joint frowned, "Why would I randomly say that? Because I'm black? Because I'm a black man and only think about sex?"

"No; naw, no; no," Johnny said and rubbed his head sheepishly.

"It's because of that," Jack said.

Sungi bounced on her toes next to the Tom Turtle Shell Deep Sea vehicle's face. He grinned like a cartoon wolf chasin' after Red Riding Hood.

Her titties flew in a ballet which any man would pay to see.

"Damn, them is some titties!" Joint said.

"Perfect," the director shouted, "And cut!"

"Wait!" Johnny interrupted. He looked around at the Mega Shark Killing Team. "Sungi- super awesome tits, then we got Jack- some dude, who gives a shit, and Joint- another dude, and the Bruisers, huh? I'm thinkin' that this story don't have enough titties in it. Nope; nowhere near enough. Joint you's gonna' become a woman."

"Uh, which woman?" Joint asked.

Johnny put his hand to his chin. "Hmm, well your black, so let's make you that black chick from the Walking Dead."

"Michonne?"

"Yeah, her *and* … you'll be topless. And, you, Jack, you're gonna' be Babs Bunny."

"Do I have to?" he asked.

"Yep and-,"

"Topless; yeah I got it," Jack said.

BING!

"Now we're talking," Johnny said and rubbed his hands together. Joint in an instant changed to a topless Michonne and Jack into a topless Babs Bunny. They each wore tight black yoga pants with a logo on the side that said 'Da' Meg Shark Movie Babes'.

Hell of 'a Copter Fishin'

"There it is," Johnny said.

The Chopper soared over the vast water.

"Yeah, I see 'em," Michonne said.

Her bad ass Mad Max death boat sped across the open waters. Babs Bunny took to the turret gun on the back.

Her cartoon pink tits did a marvelous dance unfit for Saturday morning cartoons. Sorry ya' little kids; this is an adult network.

Johnny radioed to Sungi. "Get close, but not too close, dat shark is big, ya' hear me, BIG! So, get near it, but not too near it; like, maybe as close as you would get to a Tiger, if a tiger were *REALLY* big!"

"Right, will do," Sungu plunged the dark depths in the awesome TMNT vessel.

The shark broke the surface.

"Whoa!" Johnny's hero eyes went wide. "Did you guys see that?"

"Yeah," Babs said. "That shark has the face of Meg Ryan. Can you believe that? Meg Ryan? That just seems impossible; almost as impossible as a cartoon doin' shit in real life. Oh, and my breakfast cupcakes are hoppin' all around. Did ya' see? Did ya' see, huh?"

"Meg Ryan?" Tom Helicopter Hanks asked with a WHOA! Gasp. "Oh, I'm going in for a better look ya'll; Meg, Meg? That be you?"

BOOOM! The shark jumped outta' that blue water.

"That's right; it's me, Meg Ryan Shark, hahahah! Mwuahahaha!"

Her face was CGI and mixed together with the shark's.

Razor teeth gave her a shark grin of delight.

Johnny got behind the turret.

"I'm sorry Meg Ryan; you were delightful in 'You Got Mail', but-,"

His eyes became slits.

"-You're about to fuckin' die because you're a no good shark!"

CLAKKK-KKKK-KKK-Kay-Kay-Kay!

Bullets popped on the water's surface.

HISS! The hot rounds pelted Meg Ryan Shark's face. She poured on the speed.

Johnny shouted over the intercom, "Michonne cut that Meg Mutant Shark thang off. If we don't stop her and she is able to swim, like eight hundred thousand miles or so, she'll be at London's Bridge. We cannot, and I mean cannot have London's bridge falling down. The human casualties there will be catastrophic!"

"No problem," Michonne said. She thrusted that speed boat's throttle to the max. Them black titties went skippa' ma rink 'a dink 'a dink, skippa ma' rinky doo! All around as the boat hopped them wild Chinese ocean breaks.

Meg Ryan Shark heard the engine. "Damn them; all I wanted was a meal that made me go, YES! YES! YES! Like I orgasmed hard and made me drip that sweat Harry puss juice."

Michonne caught up. "Babs, lay down the heat."

"Roger that, Ghost Tits. Do ya' like that, Ghost Tits? It's 'cause you be black; blacker than da' night, and them titties be near impossible to see in a bedroom with the lights out."

"Yeah, whatever; just fire them missiles, ya' furry bitch!"

FLIP! Babs opened the toggle switch with her thumb. She grabbed the missile's controls sticks. "Take this fish breath! No wait; take this blonde midget tittied bitch mixed with a shark!"

SHOOOOM! The missile fired.

Johnny watched with his eyes, because they see well 'n shit. *Yep, far better than my ears see, that's fo sho'.* He almost creamed his pants like he does for most any action sequence.

KABOOOM!

The Shark roared.

Part of Meg Ryan's CGI face was blown off. Nasty white skull showed beneath where her left eye used to be.

Johnny tuned back to the Bruiser Bros. "Your turn guys. Give it to the bitch; give it to her real good!"

The two bros did a bro-thing where they hit their forearms together in a sign of unity and singular purpose. They had been doing this move since Kindergarten.

"Let's go, brother."

"Yes, let us go in haste."

They positioned themselves in the bay door.

Johnny said to the pilot.

"Get us over da' freakin' shark!"

The pilot nodded, and then, KLAK! His head kicked to the side, and blood sprayed the chopper's windshield.

"What da' fuck?" Johnny looked to the water.

Meg Ryan Shark smiled and slipped a pistol back in its holster. "Good luck now, fuckers; mwuahahaha!"

"Let's do this," Bruiser said.

The two jumped out all spread eagle and action hero like; but in a WWF way, if that means anything. *OFF THE TURN BUCKLE!*

Meg Ryan Shark saw the men coming and carved a hard turn in the water. She submerged and then came rocketing back up, SPLASH! Outta' the water- mouth wide open like a porn star earnin' money for rent.

The bruiser bros, in an epic freefall, cocked back their fists because they were badass dudes and also a metaphor for cum. They were super badass dudes and I'm not sure your gettin' it, like, they eat raw oysters for breakfast 'n shit.

"Let's do this brother," Bruiser said.

"Yeah, let's give 'er them big 'ol fists of fate."

Their fists sparked and ignited with power gathered by their rocket-speed-descent which brought them to the shark's face.

POW!

Meg Ryan Shark was knocked aside. She wiggled, and, SPLASH! Hit the water.

The helicopter started to spiral outta' control.

Johnny hurried to the dead pilot. "Rest in peace my no-name friend; and don't worry, I'll take care of yer wife for ya; take care of her *real good*, if ya' know what I mean."

The dead pilot said nothing.

"Like, by take good care, I mean sex; I'll fuck yer bitch for ya'- now that yer dead 'n all; but your daughter, well, she'll be on her own. No way I'm raisin' no other man's kids."

Johnny took the pilot's wallet, so he could find the guy's house and also, he could use a few bucks. This ordeal was bound to end with him needing a cab.

RUN! RUN! And, DIVE! Johnny did a huge swan dive from like eighty feet above the water.

Meg Ryan Shark shook her head, "Damn, this shit really hurts." Blood pooled around her.

Michonne saw the awesome leap and kicked the boat to life. *Don't worry, I gottcha'!*

Sungi, who I pretty much forgot about until now, raced in towards the shark. Her guns were ready.

"I'm sorry Meg," Tom Turtle Shell Deep Sea Vessel said, "We were great together in 'You Got Mail' but that's the past. This is my awesome Blockbuster future, YEE-HAW!"

Tom Turtle Shell Deep Sea Vessel's guns were hot.

Sungi gripped the controls in a way that hugged them Asian cupcake candy titties together, mighty fine. She had these nipples like, GO GO SPIDEY WEB! SPLOUGE! Web Slingin' the City!

SOB! SOB! Meg Ryan shark cried.

Tom Turtle Shell Deep Sea Vessel pulled up beside her enormous face, HALT! "Hey, what's wrong?"

"Don't talk, just shoot," Sungi said. She squeezed the triggers. "Why won't this thing fire?"

Nothing happened.

"There, there," the turtle shell Hanks said.

Meg cried, "It's all this damn Zoltar machine's fault. You might not believe, but only a week ago I was a kid. A friend and I, this pale kid with a crazy-ass red mullet and I went to a carnival-,"

"- I know exactly what happened," Tom Turtle Shell Deep Sea Vessel said. "Look, I'll tell the others and we'll work this out."

Sungi squeezed the triggers. "Fire dammit, fire."

She shook the controls; we got a nice shot of them tits wigglin' 'bout. The shot also made for a really good GIF.

PLUNGE! The Bruiser Bros sailed into the water.

"GURLE, GRUGLE," Bruiser said, and pointed.

The two swam for the shark.

The Tom Turtle Shell Deep Sea Vessel was next to the shark illuminating the Meg Ryan face with its deep-sea headlights.

SPLASH! Johnny dove in the water like a pro.

VROOM! The boat pulled up and he climbed aboard.

"Thanks," he said with his heroic vocal chords.

"No problem, so how do we defeat this shark?" Michonne asked.

Johnny looked at her tits, *damn, chocolate, chocolate PLAY WITH ME dreams. Oh yer so squishy and soft. Lemme' kiss ya'; oh, now play with my nuts.* He looked to Babs rockin' bod. She was bathing in the sunlight; her sleek furry body did thing to Johnny that only bein' raised on Saturday morning cartoons can do.

"I have a final plan," Johnny said. "I hoped it wouldn't come to this, but I *once* found this mutagen in the sewers of New York."

He pulled out a weird container marked secret ooze. It had green fluid inside.

"I say we mutate this bitch and tear her apart."

Babs hopped up and down. "Great, this sounds just great; what a plan, WOW! I am impressed by plans, and you seem to be the best at it."

Johnny said to the camera, "Damn, I like her; definitely gonna' fuck that bunny soon. Grab them ears like reins and pound that cartoon ass till she squirts rainbow anime backgrounds."

Michonne furrowed her brow and steered the boat towards the rest of the story.

Zoltar Playset

Meg Ryan Shark climbed up onto the sidewalk. Tom Hanks Turtle Shell Vehicle nudged her side and helped.

She was toast; no, not actual toast, this story hasn't jumped the shark that badly yet; yet…

"No, no, we can't help this shark," Sungi protested.

SLOP! Its heavy body laid on the hard surface.

"She's hurt and it's not her fault. It was the evil Zoltar machine," Tom Turtle Shell Deep Sea Vessel said.

Sungi climbed out and, BAM! Kicked the deep-sea vehicle.

Michonne, Babs, and Johnny pulled up on the speed boat. They lept outta' the vehicle.

"What's happening?" Johnny asked. "I have this canister to mutate this Shark. Oh, and I'll have no control as to how it mutates, but it will probably help in destroying her; probably."

Sungi crossed her arms. "Apparently, Meg Ryan Shark was the victim of the Zoltar machine."

"No," Johnny said and looked to Tom Turtle Shell Hanks Deep Sea Vessel.

"It's true," the vehicle said.

Michonne put a hand on her hip and gave a cool pose. Oh, and her Walking Dead sword was on her back; its strap slipped between her tits. "So, what do we do?" she asked.

"You Die!" came a small not scary voice.

They looked over.

Shoe Shu walked up. She pulled a wagon with a Zoltar machine on it.

"You fucks kicked me outta' this movie. Now, I made a wish; and it's for you to die! How do you like dat?"

The Zoltar machine jumped to life. "Wish granted," the mechanical face said.

BEEP, BOP, POOP! The thing transformed in agonizing cries of transformation; not cool techno sounds like Transformers make.

DOOM! DOOM! It was now a large Megazoid kinda' Power Ranger bad guy thing. Maybe twelve feet tall.

Johnny thought fast. "Tom get on top of Meg Shark!"

The Tom Turtle Shell Deep Sea Vessel climbed on top of the grey fishy Meg Ryan Shark.

KAZAAAM! Johnny threw the canister of secret ooze.

SPLATTER! Its neon green contents spilled out.

ROAR! Meg Shark and Tom Vehicle combined, in a bent science project gone wrong.

The shark molded with robotics and grew as well as mutated. It grew long black grizzly hair off its head in a ponytail. Combat boots grew on its feet and an 80's bodybuilding tank-top appeared on its chest.

"Damn, now that some crazy shit," Michonne said.

"You bet it is," Johnny said. He was leaned up on her back and reached around, playin' with them soft small titties. He juggled 'em in his hands.

"I'm a cartoon; but shit, that is messed up," Babs said.

Johnny hurried over and got behind her. He reached around and played with them pink furry biscuits. "You bet it is, Doll Face."

ROAR! The Meg Hanks Shark Vehicle Robot stomped over and, BAM! Kicked that fuckin' Voltar Megazoid.

ZOOM! It flew back and hit the ground in a sparking impact.

"You fucker," Voltar shouted 'n shook its fist.

Meg Hanks Shark Vehicle Robot lept into the air.

Voltar looked up and screamed. Its mouth hung open

Johnny, Michonne, and Babs threw quarters in its open mouth.

SLAM! The Meg Hanks Shark Vehicle Robot stomped its face.

CRASH! It shattered.

It Dusted its hands. "Now that Zoltar is destroyed," the Meg Hanks Shark Robot creature said, "Everything should go back to normal. Right?"

Johnny, Michonne, and Babs shook their heads like sayin', we don't know. Or sayin', yeah don't count on that.

Meg Hanks Shark Vehicle Robot waited for the magic to be undone.

Police sirens called from the distance.

Johnny checked his watch. "So, uh, I'm outta' lines. How 'bout you guys?"

Sungi walked up. "Yep, want to go to your trailer?"

"Sure," Jason Statham said. "I've had this unquenchable oriental hunger."

Michonne and Babs smiled to one another. Babs shrugged.

Michonne asked, "Think we can join you?"

Joint and Jack ran up, from off camera.

Joint said, "Ladies, ladies if the film over hows 'bout we take you out?"

CHOMP! Meg Hanks Shark Vehicle Robot ate the two supporting actors.

"Thanks," Johnny said. He jumped really high.

SLAP!

He high fived the twelve-foot mutated Shark Vehicle Thing which once had gotten mail.

"You're my nigger; don't ever forget it," Meg Hanks Shark Vehicle Robot said because that Tom Meg Mutant don't give no fucks about censorship; NO FUCKS, YA' HEAR, NIGGER?

END

TORNADO

BRIDGET CHASE

TORNADO
Bridget Chase

Pussy Twister

"Uh, you'll have to stop; weather's really bad."

POP! James pulled his fingers outta' Jessica's kooter. Stringy liquid dripped from her old lady puss lips.

"Yeah, we should probably stop for the night and get outta' this shit," James said, he wiped his sticky fingers on his black jeans.

The windshield wipers beat death.

Rain pounded the car like a golden shower.

The wind rocked the reasonably priced sedan around.

"That's not a twister, is it?" Jessica asked.

Jessica was driving. They two were passing through a small town in Kansas headed to a Comic con.

She was dressed as Wonder Woman. Oh, and Jessica was like sixty-five or some shit. So, imagine an old lady in a tight, revealing costume. Her doughty tits pressed heavy at the corset.

James didn't mind.

Did James have a thing for Grannys? Maybe; *naw, it's probably just the costume that's getting me hot. Oh, and the fact this bitch gobbles cock like it's a Luby's early bird dinner.*

The two had met at a Chili's happy hour.

Jessica had dressed really slutty, and James, having struck out with the other chicks, went for the sure thing.

Lightning struck.

He leaned forward and looked through the sheets of rain.

Dark clouds were everywhere, and one was a twirling purple funnel. Green neon lights popped inside the funnel cloud.

"Yeah, that looks like a twister. Prolly paranormal too, or something. We better find shelter," he said.

CRASH! POW! The car came to a very sudden stop.

Jessica held her head, *Ouch.*

James pushed the airbag outta' his face. He looked over and asked, "Are you okay?" He also noticed one of her saggy flapjack titties came out. James looked at the dark nipple. *Come to daddy!*

Jessica looked out the front. A tree branch sat on the hood and a street light crushed the front of the car like a beer can.

"Damn, what are we gonna do?" she asked.

Crash! Neon green lighting lit the world.

"Over there," James said. He pointed.

Across the street, and standing alone in the darkness, was a building. The neon sign read 'Pussy Twister'. Below there was a neon girl with blinking LED lights that made her tits look like they were hoppin' around.

"Geez, a titty bar? Should we?"

"Beats a ghostly twister. Shit, look at that thing," James said.

The twister looked like it was folding dimensional planes. It blinked in and out of their reality.

Demon Hot Wings

"MOOO!" A cow was tossed into the street, hard. *DIE HARD!*

SPLAT! Its body exploded when it hit the ground. The cow became pulpy meat.

A few McDonald's workers with snow shovels came over and saved the biz a few bucks on meat.

"We better move," James said, "Shit's gettin' bad."

They both got out of the car.

I hate to get my Wonder Woman costume wet but; Jessica ran. Well, didn't exactly run because she was old as fuck.

CRASH! Lightning and thunder ran the sky.

BURP! SPIT! Debris rained down.

The twister circled the small town, deciding where to begin its ultimate destruction.

Jessica and James entered the club.

Dancing lights, tits, and smoke-y air greeted them.

"Well now, I'm home," James said. He grinned happily and licked his teeth. *Oh boy, oh boy; daddy's gonna' play.*

"Welcome!" A cowboy dude came up. "Have some hot wings, why don'cha?"

He raised a hot ass plate of them suckas.

"Don't mind if I do," James said.

"Eh, why the hell not? Shit, we all might die in a twister here or something. Also, I haven't eaten in the last few hours." Jessica took a wing as well.

"Oh, yes you did, baby." James made his eyebrow hop.

Jessica smiled. "Okay, I ate cum but that's not a meal."

"Well, I'll be," the cowboy said. "Welcome, the two of you be all right. All right indeed." *Damn, this bitch guzzles cum? And she landed this young guy? She must suck a good a good Tom Hanks, that's for sure cuss she's a fuckin' OLD BITCH!*

"Lone! Lone!" A big tittied girl ran up shouting. Her Sea Biscuits flopped all around like god made 'em. She wore a small pink skirt, pink high heels, and that was it.

"What's the matter?" Lone asked. He squinted at her from under the dirty brim of his hat.

"That twister is coming down the street, and well, you won't believe this, but it looks like it's opening a portal to a dark dimension and spittin' out nasty demons." She looked at James and Jessica," Oh hi; would either of you like a lap dance? I got great tits." She grabbed them Pillsbury Dough Boys and jiggled them.

"Hi, I-,"

Jessica elbowed him. "Hi, we're fine right now, thanks."

"Demons, you say? Let me see this shit, YEE-HAW!" Lone pulled out two pistols. He fired those guns and danced around on them boots of his.

Lone stopped; he look at James and Jessica, "Oh, why don't the two of you head back to the VIP room, have yerselves a good fuck. I'll take care of this demon nonsense. Lone's been down this road before, yes sir!"

James smiled at Jessica. Hot wing sauce coated his lips.

She shrugged her shoulders.

The two walked off.

Lone shot his finger in the air and said, "Show me them demons you Big Tittied Stripper!"

"This way, boss." She ran ahead. But couldn't run well because of the heels and her large tits.

Lone followed. *Damn, have to get me a lay soon, too. Would ya' look at that ass? My Lone Ranger's getting all eager for an Indian adventure.*

They snaked through a back hallway.

Girls were packed up to the rear door and peekin' out.

Glittery asses greeted him.

"Let me through," he said.

He looked into the dark night.

(No, not Batman, he isn't in this story; sorry. I said dark night, not Dark Knight.)

"Well I'll be damned. Wes gots ourselves an apocalypse, or some shit." Lone turned from the door.

"Samson," he yelled to the bartender, "Free drinks for everyone. We's about to die 'n shit. So, best to get fucked up right."

Samson' head appeared at the other end of the hall, "We're gonna' die?" A worried look was on his face; but his white man afro still looked great.

Suck My Plot Line

"There you go baby, take it all in."

Jessica was on her knees.

She slurped James' junk like it was holy communion.

Jessica was an old bitch, but old meant experienced.

YEE-AH BABY!

Yeah it does. James thrusted into her wrinkled face.

"Do you like how I suck it?" she asked.

"Yeah baby, I do."

"Yeah, come on, you stud, gimme yer cum. Give it all to Wonder Woman granny."

"Okay sweet thing, I'm working on it. Just keep sucking."

People's screams filled the building. The whole structure shook by the powerful forces of the tornado.

"Oh, this twister is getting me all hot," Jessica said. "My puss is squirting."

Her old school tits lept around as she fucked that stud with her face.

"Me too baby; we could die at any moment." Death made James' nut swell with steamy loogies.

Weird cries and calls ripped through the walls.

BOOM! Something slammed the door. It shook on its hinges.

"Climb on the bed you slut. This young bucks gonna' fuck you like Pee Wee Herman."

SLURP! Jessica pulled the thick cock from her lips. She smiled. "Rail me good daddy." She climbed up on top a coffee table in the VIP room. Its surface had seen more jizz than Jenna Jameson.

James came up behind her and pulled the blue Wonder Woman panties down.

He beat his meat while looking at that sixty five year old ass.

"Give it to me," Jessica said she was impatient. Her hairy cat quivered in anticipation of being stretched like a yoga instructor.

"Here comes the meat, Pet!"

BOOM! The door rattled, and people screamed.

James pounded that ass. A huge nut rose at the base of his shaft.

CRASH! A wall exploded.

"I'm gonna' nut baby!" James yelled. "What's this now?"

He turned, and his sweaty meat slipped out.

ROAR! Two dark creatures with spindly limbs and red eyes ran at him.

SPLOOGE! James shuddered. White marshmallow cream erupted from his cock.

SPLAT! The cum hit a dark creature in the face. THWAK! Another wet round hit the other in the chest.

"What are these things?" Jessica cried. She snuck her hanging titties back into the top.

"I don't know, but we better move while my cummy, cum, cum, cum slows them down." James slipped his pants on.

The creatures wiped frantically at the jizz on their bodies. *It burns. It burns. It burns.*

"YEE HAW!" CLAK! CLAK! CLAK! The cowboy came rushing in, "I love killing me some demon ass." CLAK! He fired.

BLAM! The round went through a creature's head. Green goo rocketed out.

SPLAT! It hit James in the face. FACIAL!

"Oh, yuck; bloody hell," he wiped it away with a hand.

Jessica fixed her tops and slipped them panties back on her dough thighs.

"Sorry to disrupt you's fuckers," the cowboy said, "But these varmints be onry."

One came flying in the door. It landed on the Lone's back. He was knocked to the floor.

BLAM! The creature rang the cowboy's head off the tile floor.

"Don't be messin' my motha fuckin' hat up. Damn devils!"

Lone rolled. He got to his back and dodged a heavy claw.

RIP! The claw tore furrows in the floor.

James hugged Jessica. She had her hand down the front of his pants and stroked that jerky in fear.

Lone brought his revolver under the thing's chin, CLAK!

Devil brains rained down.

"Do you have more guns?" James asked.

"Sure do; go on. I got Daphne at the bar; she'll give ya' a weapon." Lone rolled the devil body off him. He got up. "She's also a hot piece of stripper ass. Like really hot. Fuck me hot. If you wanted to set up a little rondeau with her later, you can do that too. Both ya'." He smiled.

"Cool, thank," James said.

Jessica slapped his shoulder. "When this it over we are finishing what we started. Nothing makes my puss more angry that bein' denied a decent bath in jizz."

"Right," James said. "Kill the demons, then fuck Wonder Woman. Too the bar!"

Demons Earn a Buck

"Well ain't she a pretty thing," Lone laughed. He kicked back in a lounger chair.

James threw a drink down the gullet. Blood trickled from his temple. "Woo take it off, honey!"

Jessica sat beside him. She strangled his turkey with one hand, GOBBLE GOBBLE! and enjoyed a pink drink with the other.

The demon got up on stage, grudgingly. It wore a blue sundress. The creature acted shy and embarrassed.

"Go on now," Lone said "Give us a show or die."

The creature gyrated timidly and pulled a dress strap down its shoulder.

A few of the other patrons, that looked like truck drivers, hooted and hollered.

A few hot, naked strippers dragged a dead stripper out the door.

The twister waited outside in a line.

He turned to the girls behind him, "Geez, when will they let us in?"

The girls snickered," Don't talk to use creep."

The twister lowered its head in shame. *Damn, its so hard getting a woman when you are nothing but high velocity gas.*

"Geez, would you stop," one girl said. She was super hot. Like, cut off your dick and run down the street bleeding, hot.

The women in line held their skirts down.

The bouncer watched. *Maybe I should let that tornado in. I mean, he did wipe out all the other bars in town; so, he did us a favor.*

Lone leaned his head out the door. "Don't let that fuckin' twister in here. He'll ruin everything." SLIP! The cowboy went back in and sat down.

The dark demon let the dress slip down its body. The creature had small ham sandwich breast. It kneed them and played with its beyond-black nipples.

Me threw dollars. YEAH BABY!

The demon wore red panties. It pulled those fuckers down.

Everyone gasped.

"Now that's the biggest snatch this cowboy's ever seen.

"WOO HOO!" The men cheered.

It was a hairy, gnarled genitalia.

A man came up behind Lone," How much to fuck the demon?"

"What you got brotha'? She's a prize for sure."

James felt the Happy Time sensation in his toes. "I'm gonna' nut baby."

Jessica leaned down and vacuum sucked that stringy snot outta' his balls.

James trembled. *Damn, she's gonna pull my nuts through my cock.* He pumped and contracted his anus. *Swim boys swim, all the way to her belly.*

The dark demon began to finger itself on stage in a fit of passion.

"Hey, whoa," Lone said.

The other hot strippers grimaced.

SPIT! SPIT!

The demon's puss spit hot juice.

SPLAT! "OH GOD HELP!"

Pussy juice hit a man in the face. The acidic genital juice ate his face.

He screamed, and his kin melted off. Leaving a screaming skull.

Lone grabbed him. "Go on, have a seat; you be fine." A hot stripper brought over hot wings.

"There ya' are; got you some hot wings. Ya'll feel much better soon."

The skulled man stopped screaming. Red dark matter dripped down his boney cheeks and oozed from his eyeless sockets. He looked at the wings and picked one up. He nodded approval to Lone.

SPLAT! HISS! A chair was eaten by acid puss juice.

Lone pulled out his gun, CLAK!

A bullet went through the demon stripper's head. It fell down dead; them titties leapt around like whipped sausages.

"James, think ya' can go back stage and kill the two others we kept? Can't have this weird acid puss demons beatin' their clits and killin' people."

James was fucking Jessica from behind. He held her sweaty flapjacks in his hands. "Yeah sure thing."

Lone gave him the gun.

"Go on babe, walk," James said.

Jessica walked forward bent over while James plowed that ass.

Lone sat and at a hot wing with his happy skull friend. He looked his strippers and decided tonight he would fuck Daphne. *Because she's hot.*

END

VENUM
Bridget Chase

Internal Narration

He walked down the street. Rain guided him. Eddie was a little weird; also, he talked to himself regularly.

I'm Eddi Broccoli, and I'm a reporter. I talk to myself regularly and sometimes find myself questioning things the government might not be looking at.

Like this trash can.

Eddie examined its grungy tin exterior.

You might think this an ordinary garbage bin; but me, I see a story. That's because my name is Eddie Broccoli and I'm a reporter.

He lifted the lid and looked inside.

There was garbage.

Okay, so maybe no story in this garbage can; but I'm Eddie Broccoli and I'm a reporter. I find myself questioning things that the government isn't lookin' at.

He walked down the sidewalk. Eddie was fucking weird. Like, he shouldn't be that weird, but he was. He could be normal, but for whatever reason he's adopted a pathetic slump-y spine and bitchy demeanor.

Oh, here could be a story, which is good because I'm Eddie Broccoli and I'm a reporter.

A hot blonde walked down the street.

She was wearing a red rain coat n' shit; that's news bitch!

"Hey," Eddie said as she passed by.

"Hi."

Damn, man; she just kept on walkin'. Must be one of them prize bitches you gotta' chase. She's fine though; so, I'll go talk-up that bimbo.

"Hey, wait; my name is Eddie Broccoli; I'm a reporter. I just wanta' talk to you."

"I'm not worth reporting on," she said.

"Oh, yes you are. I have this brilliant idea for a story about fuckin women on the first date. The headline, is it worth it- yes or no? Should be ground breaking." He ran after her.

"Oh, yeah?" she stopped. "Okay, Mr. Reporter; if you're looking for a story, well, do I have *one* for you."

"Oh great!"

"Well, that is, if you like looking at things that the government doesn't look at?"

Yep, I's in love alright; she was speaking my language. She was a hot piece of ass with titties like, HOT DA-YUM, GIMME GIMME!

Eddie smiled. "Hit me. What's the four-one-one 'n such? Damn, and might I say, you be pretty girl." He mused his hair. "Think after our little reportin' session I can buy you like, a piece of pie or som'fin?"

"We'll see," she said and smiled, "Follow me; we're going this way, back to where I work."

"Where's dat?" He asked.

"VENUM Symbiotic INC."

"Whoa, sounds high tech 'n shit; you's a smart bitch, huh? But, really, never heard of it."

"My name is Anne and I'm a lab technician; and, I like to talk to people who others ignore."

"Eddie; Eddie Broccolli; I'm a reporter. I sometimes find myself lookin' at-,"

"'Yeah, you said that already."

"Cool, well, I'm gonna' put my hands in my pocket now, like this-,"

He slid his hand in his pockets.

"-And we can walk together. And I's thinkin' the camera can film our backs as we go; thereby makin' it look like 'ol Eddie here, has himself a new girl."

"You're a little strange, huh?" Anne asked.

"Maybe," Eddie said, "Mostly it's 'cause I'm a reporter and sometimes I find myself looking at things that-,"

-The two walked the dreary streets together. Light from the street lamps built the reality ahead.

I Got 'N STD

"Oh baby, yer kooter is drivin' Mr. Stan Lee crazy."

Eddie was between Anne's spread legs. Her feet were in the air and panties hung off one foot.

"Err, err, err; I'm gonna' have to report 'bout this. Damn, Stan Lee's in there; in there, DE-EEP!"

"No, please don't," Anne said.

Her puss tugged his junk. She was a tight white bitch that shaved her yogurt suckin' snatch for them boys to enjoy.

Eddie slobbered on her neck. He got down to his elbows an reached a hand to her chest.

Oh, man these puppets are just great, mmm hmm; man 'o man her cloth pink nipples! Kinda weird lab though. He looked around. Wonder why we's fuckin in this intricate billion-dollar research laboratory? Feel like I need to wear a Spock condom or some shit. OH, HOT DAMN, A CONDOM!

"Fuck me harder" Anne said. "Make My Little Pony bleed. It's been a bad equestrian. Naughty; it's so naughty!"

"Yeah it is. Alrighty then." Eddie set his ass cheeks to Pound Town. "Ya know, maybe I should have a look around here after I nut in ya'. Seems this might be a place the government doesn't look at, but I might, because I'm Eddie Broccoli, and I'm fuckin' a gawd damn woman TONIGHT!"

Eddie's head beat Anne's gland. She quaked. "Fuck I'm gonna' cum!"

He grabbed her and rolled to his back. "Go on now, ride me bitch, and get your rocks off just how you like."

Anne did ride him. She got to her feet and dropped that ass like a jack hammer on a baby's face.

"Oh man!"

We both wound up comin' sew-pa hard. It was a good 'ol nut for me. Second one that day. It's one I might have to report on. I'd eaten a lot of Taco Bell this week and the hot loogies I shot on her chest were really lumpy and thick. Too bad, I didn't take a picture.

"So, that was great," Anne said, "We should prolly go before the janitors come in for the night."

"What? Huh? Thought there was a story you's gonna' show me?"

"Well, it's been real. Come on, get dressed."

Anne used Eddie's shirt and mopped the stringy sour cream off her chest. She handed it back to him and then put her shirt on.

Eddie watched her button the buttons.

I watched her button them buttons. I'll miss those cum rags. They certainly were nice. I got to thinkin' that, maybe this bitch loved me; and that I found my future wife.

"Hurry will ya?" she asked.

Eddie put the cum drenched shirt back on.

Outside the door-

Anne locked up. "Okay, see ya."

"Seez' ya," Eddie said.

I was super happy. I mean, I know we had to say good bye, but it was just for the night. She was into me. Now I'm gonna' go and report this shit in my diary.

He watched her ass as she walked away.

Go fuck her again. Go on!

I heard a strange voice and I looked around like reporters do when they hear voices in their heads.

Eddie buried his hands in his pockets like he learned in Pants-Wearing-School.

I'm not losing my mind, am I?

No, we are more sane than ever. Now, how 'bout we smell yer fingers. Damn, she was tasty.

The night passed, and I was tormented by a strange new voice; so, I decided to go find Anne. She'd have answers.

It took most of the day, but Eddie waited outside her building for her.

Anne came out.

"Oh, hi; um… Jefff, right? Jefff with three F's, was it?"

"No, Eddie, Eddie the reporter, with no F's; well, not since elementary school, but that's 'cause I had dyslexia," He said

"Oh right. So, what you doing here? You're not a stalker too, are you?"

Anne wore a silky top. Her hard candy nipple said, 'I have no bra on, come suck on me.' The light breeze made the thin fabric hug every curve of her torso.

"No, I'm no stalker. I quite that job last year; terrible benefits." Eddie said. "But, I had a real great time wi'cha' and I was wondering, do you have any STD's or shit like that?"

"No, yuck; why?"

"I think you gave me 'n STD."

A man wearing a business suit walked past. He grimaced.

Anne grabbed Eddie by his shoulder and in a hushed voice said. "Come on, let's go somewhere, where we can talk about this, that isn't in front of the place where I work."

We's should mouth fuck this bitch, right here. Maybe find her boss, and we'll both gang rape her a bit. She'll love it; you'll see.

"No, shut up," Eddie said.

"What?"

Eddie rubbed his head, "Nothing, nothin'. It's this damn STD."

Don't rub that head. Whip that dick out and rub the fun head. We need to rub the fun head.

"Okay, there's a diner down the street. Shall we go?"

"Sure."

The two walked down the packed New York side walk.

I walked beside her and couldn't help but remember how great them titties was.

We could cut her head off, and fuck her neck stump?

No, no, leave me alone.

Eddie looked at Anne's neck.

No, I couldn't.

Her head would look pretty on a shelf and her body could be our toy.

Diner Parasite

"So, what's the matter?" Anne asked.

She sat across from him in a small booth. Anne had a sandwich and Eddie, a piece of chocolate pie.

He rubbed his chin. "Well, I'm hearing a voice in my head."

"Okay."

"It's sayin' really awful things."

"What's it saying now?"

Well, what are you thinking, new voice?

We are thinkin' that we want a blowjob from her while we enjoy this pie.

Eddie laughed sheepishly. "Well, it's sayin' we want a blow job from you while we eat our pie."

Anne raised her eyebrow. "So what, you're a dude. What? You got a dude voice in yer head?"

Then, we hold this place hostage and ass fuck every woman in here, with no lube.

"Umm, and then it wants to ass fuck every woman in here."

"So, you're a pig and obviously a sex addict."

After, we can open each of them bodies up and take a look at their insides. We could make a booth out of tits; we could cover the wall in skinned faces. We could cover the windows in pussy lips.

Eddie hung his head. "There's more, but I really can't say."

"It's okay, it can't be that bad."

"It wants to-," (clears throat) "-Cover the windows in mutilated pussy lips."

Anne's eyes went wide. "Eddie, I think I should go."

"No!" He grabbed her arm, "It's not me. It's something new, I swear!"

Anne thought and then sat.

"Hmm, it's possible, but I don't know. The lab I work at has this parasite; it's alien thing 'n shit. Actually, one scientist was infected by it and went on some weird quasi vigilante slash villain trip. Cops eventually took him down. He was killed in some church's bell tower. Do you think you were infected?"

Eddie rolled his sleeve up. Black oily licorice moved in stretching strings on his arm.

"Yep, that's the parasite. Shit, hope I didn't get it."

"Does this mean we can't fuck?"

The Evil Dr. Bad

"Are you ready?"

Evil Dr. Bad stood in front of the glass partition.

A terrible inmate who wanted to bring nothing but carnage to the world, stood on the other side.

"Yeah, let's do this comic movie plotline, thang."

The inmate was a rodent looking dude with a thin face, hooked nose, and long oil hair. The room he stood in was mostly empty except for a pass-through slot.

"Add Agent V," Evil Dr. Bad said.

A scientist carefully carried a canister. It looked pretty-cool and some designer somewhere, got little to no money for the concept.

He inserted it into the perfectly fitted link-point in the wall. The scientist with questionable records nodded to his associate inside a sealed booth.

"Active," he said.

The other scientist typed on the computer. The screen did some eighties hacker green retro simulation thing.

Evil Dr. Bad watched.

The inmate looked around. The pass-through slot opened, and lurching spaghetti strings of bile looking-stuff leapt out.

"Wait, what's this? Gross, what is this? Help! Help!"

It crawled his arm and then the inmate began to convulse.

"HELP! HELP! HELP!"

Evil Dr. Bad watched. A grin spread on his cheeks.

Yes, I'm the most *evil Doctor there is. No doubt about that. I don't even care this guy is in pain. All I care about is the results. Geez, I sure hope this guy doesn't escape. It sure would be bad.*

The inmate mutated. His body changed, and skin looked like wet tree bark mixed with snail flesh.

"We are Carnage," the inmate said. "We are Carnage!" In a quieter voice he said, "For those that didn't hear the first time." It pounded the protective glass.

Evil Dr. Bad looked at the scientists.

One frowned his lower lip 'n shook his head.

Evil Dr. Bad looked back at the inmate. "Guess it'll hold."

SMASH! Carnage pounded the glass with his fists.

CRACK! The glass splintered.

"Oh, shit!" Evil Dr. Bad said.

Robber for Dinner

Well, I was just grabbing a bag of them good old Doritos, chedder cheese kind. You know how I do. Now, this cravin' was me, and not; who are you again?

We are Venum.

Right, I wanted it, not Venum.

We are the same.

Eddie took that delicious bag to the checkout clerk. He was ready to head home, watch a little tv; maybe jerk off a bit.

"Gimme the mothafuckin' money," a Hispanic guy said. He held a gun.

And, look at them tatts. We need tatts. Venum needs tatts.

No, no tatts for you! I mean me. Or us. No, no tatts for anyone.

Damn, Eddie waited impatiently. *Just finish robbin' the bitch already.*

The robber waived the gun in the face of some Asian chick. She was a bit older but-

-We'd eat that pussy. Have you seen our tongue? Damn, we'd make that oriental bitch cum. She'd be so grateful, like, 'I'm so grateful, I'll sucky wucky you all night wong.' And we'd say, 'Sure bitch, but only the way I like it.'

Easy now. I'll just be patient this will be done soon. Eddie waited.

The Asian lady trembled. She poked buttons and whimpered different Asian noises.

Venum is ready for our Doritos.

Hold on man. Geez, so impatient.

We are ready, now.

What the?

Eddi looked at his arms. The black oily goo grew quickly and covered his body.

The robber turned. "What da' fuck?"

A huge, black monstrosity stood there. It had weird eyes like car headlights except without the light.

"You are a bad person," Venum said with a voice like swiss cheese. "We, were only wanting Doritos, and maybe to eat this bitch out." His words rolled in hisses.

The Asian lady looked at it. *Hmm, maybe; I've boned worse.*

"Now, we're hungry, and mad."

The robber quivered; he lowered the gun. "I... I'm sorry man. Just, here, you go first. I'll rob this bitch when you leave."

"No," Venum said, "You're a sorry excuse for a person. We're gonna' eat yer arms, yer legs, yer face and yer Hispanic foreskin."

The old lady grimaced; so did the robber.

"Then, we're gonna' toss you in the street where you'll wiggle like the turd you are; but not a good turd fit for a toilet. No, a sidewalk turd. The worst kind of turd."

"No, please man." The robber protested.

No don't! Eddie shouted in his head. *I don't want to eat foreskin, that sounds really gross. Plus, this guy is from Mexico; so he's prolly dirty 'n shit.*

Venum smiled, "I hope there is cheese in that foreskin."

ROAR!

The robber screamed.

The Asian lady covered her eyes. She heard dripping and tearing sounds. *Dear Asian lord, I hope I am not bot'ering you. If you can, pwease make sure he don't hurt me next. Best wishes, Asian Chan.*

After the gurgling and crying stopped, she looked.

Eddie stood there. "Sorry Ms. Chan-,"

"-I have an STD."

She placed a hand to her springy, age defying Asian chest and looked over the counter. There was a bloody torso-stump on the floor, twitching.

Carnage Date Night

What are we?
Oh, we are something new and strange.
Cool.
Carnage walked down the street.

People screamed and ran, cars crash into one another, as well as hydrants, and one very old store, with a display of ridiculously old tv's in the window, got looted.

So, what should we do?

Ah, whatever we want.

Carnage saw the movie marquee ahead.

How 'bout we see 'Murder She Wrote- Apocalypse'? It could be a cool date night. Just you, me, this parasitic bond that brought us together.

Ah, yes; Carnage would be much happy.

A woman walking a small dog shrieked and ran.

"Oh, Carnage wanted to pet that little puppy. Damn, bitch; why'd she run off?"

It walked to the ticket window.

"Oh geez," the ticket clerk said. "Um, what can I do for you?"

"One ticket to 'Murder She Wrote- Apocalypse', please," Carnage said. Its voice sounded like an old swing set.

"Sure, sure." The clerk's voice trembled.

Carnage entered the establishment.

And, let's not forget the popcorn!

Movie Battle; Movie Theater

"I'm glad you came out, and that you didn't judge me too harshly for what Venum said."

Anne and Eddie held hands. They walked down the sidewalk together going to the movies.

"It's fine; especially after what it did with its tongue. Maybe, I *shouldn't* take you tomorrow to meet my boss and have the parasite removed."

Eddie smiled

Venum cloaked Eddie's body. "Maybe next time bitch, you'll try swallerin' to repay us!"

Eddie mutated back. "Sorry."

"No problem; maybe Venum is right. How 'bout after the movie I milk yer junk till yer pumped dry?"

"Oh, Id' like that," Eddie said.

An alien-vine thing, with Venom's head, came off Eddie's shoulder. "Make it twice, and well call it even."

The thing had sharp nasty teeth and a voice like sardines in oil.

Anne patted it on the head. "Sure thing cutie, twice; but, *after* we see Murder She Wrote- Apocalypse."

The head shrunk and disappeared.

Anne was a real nice gal. I'm glad she came out. I'm hoping after all the weird shit I did today, including eating foreskin, that we'll just have a normal nice time together. Yep, bet nothin' weirds about to happen.

"Two for Murder She Wrote," Anne said. (Cough)

She looked at Eddie.

Venum's head came out. "She wants us to pay."

"Oh, right," Eddie said. He pulled his wallet out.

The ticket clerk grimaced. *Man, what a night; so many weirdos.*

And, we are the most weird of all, a new voice said in his head. The ticket clerk shuddered.

Well, Anne and I entered the theater. She was a hot piece of ass and I thought there was a chance I could play with them titties a bit.

Yeah, we will!

"You start the damn movie, already!" someone shouted.

"Geeze," Anne said, "They are sure loud."

"Mov-E! Mov-E! Mov-E!" said the voice.

Popcorn flew at the screen.

A random douche guy got up. "Hey man... Oh, I'm sorry." He nudged his girl. She looked at the row behind them, jumped in her skin, and the two left.

Eddie and Anne took a seat.

She smiled at him. He smiled back.

I'm Eddie Broccoli and I'm a reporter; and, reporters love nothing less than a good movie.

He put his hand on her thigh.

Anne wore a super short skirt.

Now, slip them fingers in and churn a little butter.

Maybe later.

The Venum head appeared. "No, finger this bitch now!" it shouted.

Everyone in the theater turned.

"Yeah, finger that pussy," came the loud obnoxious voice from the front.

"Hey, I can handle this, don't egg him on," Eddie said.

The voice from up front said, "Don't be a pussy; finger the bitch and get your balls touched."

The Venum head said, "Ooh, I like this guy. Listen to him."

"No," Eddie said, "She's a lady. A real lady; and I'll treat her as such. Shit, when she blows me, I don't even push on her head or nothin'. Right Anne, you're a lady?"

He looked over.

She smiled and bit her lip. She was topless and had her hair up.

"See? She wants our cock."

Murmurs went through the crowd.

Some guy said, "Shit, come blow *me* bitch!"

Eddie bolted up. "Hey man, not cool."

People started snickering and laughing.

"Don't laugh; I'm Eddie Broccoli and I'm a reporter. I look at things the government doesn't look at."

More laughter.

"That's it," the Venum head said, "We're taking over."

The black tar ripped through Eddie's clothes. "Hey man, these were my best clothes." And covered his whole body. He was now a swoll-ass STD dude.

ROAR! Venum flexed like a Flex magazine cover. It was homoerotic and straight men ate it like chocolate flavored protein shakes; because man; nothin' says bad-dude like dessert flavored sports enhancement drinks.

People screamed and ran.

A dark figure in the front stood. "Hey, you're like us. You got the STD too?"

Venum looked at that loud punk. "Yeah, but you are much more puny. We're big, and hulking, because... Well not sure why; but we ARE!"

Part of the mask peeled back, and Eddie said, "Hey don't piss this dude off."

"Oh, too late for that. Carnage is already pissed."

It looked at Anne. "Hey bitch, why don't you come home with Carnage. We don't have a real home. Shit, this guy Carnage took over has been in prison for twenty years, but we can find us a nice place. We'll support you and listen to you too, if you'll drool on our dick every night. What do you say?"

Anne thought.

"Anne!" Eddie said.

"That's a bitch," Venum said.

"I am not," Anne said, "And as for you, Carnage. I would never. You'll never have me, or my tits. And, they have names, and you'll never know their names either!" She stood and wiggled them around.

The men fleeing the theater stopped and starred. Wives slapped husbands and girlfriends pouted that their boyfriends looked.

"See them hot tits. And, not *one* of you is worthy." Her girls warbled and danced like Smurfs on an ice rink.

Wait, what's happening?

"We are scared," Venum said.

Anne started to change. A dark liquid cream poured over her skin.

"Yuck," Eddie said.

"Yuck," Venum said.

"Yuck," Carnage said.

"Yuck," the other men said.

Anne became a hulking monster. Like a black bodybuilding woman. Even her hair was jerry curled.

"We are Period Blood," the thing said, "And you've insulted us; so now, your nuts, are ours!"

Venum looked down. *Hmm, where are our nuts?* "Geez, they don't seem to be anywhere. How weird it is; almost as if a very childish Hollywood movie studio designed us in a really dumb way and still thought people would find us scary. Hey carnage, do you have a cock?"

It looked. "No, what der fuck; where are our cocks?"

Venum asked Period Blood, "Do you have a kooter? We mean, you have tits, but do you got that factory downstairs as well?"

It looked past its beefy tits and stretched stomach. "No," it said.

Period blood fished around its pubic region with exploring fingers. "No, we don't!"

Carnage scratched his soggy oil head. "So, do we still fight?"

They each looked to one another.

The movie started.

Premier

"Is that grilled cheese?" Carnage asked.

"Yeah, you want a bite?"

Carnage nodded.

Venum handed half of the grilled cheese over.

Carnage's teeth sank into that hot, delicious meal. "Mmm, that's good."

"Yeah, this place is the best," Period Blood said. "And to think, the New Yorker gave this diner only two stars."

"Well, that's rubbish," Venum said. "So, what do you all think is going to happen in the movie tonight?"

"I still can't believe you were able to score tickets to 'Murder She Wrote- Vegas Lockdown'."

"We have connections," Venum said. "we know a certain Tom Hardy."

Period Blood drank its strawberry milkshake. The ice cream coated its oily upper lip.

It smiled.

END

WEIRD PHYSICS

Bridget Chase

Weird Physics
Bridget Chase

Compute Tits

"Vroom! BRRR… CHING! CHING! GRRRRR! BOP! BOOP!"

"You don't have to make those dial up noises," Gary who was played by Russel Crowe said. He was like fifty 'n fat but played a teen boy because Hollywood knows best about representing reality.

"Hey, what does it matter?" Wyatt, played by Danny De Vito, asked. He wore a VHS Culture shirt.

"Cause it's a little annoying."

"Oh, fuck off; BEEP! BOP! BOOP!"

"Look, just stop, okay? We're both sexually frustrated and about to blow; tensions are high; but, we need this to work. So, *work* with me here; soon our dicks can spit their white milk till their ain't no more cum in our bodies."

"Well, that's 'a hell of a lot of sperm! My nuts are industrial factories- hot 'n sweaty like 'em too!" Wyatt couldn't wait to rip his sweat pants off and shove his wand in some poop shoots.

"We have to make this work; we can't do those blindfolded sleep overs no more. Last time, I could barely cum in yer hand. We have to get laid; nay, we *MUST* get laid, by a chick. Seriously, we can't keep goin' on with life only fantasizing what them titties feel like. We have to know; we will know; we *MUST* know!"

"Cool, can't wait to climb me a bitch; here, scan this in," Wyatt held a cut out page of a magazine in his grubby hands, and handed it to Gary.

"Nice! Emmy Rossum's face; man, we are gonna' be the luckiest guys to ever build ourselves a woman. By the way, how the hell did we even come up with this idea and decide it was even possible to make a real-life female with this lame eighties computer?"

"No idea; think it was on the back of a soup can or some shit," Wyatt said, "But don't matter, none. Here, here's a bra to wear on your head. I like to wear these to cover my bald spot. He handed Gary one and leaned down and pointed to his bald spot.

They both put them on.

Russel Crow wondered why he hadn't worn a bra on his head before?

"Let me tweak this," Gary said, "And, well, should be about ready." He pressed some keys and the unsophisticated equipment did a poor wire-frame-mockup of a woman's body- naked body, naked; oh, so naked- CRUNCH! CRUNCH! SQUERREL!

"I'll just go ahead and hit enter, like so."

The two sat hunched over an old computer in Gary's teen bedroom, which had a poster of Wyatt, wearin' red panties, on the wall.

The room looked like TJ Max or something.

Gary hit the button- enter.

DING!

Smoke rolled from under his bedroom door and then, BANG! It burst open.

There in the doorway stood a phenomenal woman.

"Oh gawd; I'm gonna' ice cream my shorts," Wyatt said he put his hand down the front of his pants and fondled the tip of his Woody Wood Pecker. This wasn't in the script; it was just something that Danny DeVito did.

"You and me, both."

"Hiya boys," she said.

This computer made chick looked like a mix of Emmy Rossum and Anne Hathaway. She had a great face, large eyes, full lips, 'n cheeks that made ya go, SWEET JESUS! Tits like flyin' saucers hidden underground at Area 51 and an ass like a tire truck from the nineteen twenties.

"So," she asked, "Who are you? And, hmm, who am I? And, why do I want to fuck you both so badly?"

The two, old men teen boys, drooled.

Several Grams

Well, they both got blow jobs and took turns fuckin' her.

Wyatt took her missionary and Gary like somethin' called T-Bar-ing.

They named their sexy creation Hot Dayum-Liza and she swallered all their jizz again and again, as much as the two dudes wanted.

Hot Dayum-Liza had lips like a hoover vac and them boys' foreskin was peeled way back and blown like a fire hydrant in New York by poor black kids.

Tech Giant

Seth Godin, the King of Blogging, couldn't believe what he'd seen online. Two little lame kids built a woman on a computer.

"How did they do it? I need that technology! I want that technology. I'll get that technology. I'll have that technology!"

He sat in a busy McDonalds at a small table 'cause he needed the free wi-fi 'n shit. Seth ate them salty fries and thought about what he'd seen.

Two boys on YouTube had revealed a marvel of technological innovation and creation by making a real life flesh and blood woman from a computer. And, not just any computer, a Commodore.

Even more impressive to Seth and other viewers were Hot Dayum-Liza's cupcake space tits.

"I must know how they made them beautiful breast-ises look like they are in zero gravity all the time."

The computer creature-woman had tits that behaved like she was in water or space 'n shit. They didn't hang or sag; but seemed to be perpetually floating 'n wigglin' about. It was awesome!

"I'm going to kidnap this beautiful bitch-technology woman!"

The people around him, looked over with disapproval. A woman, with a child, shook her head and sighed disgust. She pulled her young daughter away in haste.

Eek! Oops; He lowered his head and resolved, *I will steal her.*

Seth took out his phone and dialed.

"Yo, what's happen', brotha?"

"Nada," Seth said, "Hey, I have job; you free?"

"Sure nuff; what's up?"

"There's a dame in need of an escort."

"Kool Aid; ya, want her dead or alive?"

Seth cleared his throat. He looked around. No one seemed to be interested in his conversation. He spoke quietly "I want her alive this time."

"Ya' sure? I know how ya' likes 'em dead."

"No, alive please."

"Okay, if ya' is sure. Damn, easier to just kill 'em. Sure ya' don't want me to killer her?"

"No, alive."

(Cough)

Seth looked up.

A lowly McDonalds manager stood in front of his table with her hand arranged disapprovingly upon her hips. She shook her head.

Action Pack

His face was a wrinkly testicle. Prune Face put down his phone and broke the seal on his packaging. He pushed aside the plastic housing, which tore part of the carboard backing.

Fresh air greeted him. His apartment was a fuckin' killer bachelor pad fit for the mob.

So, what weapons do I have, huh? He looked at what his figure came with. He already had clothes molded to his body. A white button up shirt, and green pants*, that'll do.*

Well, looks like I gotz me a nineteen thirties tommy gun and some dynamite. That about covers it; I don't really need anything else to be a criminal.

He went to his dry erase board and copied the location of said dame off the text from Seth.

I'll bring the gun and dynamite. Yep, that's about it. Prune face was ready.

Capture Dew Process

"I want to die."

"What's the problem, Gary?" Wyatt asked.

"I thought having a chick suck my Louis CK would somehow make my life worth living."

Wyatt sat next to Gary on the twin bed.

Hot Dayum-Liza was in the shower.

"I'm sorry, buddy," Wyatt said, "But I don't got time for no emotional bullshit; I gotta' get in that shower Hot Dayum-Liza is soaping up. Soapin' up, MAN!"

"Okay, buddy; I understand. I'll be here, sittin' on this bed, with my pistol to my temple. Go on now 'n have your fun."

"Okay, here why don't you read this nonfiction book by Bridget Chase; him being depressed and subsequent death. Oh, and, umm… you got the safety on, here." He turned the safety of for his friend.

"Thanks; you're the best friend I have," Gary said.

Wyatt smiled and dropped his towel to the floor. He was naked. "See ya'." His white wrinkly ass went runnin' off. "Hey, Hot Dayum-Liza, daddy's comin' fer ya'!"

Gary opened the book.

Well, Gladiator was good, I have that. That Mummy reboot with Tom Cruise sucked; maybe I shouldn't have done that flick. Oh well, it's my time.

He read the first line, and only sentence in the book. "I came like death; her mouth was open."

Gary put the book down. T*hat was good! I like cummin' in girl's mouths, and guess… yeah, guess orgasms are a kind of a death; especially fer those million or so sperm in the chick's belly. Hmm, but maybe the author meant more? Naw, he meant blowjobs fer sure!*

He picked up the pistol and put it to his head. "Wait what am I thinkin?"

Gary lowered the weapon

"Dem titties make my cock drip. I want to live! I want to *LIVE* I say!"

He hardly noticed when the bedroom door opened. SMACK!

Gary was knocked unconscious.

Is That Blood On My Pee Pee

Wyatt dried his hair with a fluffy Bed Bath and Beyond towel.

"Here are my ten tips for *living*," he said.

"Dude, what the fuck you talkin' about?" Gary asked. "We need to save Hot Dayum-Liza." He combed his hair and his beard.

"Right; except we have no idea who took her."

Gary touched the lump on the side of his head. *Ouch! Whoever that fucker was, got me good, he did.* "Well, something like clues or suspects won't stop us. To the Bat mobile!"

"You have a Batmobile?"

"Yep, sure do. Let me show you."

The two left the bathroom and went to the kitchen. "See."

"Oh well; yeah, I see alright."

A small Hot Wheels Batmobile sat on the counter. It was encased in a small plastic bag.

"Got that sucka' outta' the cereal box today; can you believe the world we live in? A fucking Batmobile car in a cereal box. Damn, can't believe people aren't goin' ape shit 'bout it. I'm gonna go buy me like, ten boxes or some shit; build a shoe box garage for 'em. I'll be the richest man alive!"

"Dude," Wyatt picked up the Hot Wheels. "We can't drive it. There's no engine and we are too big!"

"Ah, I see; you're not bein' a Jedi," Gary said, "To the eighties computer!"

After doing some shit where they scanned in pictures of engines and hooked tweezers up to the tiny car, they were able to make it grow to actual size and functional.

BAM! Lightening!

Wyatt looked at the wrecked room. "We should have done this outside. I mean the car is stuck in this room. Yer mom's gonna be pissed and I'm tryin' to get in good with her. Hopin' to lick that pooper 'a hers."

"Good point," Gary said. "Hold on."

He went to his closet and pulled a chainsaw out.

BRRRRRR! He yanked it to life.

"JUST GIVE ME A MOMENT!" He started cutting through the bedroom wall.

Wyatt said, "Gary we're on the second floor."

"WHAT?!"

"WE'RE ON THE SECOND FLOOR?!"

"SO?"

"SO... WELL, OKAY... NEVERMIND."

Prune Breakfast

"You sure you don't want to fuck me?"

"No," Prune Face said.

"Certain?"

"Yes, certain."

Hot Dayum-Liza frowned. "But, I was made to fuck; and your face looks like balls. So, now I'm all turned on 'n such."

"I don't care. I don't want you. And, would you stop rolling around the bed like that and touchin' yer tits?"

"Okay."

"No! Don't rub yer pussy either; that's not what I meant. I'm tryin' to work. Do you know how hard it is running a business?"

"No."

"Of course, you don't. Well, it is hard; even when it involves crime, it is hard as fuck. Like, eighty five percent of small businesses fail, even crime businesses. Now, I got emails to answer and invoices to process, if you'll excuse me."

"Okay, well, don't mind little pretty me with my soft lips and a deep throat."

"Hey! No! Get away from my lap. Stop! Don't undo my zipper. Okay, that's it. I'm tyin' you up."

"OH great! I love to be tied up."

Hot Daym-Liza jumped up and down.

F-ZERO

"Wounded people write better stories?"

Gary tossed the book to the passenger seat's floor. "Why does Bridget write this crap that is clearly untrue? Wounded people write just like everyone else, with words 'n shit."

Wyatt reached by his feet and picked the book up. "It's based off a TED Talk. And, you're right; the idea is ridiculous crap; just catchy shit people say to get themselves selected to get a talk; doesn't matter if it's true, just has to have a catchy title." He tossed the book out the window. The devil laughed. Bridget sat up in bed.

"So, here is our exit," Gary said.

Wyatt asked, "Why would Hot Dayum-Liza be kidnapped and taken to a Baskin Robbins?"

Gary had come up with the idea for checking Baskin Robbins for Hot Dayum-Liza after having called Bridget Chase.

Bridget was jerkin' it in the shower with a slippery Fleshlight. Seein' that the author had no time for clever places; he told Gary to head to the ice cream establishment. Really any location was just as good and just as plausible.

"No idea," Gary said, "But, it would be better if we pretended the Baskin Robins was a castle or some shit."

"Yeah, and how do we do that?"

"We use our imagination, geez! Wyatt, it's like we haven't been friends for sixteen years and our characters are only now learning 'bout one another. Like in movies where the mom reprimands the kid sayin, 'Johnny we go through this every morning'; when what she is actually saying, 'Johnny, if I reference the past it will for sure make this a more believable world and family'."

"No, untrue; so untrue. We've definitely had a sixteen year friendship, and the fact that in movies friends get surprised by one another's behavior is very plausible. Okay, let's get Hot Dayum-Liza back. I got a boner."

"Dude, me too."

The Batmobile pulled up to Baskin Robbins.

A kid was having a birthday party inside and all the kids ran out, shouting about the Batmobile in the parking lot.

Gary looked at the boner pressing his pants. "Let's wait a minute before we get out."

"Yeah, good thinking; what do we do about these boners?"

"Do you remember the F-Zero game?"

"Yeah, what was that, Super Nintendo?"

"Yeah, that was a fun game. I wonder if it still holds up?"

"Probably not," Wyatt said, "I think even as a kid I knew the mechanics weren't pretty illegitimate.

"Do you remember the different levels? For me it kinda all blended into one single track."

"Yeah, can't recall any. Hey, guess what; boners gone."

"Cool. Let's go!"

Ice Cream Clue

"WHERE'S THE MOTHAFUCKIN' COMPUTER CHICK WITH SPACE BOOBS?"

Wyatt shouted in the Baskin Robbins worker's face and held a Robocop pistol to his temple. Insanity played in Russel Crowe's eyes.

"Easy, Wyatt." Gary put his hand on the gun.

The Baskin Robbins guy had his hands up. "Dude, easy; that zero-gravity-boob-chick was here with some guy. I had nothing to do with it."

Wyatt's hand shook. "She was so hot! You have no idea what it's like to have her stolen like a mint condition baseball card. Shit, they could be doin' anything with them titties. ANYTHING! Tell me what you know!" He pressed the gun harder against the ice cream worker's temple.

Gary said, "Better do as he says."

"Okay," the Baskin Robbins minimum wage worker said, "Look all Iz know, is this guy with a face that looked like balls came in with this super-hot chick. After a few minutes some dude came in 'n met them. Then, they left."

Wyatt asked, "Did they say anything?"

"I mean, I think I heard the name Seth several times."

"Oh, that was Seth Godin," a voice said.

The two horny teen boys that looked middle age, turned.

A demon man sat at a small table and licked on an ice cream cone.

The two boys asked, "Freddy Krueger?"

"Yeah."

"What are you doing at Baskin Robbins?" Wyatt asked.

"Fellas, this is *my* joint. I can't get me enough of this ice cream. Shit, a feller can't be all kill, kill, laugh, laugh, laugh, hahaha."

Gary stepped forward, "So who was it?"

"Seth Godin, king of blogging."

Wyatt said, "Well, now we have a lead. He turned to the worker. "And, give me two scoops of dat chocolate Ice cream, bitch." He still held the gun in the guy's face.

Freddy popped that last delicious bit of cone in his mouth. You know that last bite where all the melted goodness gets absorbed and makes the cone a little soft. He stood and said, "So, guys, ya' think I can join yas in this man hunt? I know where they was goin."

Gary asked, "Why do you want to come?"

Freddy smiled. "Cause that bitch be super-duper-HOT! Maybe if I help yous fellas, you can make me one. Horror monsters get lonely sometimes and necrophilia can get quite borin' after'a while."

Wyatt tuned with an ice cream cone in his hand, "Sure thing, but there are only to seats in the Batmobile."

A few minutes later.

Wyatt licked that cone.

"Hey, watch the drips," Freddy said, "Shit, I hate goin ta dat laundry mat."

"Sorry," Wyatt said. He sat curled up on Freddy's lap.

Gary drove. He wore black leather driving gloves with the fingers cut off and metal studs on the knuckles.

Barnum 'N Blood

Men gawked and jizzed their pants. Boys trembled and found out what erections were, right there in that gawd damned circus.

"Do you think this is wise?" Prune face asked. "She is drawing too much attention."

Men starred at Hot Dayum Liza. She wore a red bandana for a top and those Daisy Duke shorts like the Dukes'a Hazard. Her hair was gorgeous, lips sensual and hips full.

Men, and boys ran into each other; some trip and fell. People were stepped on, and wives fumed- jealous in rage.

Hot Dayum Liza's tits floated like bubbles in a hot tub.

"Yes," Seth said, "It is fine. Besides I like combining several tasks to maximize my day. This will just be an hour or so. I do love me Barnum 'n Bailey's circus."

"Couldn't you just-"

"-No," Seth said, "Why don't you grab a popcorn or whatever you want for the show."

Prune Face grumbled.

Seth handed him a wad 'a bills.

Prune Face walked off.

"So, Miss Hot Dayum Lisa, how is it that those boys were able to make you?"

Her tits were barely held by that thin fabric. "Well," she said, "I suppose their sexual frustration was manifest into some kind of cosmic power which they funneled through an old computer."

"Interesting," Seth said, "And your tits? How on earth are your tits able to defy gravity?"

"Well-." Hot Dayum Liza looked down at her cleavage. "I suppose all those airbrushed and photoshopped magazine pictures were somehow translated into physical form. It's what everyone fantasizes about, and here they are; by the way, are we gonna fuck? I really need to fuck!"

A man passing by was eating popcorn. He over heard her and choked on a kernel. He coughed and wheezed for air. His wife patted his back. *Damn, that bitch just said she wanted to fuck! I can believe it. Wait.. am I choking? Am I losing air? Man, what lucky guy gets to empty his cum sac into da likes of her.* The man looked at her ass while his wife smacked his back. COUGH! GASP!

Hot Tub-in'

"Wow, this is wonderful," Hot Dayum Liza said.

"Yep, my hot tub is where I do most of my blogging from. You'd be surprised how stressful it is. If I had known, I wouldn't have built my career on the promise of one blog post a day. Hell, I'm so burned out, yesterday I blogged about my shampoo." Seth had his thin arms draped over the sides of the hot tub.

"But you're bald," she said.

"I know… I know." He shook his head.

Prune face smiled and sipped a cocktail. His prune face was even more prune-y than usual. "So, ya' thinks I can get paid now n shit? I mean, I gone 'n done yer kidnapping for ya'."

"Soon," Seth said, "Soon."

Prune Face thought, *damn, this dude is worse than drug dealers where yous got ta hang out with dem for like the whole afternoon 'n shit.*

Hot Dayum Liza stood up. "I should really be going now. I'm sure Wyatt and Gary are worried about me; plus I'm horny as fuck for some comedy teen cock." She wore a leopard print bikini that was hot-dayum-oh-my-god-my-balls-are-as-swollen-up-as-a-shake n-up-beer.

"Not so fast," Seth said and grabbed her arm. "I haven't done any experiments on you. I'm gay, so none of them will be sexy experiments. No, more the alien abduction kind where you are probed coldly like a cow."

Suddenly an alarm went off.

"We got visitors," Seth said.

Prune Face hopped up. He wore board shorts kind a bathing suit. "Cool, let me get my gun and red sticks of dynamite and I'll take care of them. I bet it's those twerps I drop-kicked earlier!"

Meanwhile, our ill-casted heroes arrived.

The Batmobile tore up the road.

"Whoa! Seth lives in the Eternia Castle?" Wyatt asked.

"Yep," Freddy said.

Gary gawked. "How cool!"

SCREECH! The Batmoblie pulled up to the front.

The three hopped out.

Wyatt yelled, "Hey, Booger Blogger, give us Hot Dayum Liza, back!"

Gary followed suit. "Yeah, and yous better not'a fucked her repeatedly and ruined her for us!"

Freddy said, "Yeah, 'cause they are making me one next. I don't want ta sit around while they make a replacement first! Little Freddy's ready ta' part-EA!"

Seth peeked his head out a chamber window like eight floors up. "No, you can't have her; sorry. Please leave. See ya' later boys."

The two middle age men with teen haircuts and horror icon, looked at one another.

"We can storm the castle, right?" Wyatt asked Gary.

"Sure, I mean, he said *no* but we could fight."

Freddy said, "I like me a good fight. I'll be all like, 'Iz gonna cut you bitch, SHI-SHA!'" Freddy did some clawing of the air with his finger knives.

Wyatt said, "So we fight for her."

Gary nodded.

The draw bridge lowered some revealing Prune Face "Incoming!" He yelled.

"Dynamite!" Gary shouted.

Freddy jumped for cover.

KA-BOOOOM!

Blood sprayed.

Dust twirled a horrific death.

Freddy lifted himself off the ground. "Dear Fangora!"

Next to him, Gary and Wyatt wiggled on the ground. They were missing limbs and bleeding everywhere. The two boys gurgled wet labored breaths.

"Shit, those boys've been blown ta pieces!" Freddy said.

Prune face laughed.

Seth watched out the upper window. "Damn, I'll have ta' hire some people to clean that up. Can't have my lawn with limbs and guts rotting. Although, there might be a possible blog post in there some where."

Hot Dayum Liza shoved Seth aside. She looked out the window. "WYATT! GARYY! PENISES! NOOOOOO!"

"Hahah; they are dead and now you are mine!" Seth said. *Man, I love winning; just fuckin' love it!*

Freddy ran to dat Batmobile. "I don't know what I'm doing but these boys brought that computer with 'em. Hell, maybe it can save their lives.

The horror icon set the old 80s computer down on the ground. He hooked the jumper cables up to the boys bodies and plugged the cord into the car.

Dat computer dialed up.

Freddy stepped back.

"What on earth?" Seth watched as green neon lights came out for the computer and boys. *This can't be possible. No way a lame computer can emit healing green neon lasers. It just isn't possible!*

The light show became bright; so bright that the computer and boys couldn't be seen anymore.

After moments the light dimmed.

"Well I'll be damned," Freddy said.

A massive figure stood in the clearing.

Hot Dayum Liza squeezed her head next to Seth's. "They mutated together. Wyatt? Gary? You guys alright?"

Gary and Wyatt's bodies had merged. They shared one body with two heads. Nasty stitching held their bodies together and each head controlled on arm and leg.

"Whoa!" Wyatt said, "We are some kind of awesome mutant."

"Sure are," Gary said, "I bet we can kick some serious ass now." He shouted to Hot Dayum Liza, "yeah, I think we are okay!"

"Wait, what about?" Wyatt pulled out the waist band of their pants. "Gary!"

He looked down. "Well, we won't have any problem with double penetration."

Hot Dayum Liza saw the double cocked mutant boys. "Come save me she shouted, "Im so horny, now!'

The mutant boys looked up.

"Go get her," Freddy said, "I think you'll got this taken care of."

Series Finale

Seth was a pile of gore. All of his bones were crushed.

Hot Dayum Liza rubbed her gawd damn body all over that mutant's body with two heads.

"Why is that chick so slutty?" Prune Face asked.

"We gave her the brain of Albert Einstein," Wyatt said.

"Yeah, I have the brain of a genius. Didn't you know?" Hot Dayum Liza said.

Gary said, "Yeah, that dude was a magical nympho."

The two boys held Prune Face by the ankle and dangled him from atop Eternia; then, DROP! They let him go.

His testicle face splattered the cement.

"Any last words?" Gary asked and laughed.

"Good one," Wyatt said, "He's dead but you asked him for last words."

They high fived one another.

Prune Face lifted his head off of dat ground and asked, "How's your sister, Gary?"

The mutant boys gasped.

END

MURDER
She Witnessed

Bridget Chase

Murder She Witnessed
Bridget Chase

How'd you know I gone 'n done it, Bitch?

Oh, that's good, give it to me; just like that.

Jessica Fletcher watched the Baskin Robbins worker plop two large scoops of delicious ice cream into that golden cone.

She licked her lips. *Oh, that will taste nice; and I deserve that shit, because I'm a badass motha' fucka' at writing mysteries. No one loves that Rocky Road more than me!*

Her conservative blazer told the tale of her success in life.

"Here you are ma' am," the worker handed that cone across the counter.

Our Old-Lady-of-Word-Smithing took hold of the cone, and noticed-

-His tattoo. Oh my god, his tattoo!

Jessica tried not to show her surprise.

The ice cream clerk eyed her suspiciously.

"Thank you *so much* young man-"

"-And how much do I owe you?"

The clerk whipped out a gun, "How'd you know I gone and done it, BITCH?"

Jessica slipped a hand cautiously into her purse. *I don't want to startle this fucker.* "I don't know what you've done; I just came for the ice cream." *And the mystery!*

Her fingers searched her purse and brushed against her swollen dildo. *No don't need that right yet; but later, for sure. Ha there!*

She grasped her emergency I've-Fallen-And-I-Can't-Get-Up-Old-Lady-button.

CLICK!

An instant later...

"Police freeze! You're under arrest."

Police officers barged in the door guns drawn.

The ice cream tattooed clerk grabbed Jessica and used her as a shield. He held the pistol to her head. "Back up pigs; back the fuck up or this old lady gets it in her slutty skilled-writing head; I'm warning yous'!"

Jessica with her martial arts 'Sit and Be Fit' skills smashed the ice cream cone into the guy's face.

CREAMPIE! (wink)

Then she, BLAM! Stepped on his toe.

The guy released her and hopped around.

The police ran up and arrested the man- The terrible crook- The tattooed menace- The slinger of ice cream- The *BAD DUDE!*

"Wow, I'm the best writer ever!"

Jessica Fetcher gazed at the paper that stuck out from the top of the typewriter. Words covered the sheet. It was fiction gold. *I'm the best, bitch!*

Some shitty music starts playing.

Fingers type wildly on a typewriter.

Ink letters type out 'Murder' on the paper.

Jessica Fletcher rides her bike down Main Street in a small town, wearing a sensible sweater. She smiles, living the perfect life of comfort.

Then she climbs some stairs while carrying fishing equipment, because shit, she is not only successful, but she also makes sure to sample every aspect of joy the small town has to offer.

Wait now, hold on; she is being really active, and taking a jog in a peaceful prairie. She is wearing a comfortable 'I have a happy life' grey sweat-suit. She definitely has the right outfit for each occasion.

Wait, back to her typing again and we focus in on the fact that she has a ring on her finger. Poor lady was widowed at 50.

Letters type out 'SHE WROTE' on the paper, bringing the Intro full circle and complete.

Oh, but wait, a sail boat passes by; while Jessica is standing on some random dock. She waives because she is super friendly with everyone in the small town.

WHOA! Watch out now; she has a gun. Jessica pulls the trigger and, BANG! A flag comes out the end saying, "Bang!" Oh, (sensible chuckle) it was a fake gun. Good thing she has on proper eye wear.

What's this?

Jessica shines a light into some dark hole. It's night and we don't know what she's doing; but we can assume she is investigating for clues.

Then Jessica peeks though a door, and wait, nope; she run outside as if she were chasing someone. Doesn't she know to take it easy at her age?

Now a bunch of scary weird silhouettes of two people struggling-

-Whoops, and back to the typewriter.

The letter keys go crazy and Jessica types away like Vanilla Ice grinning with joy; she's wearing a red sweeter because, well, we will find out later.

She takes that shit and puts the finished story into a nice leather folder.

Jessica closes the folder and 'Murder She Wrote' is inscribed on its cover.

So, there we have it!

And, we find ourselves on a coastal road.

It Begins

"I can't believe my short story is being published in Hustler Magazine; how embarrassing," Jessica said. "Me, my story; How will I ever show my face in this town again?"

Michael Horton, her nephew, drove the car. "I'm so sorry I had no idea that it was sent to the wrong place; by the way, do you like my hair? I just had it professionally feathered?"

"Your hair is superb; but, how did this happen?"

Michael couldn't tell her the truth. "I don't know, must have been a mix up. I thought I had sent my story-,"

"-Your story?" Jessica perked up, "You wrote a story for Hustler?"

"No; no.. I would never." *Damn, she is a good detective!*

"Did your dirty story go a little something like this?"

The old lady smiled. Her thin lips were painted in red lipstick. Her tongue greased the monkeys.

"What are you doing?" Michael asked.

Jessica unzipped his pants. "I'm a dirt slut; gimme' yer' cocka' Wally!"

"You can't, I'm driving; and besides-," He didn't finish because her fingers were already pullin' that Slim Jim Meat stick from its wrapper.

His little tarantula grew.

Well, damn, maybe this is okay.

Jessica slurped that crispy fucker and, GOBBLE, GOBBLE! Gobbled that flesh stick up!

BOB, BOB, BOB! She head-banged and stroked vigorously with her vacuum suckin' mouth. "Gimme' yer nut you prick!"

Michael moaned, *damn I got a nut coming already? Shit, this detective is fuckin' good at vacuum suckin' midgets! I can't, I just can't cum in her belly. Maybe I should tell her I'm about to cumma, cumma. She might not be a swallawer'.*

Jessica Fetcher worked the head with her tongue, "Give me that family gravy," she said in a nasty voice.

Marshmallow cream rose. *I'm gonna' fill her mouth! Here it-*

-Michael placed his hands on the back of his head and leaned back in his chair.

He re-read the last few lines of his story.

This will make it into Hustler, for sure.

He saved the file and then went to Porn Hub.

Time to strangle the outlaw.

He grabbed a Kleenex.

BUKKAKE BABY!

DAMN, WAKE UP BITCH!

The police officer nudged the woman with his shoe. "What's wrong with her?"

His partner sipped on his morning coffee, "No idea." He leaned over and shouted, "Hey bitch, sidewalks aren't for sleeping! Damn, wake up, Bitch!"

"Maybe, we should pick her up," Officer Gorin said.

His partner, McCulkin, nodded.

They each grabbed an arm and lifted.

"Nope, she's still out," McCulkin said.

Gorin suggested, "Maybe if we put her head back on, she'll wake up?" He reached for the severed head on the grass.

"Stop, don't do that!" Jessica ran up. She held a bag of groceries in her arm. It was a paper bag because, *I'm conscientious about the environment.*

She had been walking home when she saw the yellow police tape; *I hurried the fuck over.*

"Don't touch her," she said.

"What? Move along, Jessica," Officer Gorin said.

Jessica huffed, "Can't you see that she is dead?"

"Dead?" McCulay asked. He reached down and grabbed the head by its hair and looked at it. He turned it over in his hands. "Hmm, maybe this hot old lady is right."

Jessica winked at him. "Hot huh?"

"Yeah," McCulay said, "In some weird way, yeah. Maybe, it's your take charge attitude; or maybe, that you cover up your body so much that it has become some secret fantasy."

"So, what do we do if it *is* a dead body?" Gorin asked.

Jessa Fletcher put her finger to her chin. *Hmm, I m the greatest writer in the world; so, let me use my world building and fiction creating mind here.*

She began putting the pieces together

If there is a body, it could be a murder. If it is a murder, there is a suspect. If there is a suspect, there are clues; and if there are clues, I can solve this shit!

Jessica shouted, "My god! It *was* murder!"

The two officers gasped.

"Stop lady your scaring me," Gorin said.

McCulay put the severed head down and wiped his hands on his trouser leg. "So, who gone and done it?"

Jessica needed clues, and then she saw it. The old lady pointed, "He did it!"

The police turned.

A man standing by a picnic table, in the park, was cleaning a bloody machete."'HUH?" He saw them looking.

"Arrest that man, POLICE!" Gorin shouted.

McCulay whipped out his gun. "We are the police, stupid."

"Don't shoot him," Jessica shouted

"Why? I already have my gun out," McCulay asked. "I can't *not* shoot someone now."

"Look at his chest," she said.

The man had C4 strapped on with duct tape.

"He's gonna' blow this bitch up!" Gorin said with a smile.

"I'm not," the long-haired, machete cleaning guy said, "Someone strapped this bomb on me and made me kill her."

"I'm gonna shoot him," McCulay said, "It's happening. I can't *not* shoot. I mean, my gun is out. Someone, please stop me!"

Jessica thought fast. *I can disarm this, I'm a writer!* She reached into the grocery bag, *perfect*, she pulled out a bottle of hand lotion.

SQUIRT! She squeezed out a large glob into her palm.

"Hey, watch doing?" McCulay asked.

Jessica Fletcher reached her greased hand into his trousers and started giving him a handy.

This outta' relax that trigger finger. It's worked with so many cops!

The officer grinned. "Oh, yeah, here we go."

"What about me?" Gorin asked.

"Get over here, you Black Stallone!"

He moved closer and she reached in his trousers with her other hand.

Just savin' the day, here.

She yanked those jockeys like charmin' snakes from vases.

Jessica had both men moanin'.

Their meat was hot, and Jessica was well versed in satisfying law enforcement officers.

"Please help," the machete guy said.

"I only have two hands; unless, you are okay with a foot job?"

The machete guy shrugged, "Sure."

"Then get on over here," Jessica said.

He dropped the bloody machete and took a step.

KA-BOOOM!

The machete guy jumped. "Damn, am I still alive?"

"Sorry, sorry, just me. I came hard," McCulay said. The front of his pants were blown out and marshmallow cream coated the fresh park grass.

The hefty manuscript hit the table.

Terry looked up at Jessica

She sat across a large oak desk and smiled.

"I think your writing has changed, some," he said

"How so?" Jessica asked. Her hands were clasped properly in her lap.

"I mean, you are giving two guys hand jobs at the park-," Terry flipped thought he papers. "-And, looks like you were about to jerk a guy off with your foot."

Jessica smiled, "Well, it's important to the plot."

"How?"

"How is it not? Aren't I a great top-caliber writer of mystery?" she asked.

"Yes."

"So, it's a mystery, besides-,"

Terry jumped. Her foot came under the desk and nudged his Garbage Pail Kid.

"A little sperm always makes *murder* more interesting," Jessica said and lifted her eyebrows.

She unbuttoned her blouse and set those Sea World whales free.

Our slutty Jessica wore a large bra, but not for long because, REMOVE! She took it off and threw it across the desk.

It hit Terry in the face. He licked his lips.

Jessica's tits were flapjacks hangin' down to the waist band of her skirt.

Terry realized that entertainment and semen were inseparable.

END

Mystery! SQUIRT!

PEPPERMINT
PYRAMIDS

BRIDGET CHASE

Peppermint Pyramids
Bridget Chase

Double Mint MURDER!

"Oh, honey; you's so sweet. Mommy loves you. You have vanilla ice cream skin, cotton colored eyeballs and peppermint in yer white girl viens."

Dick Tracy steepled his fingers. "And, that is the last thing you said to yer daughter who was horribly murdered along with yer husband in cold blood along the dark streets on yer way home from a carnival type thing?"

Jennifer Garner grabbed a tissue off the desk. She dried her eyes. "Yeah, pretty much."

Dick Tracy had his feet up on the desk. His office was dark and street lights radiated through the pulled blinds in quantum double-slit experiments.

He thought on this name 'Peppermint'. *It could be a good movie name that might draw in some females 'n shit.*

"Yes, Peppermint seems catchy and quirky," Dick Tracy said, "And, if people over heard someone seeing a movie called Peppermint, particularly a male seeing a movie with that name, they might inquire as to the contents of said film."

Jennifer Garner adjusted her tits. She wore a S&M Electra costume that held similarities to Vampirella's costume with regard to the deep-V that let them titties spill out real nice. It was a red sleek number and super tight. She had them sexy high boots that came up mid-thigh, red gloves that came up past her elbows, a choker and the one-piece bodysuit was cut high on her hips and disappeared in a nut busting curve between her thigh gap.

Dick Tracy was more than happy to help. *Yeah, I was in. Any adventure involving Jennifer's tits is an adventure for me.*

"So, you'll help me track these bad, oh so bad, men down?" She asked.

"Sure nuff."

"Oh, this is great," Jennifer said, "You wouldn't believe how hard this whole thing has been. It's just been a nightmare. This gang payed off the cops, judges, everyone! I went to court, and the three men responsible got off Scott-free; a cop tried to buy my silence, and the judge, well the P.A.R.T.Y gang owned the judge. I'm *so* glad you'll help me. Where do we start?"

Dick Tracy explored his ear canal with his finger. Finding nothing of interest, he said, "How 'bout showin' me them titties to start."

"Okay."

Jennifer began to unfasten the garment's clasp behind her neck.

"No wait. Let's not, yet. I mean, I'm for sure gonna' fuck you, but I think on this assignment I'll delay gratification a little."

"Are you sure?"

"No, but I'm gonna' try somethin' new."

"Great, I can't wait to take revenge for my peppermint daughter. May she rest in peace; and I hope she sees me kickin' ass and killin' them bad guys for her. Yep, hope it makes her smile real-big in heaven seein' mommy dripping with blood and going on a murderous rampage for her."

"Yep, that would make most any daughter proud. On second thought," Dick Tracy said, "Lemme' see them titties."

Jennifer stood up and peeled that second skin suit off. She bounced on her toes and made 'em hop-scotch.

Them cupcakes were delicious lookin'.

Dick Tracy was now ready.

Egyptian Gangs of Egypt

"Ya' killed my motha' fuckin' daughter, you gang bastard!"

Tears and drool dripped off Jennifer's face onto the gang guy she was screamin' at.

He grimaced and tried to turn away.

Her hair was all sorts of fucked and wet, and the veins in her neck stood out.

"How could you? You'll pay; I hope da' Devil tongue punches yer shit box and a horde of parasitic elephants ass fuck you and then have that video sent to yer mom and yer church!"

Dick Tracy watched.

This was a crazy scene for sure.

They had found one of the gang members involved and held him prisoner in a warehouse where they gave him cement shoes.

The dude was naked and tied to chair.

Jennifer paraded around him, pistol whippin' him 'n shit, while sayin' all kinds of motherly mourning abusive nonsense.

The gang dude wept. He knew the end was near.

He was so upset, and you'd have to be super upset, that he didn't care 'bout Jennifer Garner in that hot-ass outfit.

The gang guy barely noticed them titties swingin' about in his face. Again, this was amazing because them are some perky white girl celebrity titties.

Dick Tracy took a moment 'n mused on them. *All buttery homestyle biscuits, HOT DAYUM! GIMME! GIMME DAT NUMBER 5 Breakfast meal! Them nipples can't hardly hide under that thin fabric.*

"Where's the fuckin' gang headquarters, you mule intestine motha' fucker?" Jennifer asked. She held the pistol to the guy's nuts and, CLAK!

"Whoops!"

The guy screamed.

"Whoa!" Dick Tracy said, "Yer supposed to let him answer first."

"I don't give a fuck." CLAK! Jennifer sent a bullet through the dude's abdomen.

"Let's go," she said, "We'll get our answers elsewhere."

The gang guy blew blood bubbles and gurgled bile.

Dick Tracy joined the revenge drunk bitch and they walked to the warehouse's metal sliding door.

"Please," the gang guy said in a shallow, I'm fucked, voice.

Jennifer turned. "Please, there is no please. Give me my daughter back; oh, and my husband too, I guess. I mean he was cool n shit; payed for the house and my shoes 'n such; but you can't, can you? You can't give me them back!"

"I…" the gang guy could hardly speak. Blood dripped on the floor.

"That's what I thought."

Jennifer slid aside the door.

A werewolf stood on the other side. Its red eyes glowed in the night.

"Get him; he's all yours," she said.

ROAR! The gnarly beast thing in grizzly hair tore up the ground in a sprint toward the captive.

"NOOOOO!" the gang guy's cry carried over the air.

Jennifer and Dick Tracy headed to the awesome nineteen fifties police car.

They slipped into the comfortable leather seats. A gentle scent of luxury greeted their noses.

"Oh, sorry ya' got some blood on yer hat, there," Jennifer said.

She pulled out a handkerchief (from nowhere), brushed it on her tongue, and dapped the spot on his yellow hat.

He peered over at them tits wigglin' on her chest.

Yep, mighty fine weight 'n shape to 'em; no wonder Ben Affleck is in rehab all the time. Can't imagine loosin' a chick like her. Fillin' her belly with cum, and then one day she's my ex; yep, I'd do some drugs to. Damn, bet them lips yank a good cock they do.

He said, "Did you see that guy's tatt?"

Jennifer sat back and adjusted them birthday cakes. "This top is near impossible to keep my tits in. There, I think I finally got it to cover my nipples. No, what about the tattoo?"

"Egyptian," Dick Tracy said, "I think we better research its origins 'n shit."

"Cool," she said, "Maybe I could do some awesome training for our audience to watch while you do the nerdy shit. Maybe I'll train in a bikini by the pool."

"Sound like a good plan."

Dick Tracy turned the ignition key.

The headlights burned over trees 'n underbrush as the car made its way across the dirt road and back to the bustling city.

Train in Oil

"So, we aren't showing my training footage?" Jennifer asked.

"Naw, it got cut," Dick Tracy said.

"Hmm, even when I trained with the shake weight topless? I mean that was super-hot."

"Yep, even that."

"Well, let's hope this train scene is worth it because I really think men would've wanted to see me training naked in the lake doing them explosive jumping jacks."

"They for sure, would have. I know I sure liked watching you."

The train barreled down the tracks. Its path wound through the mountains like a Lone Ranger episode filmed with miniatures.

"So, what's the plan?" Jennifer asked. She had boarded the train without question.

Dick Tracy opened his briefcase. "From what I found out, this New York gang originated in ancient Egypt. So, we are headed to the only man who knows anything remotely true about ancient Egypt."

"Who's that?" Jennifer asked.

"I can't say. But, seeking him brings much danger."

"Really? Like that kind of danger?"

A severe looking cop walked down the isle of the train car. He had them royal blues, black pants, a motorcycle cop helmet, and sunglasses.

"Shit," Dick Tracy said, "I knew this would be trouble, but not *that* kind of trouble."

"What kind of trouble is he?" asked Jennifer. "Here, I have guns."

She stood up and, WOOSH! Threw aside her long dark coat. She wore that Electra stripper costume and, DAYUM! If her body wasn't loaded up with guns 'n shitocracy underneath. All strapped on tight; like, FUCK ME! Tight.

Dick Tracy called on his watch. "This is Dick Tracy; Sam, Sam Catchem, you out there, buddy? Bring that orange hat 'a yers; we need your help. Oh-," He glanced at Jennifer's chest. "-We have tits over here too, over; do you copy? Tits. Like, female tits, ya' know; the kind that are fun to play with 'n shit."

"Yeah, hear ya' loud 'n clear; I'm on my way. And, don't let them tits go nowhere. I'm bringin' my camera."

"Sam's comin'," Dick Tracy said.

"Good, is this cop that bad?" Jennifer asked.

Dick Tracy's eyes became slits, "Yeah that is a Terminator."

"It doesn't look like a Terminator."

"It is."

"Are you sure?"

"Yes."

"Positive?"

"Yes."

"Okay, 'cause it doesn't look like the ones in movies."

"No, this one's from Terminator 2 Future Wars- action figure line; this dude's face falls off and reveals a missile launcher 'n shit; you'll see."

"Oh, I don't think I want to see. What do we do?"

"Come with me if you want to live."

They got up outta' them bench seats, which was unfortunate because thus far it had been a delightful train trip across the continental United States of America.

"Freeze!" The Terminator charged and, ZIP! ZAP! His face and chest peeled forward revealing a gnarly super-awesome weapon.

ZOOM! In a second, missiles fired out.

People in the train car screamed and leaned towards their windows.

The missiles flew down the center aisle.

Jennifer whipped out her swords and, SLICE! Cut the steel side of the train's cabin. She kicked the steel and grabbed Dick Tracy's collar.

He fired his pistols. Jennifer yanked him out.

The wall gave and the two fell.

WHOOOSH!

The cool air whipped at Dick Tracy's collar. He fell, looking up to the sky, and watched the train crossing the bridge suspended across the huge canyon.

Out of the train, jumped the Terminator. WHIP! WHAP! It pulled out two pistols.

CLAK! CLAK!

Bullet whizzed past Jennifer. *Shit, what we do? We are just plummeting to our deaths. I should have planned better.*

They fell some fourteen hundred feet.

Dick Tracy aimed and, CLAK!

That bullet trailed the air and, BING! Nailed the Terminator in its natural born killing eye.

"Oh shit, it's part liquid metal." Dick Tracy watched as its face was blown to pieces and then, in liquid fashion, remolded. You've seen the fuckin' movie.

The ground was coming quick.

Jennifer clung onto Dick Tracy. He looked over his shoulder.

Boulders and foliage-shit were coming fast.

Come on, Sam Catchem; come on!

VROOOM! Something tore the sound barrier.

BAM! In a flash, a jet tore by. It banked with its bay door open, and perfectly timed it with the two fallin' heroes.

WHAM! The two were caught and landed with a skidding stop in the cargo bay.

The Terminator, WHAK! Hit the ground like a cement truck.

Dick Tracy dusted himself off. "Thanks, Sam; good timing."

The cargo hold was an open expanse. Upfront Sam turned in his seat. "No problem, partner. Now where to?"

Dick Tracy helped Jennifer up. "We are going to go see the man that knows everything, Neil deGrasse Tyson."

Jennifer's cunt trembled. "That man *does* knows everything!"

The jet tore through the mountain valley and, WOOSH! Crossed the sky.

Sam asked, "Cool, so where do we find him?"

Katy Bots

The Himalayas was a vast natural paradise. Twisted trees dripped flowing white leaves. The temple sat atop its summit as a testament to divine knowledge calling upon the blue skies of heaven.

The dancing drapes parted in the temple's doorway leading Jennifer, Dick Tracy, and Sam inside.

The hike had been extensive. Sam lifted his hat and wiped sweat from his wide brow. Jennifer looked sexy and fine, like she hadn't hiked at all. Her Electra suit had changed to an alluring white.

Two, two foot tall Tin soldiers led the guests through the main hall.

"Well, what do have we here?" Neil deGrasse Tyson asked.

Dick Tracy kept his hat on even in the sanctuary of YouTube intelligence. "I have come to consult you on a grave matter of importance."

"Ah, wonderful," Neil said. He wore a flowing purple hippy tunic, "For discussing of matters of great importance we need tits 'n ass. Katy Bots!" he called out and waived his arm.

Two flawless Katy Perrys came out from the side hall and into the room. They did a lurid dance as they walked and then stopped in front of Neil's throne and continued dancing-like, slutty, really, really slutty. BET after midnight, slutty. Like pop 'n lock that ass, TWERK FOR ME BABY! Slutty.

"Wow, now we're talking." Sam Catchem grinned happily. *Yes sir, I came for some titties.*

These women ignited Dick Tracy's detective senses "Who are they?" he asked.

"Ah, these are my Katy Perry robots. They service me in whatever needs I demand. Aren't they super sexy and give you boners?"

"They sure do," Jennifer said.

The two Katys danced and shook them awesome titties and curvy asses. Dick Tracy was intrigued, them being robots 'n all. He couldn't even tell. *Nope, them tits and lips 'n ass, look all real, and alright to me.*

The robots wore… hmm, I'm thinkin' here; we need a real good outfit for them; something hot 'n shit; okay, got it! They were wearing that Barbarella silver outfit with the clear titty cups. Except their legs were bare and not in black tights. Yep so them cupcakes and sweet nipples were visible.

"My Katy Bots, come join big Papa Nerd."

Neil put on fluffy small bear ears fixed to a plastic head band. He slipped them suckas' on.

Stories 'N Time Travel

"Ya' didn't have to come with us, Neil," Dick Tracy said.

"Well, I certainly did; you never know when you'll need the man who knows everything. Science is god, science… is… God. And you, good sir, might I say; that is a nice colored hat."

"Thanks," Sam said.

"We are here," Jennifer said.

They stood in front of a Mr. Gatti's Pizza Place. It was a rundown building with an open window face that displayed arcades 'n shit, inside.

"To ancient Egypt," Dick Tracy said and opened the restaurant's door.

Kill Screen

"Hot dayum! Girl you's amazing," Neil said. He practically climbed Jennifer's back.

Nothing turned Neil on more than girls that were good at video games.

Jennifer was intently focused. *Almost there almost there.*

She stood in front of the Sunset Riders arcade game. Jennifer worked them joysticks in a way that brought all the boys and men to come 'n watch.

She was in the final fight against the final boss who was some Louisiana douche, skinny and prissy, and the fight took place within his mansion.

Visible bullets were flyin' everywhere in this shoot out.

Her fingers gripped the stick and guided it around in sexual motions. Them tits were Denny's on Sunday morning and all the men that gathered closer wanted them some pancakes with syrup and butter.

"You can do it," Dick Tracy said aloud, but without really realizing.

The tension was high.

Sam watched the artistry in motion on the game.

Jennifer stopped blinking. A few more hits and then the kill screen and time travel.

Boring

Sand, heat, and people wearing flowing white garments, greeted them.

"Ah, ancient Egypt," Neil said and took a deep breath.

"Looks like shit," Dick Tracy said.

"Yeah where are the pyramids?" Sam asked.

Jennifer put her hair up in a ponytail. The men took notice of the way her raised arm lifted them titties.

Neil smiled happily, "Well, they haven't been built yet. So-," He leaned in, "What's the plan, here? We go find a guy and rip his insides out?"

"Well," Jennifer said, "I can't really recall why we came back here. Kinda' seems like this adventure got away from us."

"Certainly has," Dick Tracy said. "Didn't it have to do with yer daughter and husband bein' killed?

"Yeah, but... well; guess I am over it. Revenge wouldn't honor their name the way I thought it would. And, I remembered that the whole Peppermint thing was fiction; she wasn't actually my daughter, I just got carried away with the role."

Sam looked around at the people. All the men were dark and looked the same to him.

Some of the local me took notice of Jennifer.

'Oohs' and 'ahhs' started coming from the growing crowd. Them tits were magnetic; which Ben Affleck knew and it's killin' him to not have 'em.

"What's happening?" she asked.

Neil said, "Looks like your titties are drawin' some attention."

"We want 'em. Lick 'dem, suck 'dem," The ancient Egyptian men started to say. They crowded around, and swords were drawn.

"Titties, now! Give us!"

"What do we do?" Dick Tracy asked, he reached inside his vest and pulled out his pistol.

"I say we leave," Sam said.

BRRRRRR! A wormhole opened, and that Terminator future war thing came out.

CLAKKKK-KKKK-KKKKK! It opened fire on everyone.

Dick Tracy, Neil, Sam, and Jennifer ducked and ran.

CLANG! CLANG! CLANG! A sound picked up.

Jennifer raised her head in time to see a large militia of guards, approach. They were dressed in golden armor and wielded sci fi weaponry.

ZZZAAAAAP! The militia aimed their glowing staffs at the Terminator and fired.

"GRAH!" The Terminator convulsed. *Power lower. Shut down eminent!* The killing machine fell to his knees and keeled over.

"Thank god," Neil said, "In 'bout two seconds I's gonna' open a can 'a educated whip ass on that robot."

Sam dusted off his hat. "I hope these guards are a good thing."

A pharaoh in an elaborate headdress, like some weird animal, approached Jennifer.

"By Shizami's Corn Hust," he said, "Those tits! Those tits are magnificent!" Which is pretty much how anyone who see Jennifer Garner's tits react. He reached his sunburned hands for them soft nibblets.

Jennifer slapped the hands away. "Hey, stop that."

Dick Tracy got in front of her. "Back up. Those tits are only for this team and me!"

The pharaoh asked, "And who might you be?"

"I'm dick-,"

Before he finished the pharaoh signaled his guards. They used their sci fi staffs and-

-It was lights out for our entire time traveling team.

Pharaoh's Shaft

Jennifer awoke.

"Oh shit, what happened?"

She looked around.

Jennifer was sprawled out on a bed and wore a flowing translucent green robe. She was butt ass naked underneath with her sleek sweet skin.

"Damn, who undressed me?"

"Ah, you're awake."

"Who's there?"

She looked around and then saw the Pharaoh. He was butt ass naked, as most men are when they approach hot women.

The King was a big man, full of carpet-y hair on his torso but he had a shaved head. His dick was rigid and angry with secret Egyptian power. It was sleek 'n shiny with essential oils.

"Who are you? What are you doing with me? And where are my clothes? You better not have-," She checked between her legs with her fingers. *Ah, phew!*

"I am king Tut, and now you are my sexy sex slave."

"Oh, I don't think so. I'm Jennifer Garner. I am a Venus that can kill any man with only my body. I am no sex slave; especially for a hairy muppet like yourself!"

"Well, I can see you're a bitch with a mouth. I will use that mouth to empty my balls at my leisure. It was foretold by Prophet Joe, back in ancient days. It's said that a woman would come with tits so glorious they would lead a king to eternal majesty."

"And?"

"And, you are these tits. I mean, look at them. Those pink nipples, WHOA-ZAM EGYPTIAN WALK!"

Jennifer looked down and jiggled them with her hands. Her fingers dimpled their soft pale skin. "Yeah, they are nice. What did you do with my friends?"

"To the fire with them; the fire of unimportant characters. They will be dead soon, if not already. Now, spread them legs; I want that little puss 'a yers!"

King Tut charged the ornate bed.

"Oh shit!" Jennifer rolled aside. Her soft tits slipped around loose in that sheer robe.

"Now, don't be tryin' to escape me. I'll give chase 'n then tie you up!"

He lept onto the bed.

Jennifer scrambled to her feet. "You better stop. The last man to slipped into my tight, cock-huggin' kooter is now in rehab. My pussy destroys weak men!"

King Tut climbed off the bed. He was already huffing and out of breath. Sweat beaded on his large forehead.

"I don't know what word you cast but all that matters is those titties; NOW GIMME!"

Where is the door? She looked around.

As our Hot Celebrity ran for the door, King Tut was on her. He jumped on her back and took Jennifer to the ground.

If only I can get a knee up. I'll take the excitement right outta' King Tut's manhood!

"Ah there!"

POW! She kneed the king in his balls.

He cried out as any man would. "Guards!" he shouted between clenched teeth.

Men rushed in wearing sparkling golden armor.

"Grab da bitch!"

They lifted her and held her by the arms.

King Tut said, "I thought you might not cooperate; the prophesy said you'd be a feisty kitten, but my Seer has given me a bargaining chip to get your cooperation."

What could he be talking about? A bargaining ship? "I'd never rub that cock a yours with my slippery tight pussy!"

"We'll see. Cancuer, bring in the girl!"

Dungeon Dance Floor

"We's gonna' kills ya anyways. So, dance!"

Neil, Sam and Dick wore sparkling sequined dresses, varying colored wigs, stuffed chests, and high heels. They were on a disco light changing platform in a dank drippy dungeon.

"I'm not dancin'," Neil said.

"Yeah," Sam said, "If I'm gonna' die. I'll die with dignity."

A massive and ugly dungeon master smiled. "We'd prefer a show and dance before wes fuck you. But hell, we'll fuck yer dead bodies just as happily."

Two other freaky men stood to each side of him.

Dick Tracy didn't like being fucked by men. So, he asked, "Why are you guys gonna fuck us anyhow? Wouldn't ya rather have a fine lady suck yer pizzle till it pops?"

"Well sure," dat dragon master said. The three of them wore BDSM leather masks. "Problem is dat king 'o ours won't give us no women. We've worked down here for years. We'll die down here. And, da only holes dat come through here, are men's butts. So, dance some 'n den wes gonna bend ya over 'n give ya our sweaty meat."

"What do we do Dick Tracy? That yellow hat 'a yers must have made men want ta bend ya over before?" Neil asked in a hushed voice.

"Give me a sec. Our anuses will not be destroyed by these infected WWF guys."

"Now dance," the dungeon master said.

Neil started a little jig and Sam stumbled spankin' da ground with his feet.

It was then that our yellow hat friend saw what he needed.

A sword! Perfect! What a long sharp blade. I'll take it down and chop off our jailers' heads!

Dick Tracy bolted for the sword.

SCHWING!

He retrieved the blade and spun in an arcing the blade.

The dungeon master and friends charged and ran into the path of the blade.

Three heads popped off in spinning blood.

"Whoa!" Neil said, "That was amazing display of both physics and gravity!"

Sam watched the blood squirt from the neck stumps and said nothing.

Dick Tracy lowered the sword. "It's over."

A pool of dark blood seeped into the earthen floor.

Motherly Instincts

"Say hi to your daughter."

Jennifer's eyes went wide as quarters. "No! My daughter? But how?"

"Ah, nothing a little Egyptian time travel can't solve. What? Aren't you happy to see her?"

"Mommy!" The girl cried and ran forward. She looked like a midget Ben Affleck in a curly brown wig.

"Not so fast."

The pharaoh caught her by the neck. The girl-Ben grimaced.

"So, now that I have your daughter, and I'll put a knife to her throat-," He put a knife to her throat. "-You'll spread them legs for me, right? 'Cause daddy's ready to cum!"

"No," Jennifer said.

"No? But mommy?" Girl-Ben started to cry.

"My answer is no."

"But this is your daughter and I'll kill da little bitch."

"Okay, kill her. She died once; what's a second time?"

The pharaoh's jaw dropped. "I don't understand."

"Well," Jennifer said, "I guess I realized my peppermint daughter was just a fictional character and means nothing to me. Do as you want with her."

"We'll see about that," King Tut said with a sinister smile.

"No, stop the," girl cried.

"Stay still." King Tut in heavy jerks ripped her clothes off.

The girl tried to hide her body. *Oh no, this man I so strong and why doesn't my mommy care about me*? "Mommy, help!"

"Eh," Jennifer said, "Have her."

"But... but... Fine!"

He stroked that cock tryin' ta get good n ready.

Jennifer examined her fingernails.

King Tut huffed. He squeezed at the girl's chest "What about now?" *Damn her, I want them titties. I don't want this little weird looking one. She is too small, has a beard and doesn't have the cosmic jugs of this futuristic siren.*

ROAR! The pharaoh charged Jennifer.

BOOM! The door flew open 'n Dick Tracy opened fire. Bullet ate the walls. The guards charged but were laid to rest.

CLOCK! Neil jumped on one of the Pharaoh's and punched him in the face.

"How do you like education in the form of black knuckles?"

The guy collapsed to the ground.

"Oh, wow! You guys came just in time," Jennifer said.

The little girl-Ben ran up and hugged her mon. "Mommy."

Jennifer brushed her off and walked over to Dick Tracy. "Thanks for comin'."

"No problem," he said to Jennifer and holstered that awesome pistol. He then played with them soft titties 'a hers for a bit.

King Tut cowered in the corner.

Neil circled his arm. "Maybe it's time to go home." A dark portal opened.

The team went through.

"MOMMY!" The little girl ran after them but, BING! The portal popped shut and girl-Ben was left behind.

The Pharaoh's guards rushed in.

"What happened," one asked.

"We lost them special titties."

"What will we do?"

King Tut thought for a moment. "We will build some titty shaped pyramids in their honor."

"What's a pyramid?" a henchman asked.

"Well, huge stones stacked up. They will be conical and have yummy, yummy pink nipples on top."

"Cool; so I think I know how to build them," the henchmen said.

"How?" This intrigued King Tut, for stacking big stones was impossible for mere men alone.

The guard opened the door and the Terminator walked in under the control of an Egyptian. A cord hooked into the Terminator's back and ran to a rickety control made of wood, stone, 'n gold.

"With this!"

Celebrity Reality

Bubbles rose around them.

Dick Tracy dried his hand on the towel and reached for his phone, which sat on the side of the hot tub.

"Oh, you're serious," Jennifer said. She was topless and them girls were all floating and slippery wet.

"Yeah, I was serious." He typed on the keypad.

Sam kicked back a beer and Neil deGrassed Tyson ate some chilled shrimp. Neil said, "He's telling the truth."

"No way. How on earth could that happen?" Jennifer asked.

"Ah, there-," Dick Tracy turned his phone and showed her. "-See we changed history; the pyramids aren't as we once knew them."

Jennifer looked at the picture. "Oh my god! Those are my tits!"

The pyramids were no longer four sided, but instead, cones. And on the top were large nipples ornate with gold.

"I can't believe they loved my titties so much that they built the pyramids to honor them."

"You bet they did," Dick Tracy said.

"Yeah; and even funnier," Neil said, "Is that historians have concluded that the 'nipple look' signified a long tradition in ancient Egypt of honoring man-boobs."

Sam laughed out loud. "Man boobs, pshh!"

"Well, I'm honored and embarrassed," Jennifer said, "But my tits do inspire lots of weird things."

"That they do," Dick Tracy said, "Them are some hot little titties ya gotz there! Mind if I...,"

He played with them wiggly water toys.

Meanwhile back in time...

The girl-Ben cried.

"Toss her," King Tut said.

"NOOOO!"

The girl-Ben was thrown off the ceremonial sacrifice cliff and into roaring fires below. "Mommy-eeee... eeee!"

END

That's all folks; hope you enjoyed. Don't forget to leave a review, tell a friend (if ya got 'em) and check out the next book in the series 'Moonshine Vol.1'/
See ya'!

Vol. 1

Moonshine

BRIDGET CHASE

Made in the USA
Columbia, SC
21 February 2023

12770411R00183